For Sale:
Wedding Dress.
Never Used.

By Michelle L. Levigne

M Zion Ridge Press LLC

Mt Zion Ridge Press LLC
295 Gum Springs Rd, NW
Georgetown, TN 37366

https://www.mtzionridgepress.com

Copyright © 2019 by Michelle L. Levigne
ISBN 13: 978-1-949564-41-9

Published in the United States of America
Publication Date: June 1, 2019

Editor-In-Chief: Michelle Levigne
Executive Editor: Tamera Lynn Kraft

Cover Art Copyright by Mt Zion Ridge Press LLC © 2019

Part One: Andy
Chapter 1

I was warned, but did I listen? Nooooo.

During my college freshman orientation, a wise and kind senior gave the girls in our dormitory the most important advice we would ever receive in our college careers:

"Stay away from the pre-sem students. You're here for your BA degree, not your MRS. Thanks to Dr. Rittsmer -- who has never been married -- they believe a pastor's wife should be barefoot, pregnant and in the kitchen. Except on Sunday, when she's wearing sensible pumps and sits in the front row, closest to the door, to take care of every emergency that happens during the service."

Then she shared with us horror stories of girls who had been duly warned but forgot that advice in the glory of falling in love with an *alleged* man of God. Just because someone says the right words and wears the right clothes, that doesn't mean they're legitimate. *By their fruit, you shall know them*...and too many guys were more nutty than fruitful, if you get my drift.

These idealistic, spiritually devoted girls earned degrees. They worked toward careers. They got involved in ministries and used the talents God gave them. They provided most of the financial support while their husbands finished seminary. After seminary, each hard-working wife was expected to abandon career, achievements and occasional nights out with the girls. She had now entered a life sentence in a goldfish bowl. Responsible for every church task no one else wanted to do. Constantly struggling to live up to the expectations and criticism of everyone, and follow *everyone's* advice. Even when they contradicted each other. She *never* shared in the praise, recognition, and credit for her husband's success, but she was *always* blamed if the church split or her husband lost his calling or became part of a scandal.

In my defense, I didn't expect to ever need such advice, so while I heard what that kind senior said, I didn't really *listen*. Two reasons:

First, it had been pounded into my head since I was three years old (when my cousin, Bill, came to live with us) that I was fat, stupid, and a family embarrassment. No intelligent man would ever want me.

Second, I had a great future that didn't require a man to validate my existence. I would work for Allen Michaels Evangelistic Association (AMEA). I had started in middle school as an assistant teacher in summer Bible day camps and graduated up to more responsibility every year. The summer before my sophomore year at SCC, I worked at the Colorado AMEA camp as second assistant director. Mrs. Zeminski, my boss, asked me to come back the next summer as her right-hand gal.

So I was flying high when I got back to Southeastern Christian College (SCC) for my sophomore year. My future was coming together. I had an AMEA scholarship. When I graduated with a degree in management, I would start low in the ministry and work my way up to wherever God wanted me. My future was wide open.

I was the Dateless Wonder, and I had made my peace with singleness that summer. What could be better than to spend my life in ministry, going where the Lord, and AMEA, sent me?

So when I met Andy and he gave me a second look, it never occurred to me to run, not walk, to the nearest exit. He could never be interested in me, Eve Miller. As a co-worker? Sure. As a girlfriend? Never.

Like someone told James Bond -- or was it Sean Connery? -- never say never.

*****

Darleen Phillips, a senior my sophomore year, lived in Pennsylvania. She had to come within twenty miles of where I lived near Cleveland, on her way back to SCC, in the southeastern corner of Iowa. (Hence the name.) She was going to be RA on the first floor in my dorm, and had to come up early for Freshman Orientation. She offered me a ride, if I could come up to campus early. Could I? It got me out of town four days early. Less chance for relatives to come swooping in for a dose of low self-esteem before I escaped their clutches until Christmas. I set up my half of the dorm room I was sharing with Tonia Esperanza and sailed out across campus to reacquaint myself with Blue Bell City.

Campus was a hodge-podge of new buildings among turn-of-the-last-century sandstone and granite, holding down a spot in the middle of farm country. The only time there was ever a traffic jam was during fall move-in and spring move-out. Campus straddled a two-lane highway, and didn't even have a stoplight to cross the highway. The library and administration building were on one side and the Student Center was on the other. When I was a student, I counted five stoplights in the entire town. Blue Bell didn't even rate a dot in most of the atlases I checked when I investigated it during my junior year of high school.

That appealed to me. I was practically invisible in my Christian high school and didn't care to vanish entirely in an even bigger crowd. SCC suited me. I could breathe, with a chance to make my own place.

I planned to sleep in late, bop around campus, and watch all the kids play those silly "breaking the ice" games I endured when I was a freshman. Orientation activities were in full swing when I strolled into the Student Center with all the time in the world. I ran into some classmates who had come in early with freshman brothers. They invited me to come with them to hit the Grease Pit for lunch. I thought about my two sizes-smaller jeans, and chose virtue over to-die-for chili-cheese fries.

I checked my mailbox, in the top row in the wall of the mail room. I hadn't grown taller, just thinner over the summer, and still had to go on tiptoes to reach inside. Then I wandered around. The freshmen were easy to spot, all wearing color-coded nametags. A bunch raced past me, giggling (even the guys!) and jabbering about bonus points as they headed for the gym. I figured it might be fun to watch someone else act like a dweeb, so I followed along. And there was Andy, right in my path, sitting on a tall stool next to the door into the gym, playing his saxophone. A big sign on the wall above him proclaimed he was the Answer Man. A table next to him held maps of the campus, schedules for orientation, coupon books for the stores in town, and clipboards with sign-up sheets for the various orientation activities.

I just gave him a passing glance. He looked vaguely familiar, but with an average population of 900 students, that wasn't hard at SCC.

"Where's your nametag?" He grinned at me and stuck out his saxophone to block my path.

Now I really looked at him. How could I not? His smile -- how could I describe it? The memory of that first smile came back many times through the years to zing me. It was part boy-next-door, part troublemaker. He had a shaggy mop of blond hair and Clark Kent glasses with no glass. I always wished I had the guts to do something quirky like that. He had on a gray Petra tee-shirt that had seen better days, and faded jeans.

With those drown-in-me blue-gray eyes focused on me, how could I even think straight?

Once I took a deep breath and replenished the oxygen in my brain, I realized why he looked familiar. I had seen him leading chapel services at least once a month the year before. He had headed up the crazy Polar Bear Games on the Commons in January, to raise funds for spring break and summer mission trips. It made sense that he would be sitting here during orientation, involved in some campus activity, and at least pretending to notice everyone who walked past. Even me, the Invisible Girl.

My self-confidence had gotten a major boost from working summer and snow camps for AMEA. The week at home between camp and college hadn't stuffed me back into my lowly position in the world because Bill wasn't there to mock and criticize. Proof that God was merciful.

However, a lifetime of criticism from Dad's side of the family didn't wear off that easily. Despite a summer feeling useful and worthwhile, and not a single crampy day from my fibroids acting up, the doubts were trickling back into my brain by the time I ran into Andy. I still had enough self-assurance to look him in the eye, instead of scrambling for an apology.

"Don't need one," I said, and stopped when I could have sidestepped the saxophone.

Dummy me, lucky me, thinner me. (Ten hours a day on my feet did amazing things for my confidence and figure.) I stopped and grinned right back at this cute guy who could *see* me.

"Oh, I get it." He rested his sax across his knees. "You don't have a name." He nodded like it made perfect sense.

"I have a name. I just don't need a nametag. Those are for freshmen."

"Thank You, God!" He slid off his stool and hit the floor on his knees, clutching his sax to his chest. "An upperclassman! I'm saved." He leaped to his feet the moment I took a step backwards from this raving lunatic.

Just because a madman was cute didn't mean he was safe.

He grabbed my arm. "Have mercy and eat lunch with me. If I have to answer one more question that's already covered in the info book, I'm gonna scream. You know how hard it is to eat and scream at the same time?"

I got this tingly feeling when his hand gripped my bare arm. The last time a guy had touched me, other than getting my attention to handle an emergency, was during square dancing in seventh grade gym class.

His name, I learned about ten seconds after he hit the floor, was Andy Carleone. A senior. He pretended to be distraught that he didn't know me, meaning he didn't know everybody on campus after all.

He won me over, right there, when I told him my name was Eve and he *didn't* offer me an apple or warn me to look out for snakes. Finally, a guy with a sense of humor *above* second grade.

Then he led me to a back room where everybody working orientation ate lunch. Andy managed to eat and talk at the same time without spraying turkey-and-Swiss across the table. I managed to eat and laugh at the same time without getting tea up my nose. He had a fifteen-minute break. It was enough time to get the important details about each other.

He was in Jazz Band and the orchestra and traveled on mission trips during fall and spring break. He had just finished up his fifth summer Christian youth band tour. The quiet of his hometown, Argo (smaller than Blue Bell), had driven him back to campus early. He finagled a work-study opportunity that paid him minimum wage for basically sitting there, toodling on his saxophone (he also played piano and guitar), answering questions and pointing freshmen where they needed to go.

Andy had a double major in Christian ed and music, and hoped to join a traveling music ministry team with an organization I hadn't heard about. He assured me it was growing and getting good feedback. Then he asked about my plans, so I told him how all my time working behind-the-scenes for AMEA was leading to a job when I graduated.

"Sounds like you have your future mapped out for you," he said, as another shift of orientation workers stumbled into the room, laughing and griping.

"I guess."

Funny, but after listening to Andy talk about his plans and the things he had done that summer, my life sounded a little blah and predictable. My Spiritual Gifts test confirmed what I had always known. I was a backstage person, facilitating everybody else. Until I talked with Andy that afternoon, I thought my future of troubleshooting and taking care of others' needs would be totally cool. Humble. Serving God without expecting any praise.

Andy made me doubt my plans, just talking over sandwiches in a room off a noisy, crowded gym.

Then, he flashed a crooked grin that made me feel bubbly inside. Andy Carleone's grin, at close quarters, was about as close to an addictive substance as SCC would ever see. Discounting chocolate and high-octane sodas.

"You know what you're going to do with your life. I really admire that. I'm still floundering around." He shrugged and picked up his glass to swirl his root beer around before downing the last mouthful.

"You're floundering? But you're into everything. You're a leader on all these mission and service teams."

"Yeah, but it's like test-driving things, y'know? What does God really want me to do with my life? It's not like He threw an instruction book down in front of me like He did with you."

Did I really give him that impression?

He had to get back to work, and I wanted to take a stroll downtown. At his assigned doorway, I said good-bye and started to walk away.

"Hey, Eve, wait up." He grabbed hold of my hand.

There were times I considered suing my parents for naming me Eve. Sunday school class was a miserable place to wear a prominent biblical name. I refused to eat apples when I was around those bozos. Somehow, coming out of Andy's mouth, Eve sounded like a great name.

"Let's meet for dinner. We'll hit the Grease Pit instead of the cafeteria, okay?"

Looking into Andy's eyes, I completely forgot about my resolves and my hard-won physique. The allure of batter-fried mushrooms and shakes too thick for straws wove a siren song through my soul, straight to my taste buds. I could feel my new jeans starting to get tight, but I didn't care.

That was the effect Andy Carleone had on me, right from the beginning.

*****

A wise man once said that a girl's relationship with her father affects all her relationships with men. That has proven so true in my life. I loved my Dad. Despite all the times when he let down Mom and me, he did love us. However, he lived in mortal fear of disappointing his family, except for marrying Mom against all their advice and wishes. Proof? He took Bill into our house when the jerk's mother, the only perfect daughter-in-law, died. Of course, maybe she was the perfect daughter-in-law *because* she died. Mom was what my grandparents had to "settle for" because Dad always made bad choices. If Mom was so bad, why did Bill's father let him live with us instead of taking care of his only son himself? Why didn't Grandma Miller take the job?

Abusive in-laws are only funny in sitcoms where everyone is stupid. How many times did Mom cry coming home from family gatherings?

When Dad died, he was the only Miller in four generations with more than a thousand dollars in the bank after funeral expenses. Bill thought, as the only male of our generation and because he grew up in our house, he was the heir. The only heir. However, Mom's wise investing created the family estate in the first place. Dad had the moral fortitude to give her full control. That infuriated the Miller clan. They cut us off when she refused to hand everything over to Bill. Why did they think that was punishment?

When I met Andy, Dad was still alive and Bill had moved out for the summer in a snit because my bedroom door was locked. He couldn't help himself to all my possessions while I was away. He had been helping himself to everything that was mine for as long as I could remember, and considered it his right.

My experiences with my Dad and Bill explain a good portion of the mistakes I made. Not all of them, but a good portion.

*****

Andy Carleone wants to eat dinner with me! went through my brain about four times while I walked to downtown Blue Bell, a four-block by six-block section of town. I remembered seeing him everywhere, and I do mean *everywhere*, on campus the year before. Andy Carleone was a mover and shaker at SCC.

So why did he want to spend time with me?

I passed up Sugarland. The combination bakery, candy store and gift shop was one of my favorite haunts the year before. My brain was in meltdown if I could walk past that place without being caught in the tentacles of aromas coming through the open door and dragged inside.

There's no one else to hang with yet. He's bored. When his regular gang shows up, I'll be forgotten.

I should have had the sense to go to the taco party that Gloria, our Resident Director, had that night, and called Andy to cancel. I could have written a paper on the brain damage caused by blue eyes and a sincere expression.

The Grease Pit wasn't actually named Grease Pit, but decades of college students had referred to the burger joint by that name, so it stuck. Even after management added healthy items, like a salad bar.

Andy and I practically had the place all to ourselves. The freshmen were at a picnic at President Van der Hoff's house. Only the early arrivals and work-study kids had to endure the pizzas from Planet Inedible in the cafeteria. A handful of professors and their spouses had booths in the back while Andy and I had a table near the windows up front. The plastic-sweet scent of the fresh green and blue paint on the plywood booths and new red vinyl seats tinted the air. The aroma of slightly burned frying oil, spicy pizza sauce, rising dough and hot fudge hadn't built up yet.

Andy did most of the talking, about his mission trip that summer and his dreams of being a youth leader -- not tied to one church, but working youth camps and traveling with a music and drama troupe. He asked about my behind-the-scenes work. He talked about friends in the theater program when I mentioned work-study money I earned last year behind stage at the Playhouse. It was like we had something in common. He asked me a lot of questions about my administrative work.

Afterward, Andy walked me back to my dorm, which was nice. Unnecessary, though. Blue Bell was the kind of town where the older generation still didn't lock their doors at night. It meant I could walk the streets of the town after midnight and not be in any danger. Plus. my dormitory was just around the corner from the Grease Pit.

When I walked into the dorm, freshmen filled the main lounge, engaged in several different team games. The uproar didn't do much to jolt me back into common sense. As I reached my room on the third floor, the thought going through my brain ran somewhere along the lines of, *Please, God, make Andy remember me if we run into each other again?*

I finished unpacking and setting up my neglected dormitory room. Milk crates to be turned into shelving, posters hung. I made a shopping list for the morning, to fill the cube refrigerator Tonia and I had agreed to rent for the school year. My head was finally out of the clouds. I went over my class schedule and made a shopping list of the books I should have bought that day, instead of providing entertainment for one bored senior. I vowed to be smarter for the rest of the year.

In my journal, I wrote, *Resolution: I will NOT run around campus looking for Andy.*

I forgot my resolution when the phone in the hall rang at the unholy hour of 8am.

Normally, that wasn't an awful time to wake up, but I had planned on sleeping late. I didn't have any classes. I had a right, almost a holy duty, to spend a day goofing off.

It sounded like there was no one alive on my floor except me. Good indication that everyone had already headed out for more freshman orientation breakfast activities. The noise when the rest of the floor's occupants left hadn't awakened me, but that phone kept ringing.

I stumbled out of bed and banged my toes on the door before I got my eyes open. I staggered down the hall to the phone nook, in the middle of the floor opposite the bathroom. I learned then why nobody else wanted the room next to the stairwell. It was a long stumble to the phone.

"Keeler third floor," I mumbled. Our dorm had been renovated just after the actress, Emily Keeler, set up our award-winning theater program, about ten years before. She had actually stayed in the dorms with the students, and all the girls insisted it be renamed for her.

"Hey, Eve?"

I recognized Andy's voice, despite my brain being on half-power. The fact that he recognized my voice shocked me enough to forget my plan to go back to bed.

"Yes."

"Hey, it's Andy. Andy Carleone. Remember, from lunch? And dinner?" He laughed, and I was a goner. Why did God have to give some guys such gorgeous laughs that melted a girl's brain circuitry like chocolate in the sun? "Could you do me a really big favor?"

I woke up the whole way, feeling like I had been dropped into an icy pond. Suddenly, I was back in elementary school, when the cutest guy in the third grade asked me to meet him after church. It turned out that Cutie (his name has faded into the past) wanted to borrow the two plush lambs Grandma Miller had given me for my birthday. He was a shepherd in the Christmas play, and Bill had volunteered my lambs as props. Bill was always asking if anybody needed help or needed to use something, and then volunteering *me* and *my property*. I always came across as the villain if I didn't cooperate with his promises. What could I do? I loaned Cutie my lambs. Then his older brother and Bill used them for bb gun targets.

Now Andy was asking for my help. I should have known. Guys like Andy never looked twice at girls like me unless they wanted to borrow our homework.

"See, Chapel Team has the first chapel tomorrow, and we're working on it today. Maybe you could help us? It's right up your alley."

"Doing what?"

Thanks to Bill, I had learned never to say yes to any proposition before hearing the details.

"I don't know." He laughed. My resolve weakened. "That's why I'm asking for your help. I have no idea what we should do. Save me!"

"No, I mean, what do you want me to do? I'm not on the team."

"Do you want to be?"

I should have said no. I should have remembered an old *Peanuts* cartoon. Like Charlie Brown, I was tired of being second fiddle when I didn't even belong to the orchestra. I should have said that to Andy. I would have saved $200 on a wedding dress I never used.

"Don't I have to get approved by the team and Chaplain Nate and--"

"Well, it's only temporary, until we get things started and you get to know everybody."

I opened my mouth to say I had plans for the day. I had to buy books and paint my fingernails and take a nap. Important things. Tonia was getting in that afternoon, so I had to stick around and help her haul her gear up the stairs.

I made the mistake of looking up at the bulletin board next to the phone. This early in the school year, it had nothing but a cute rainbow border and some nice little photographs with catchy phrases and Bible verses. One asked me to extend a helping hand, even if nobody ever extended a hand to me in return. It quoted the Bible verse about not limiting my hospitality to people who could repay it.

Okay, God, I get the message!

"Sure. When do you want to meet?" I managed not to sigh too loudly.

"We're on our way over to Chaplain Nate's office right now."

"Let me get some breakfast and I'll meet you over there."

"We'll bring some for you, okay?"

My brain finally started working once I was in the shower. When I showed up at the chaplain's office, I expected soggy corn flakes and warm milk, maybe some cold toast.

Tricia, one floor down from me, was on the team. She was one of those too-good-to-be-true people: athlete, missionary kid, top scholar, cheerleader, studying to be a special education teacher. She took care of my breakfast: French toast with blueberries, and scrambled eggs. Still hot.

My breakfast got cold because I was so busy taking notes and answering questions. They needed what I knew. It felt good to have answers nobody else on the team could come up with. Working behind the scenes around campus last year, I learned who had the real authority, where things were stored, and who had to give permission to use them. I felt like the whiz kid running around the storage rooms at the Playhouse with four hulking senior guys doing my bidding. Fun. Exhausting, but fun.

I didn't go to lunch with the team because I still had to hit the bookstore. By the time I hauled my back-breaking load to my room and got to the cafeteria, Andy and the rest were heading back to work. How could I say, "No, I want to go eat," when he hooked his arm through mine and dragged me along? Who could even walk, much less resist, with tingles going up and down her spine?

We spent the afternoon rehearsing the skit Chaplain Nate had pulled from his files. I was exhausted, and all I did was sit on the sidelines to cue people. Thank goodness the team only handled the second semester Spiritual Emphasis Week, or they would have been working on SEW for first semester from the start of the school year.

At the end of the day, we split up to run a last few errands. When I got back from returning the keys to the theater department, Chaplain Nate was just locking up his office for the night. Everybody else had left.

"Are you planning on joining the team?" he asked me, before I could ask where everybody had gone.

They had been talking about going to dinner somewhere, to avoid the picnic in the stadium, hosted by the fraternities and sororities. I had assumed that when they said "we," I was included. I guessed wrong, since nobody waited for me. At least Chaplain Nate was just too worn out to notice my abandoned-and-suffering-low-blood-sugar dazed panic.

"I don't know. Andy sort of drafted me." I shrugged.

"Yeah, he has a tendency to do that." He laughed, so I must not have looked too pathetic. "Think about it, though. It's nice to have the visionaries and leaders. But we need the people who know how to actually make it work."

"Is that a step up from the grunts who don't even get their name in the program?"

That got another laugh from him. He thanked me again and offered me a ride to the cafeteria. I didn't feel like reminding him that everyone was supposed to attend the picnic. Those of us who didn't want to be accosted by the recruiters for the fraternities, sororities, and ministry groups had the option of the Grease Pit, and various other diners within walking distance.

"I think I'll head back to my dorm. Tonia should be moved in by now."

Chaplain Nate asked me again to consider joining the team, so I knew it wasn't just politeness or desperation for some topic of conversation. We parted at the back door of the administration building, and I had a nice glow that carried me about two-thirds of the way across campus. Then the smell of the hot dogs cooking in the stadium behind my dormitory parking lot hit me. My stomach woke up and remembered it was empty. It hurt, punishing me for neglecting it.

With my luck, I figured Tonia had already arrived, moved in, and run off to the picnic. I ran through my list of options as I staggered up the stairs to my dorm room. Maybe now was the time to hit the grocery store. I could stock our refrigerator and reward myself for working on a day I had planned to be lazy. I quickly discovered Tonia had arrived and left a note on the bed, commanding me to join her for dinner at the Grease Pit.

Funny how fast I could run when I was weak with hunger.

I found Tonia at a table where she could see the door, snarfing a rack of ribs and a double helping of coleslaw. She could get away with that kind of eating since she had been born skinny as a rake and stayed that way no matter what she ate. If I didn't love her so much, I would have hated her. She gave me a big barbecue sauce grin when I waved and ran for the counter to order.

Tonia was the coolest girl I'd ever met. She had a talent for making odds and ends from the Salvation Army store look like the latest fashions. She saw no need to crush her internal organs to wear something currently "in" or make herself look three sizes smaller. She had the gift of looking equally as elegant in an oversized camouflage jacket as she did in the red silk Mandarin-style dress she wore to church. She had a coffee-and-cream complexion, and didn't wear a speck of makeup.

Today she had her hair in a dozen braids, all wound with ribbons in graduating shades, so it went from red on her left ear, through purple and blue, to orange on her right ear. A walking rainbow. She wore enough bracelets to sound like a junk truck when she moved.

Knowing Tonia's eating habits, I ordered a peanut butter malt ice cream swirler along with my dinner. I got it in front of her just as she turned to look for me. All she got out was "Hey, E–" then looked down and saw that jumbo-sized cup. She snorted and gave me a cocked eyebrow look Spock would have envied as I slid into the seat opposite her.

"So, you learned to read minds over the summer?" she asked in a fake, nasal Bronx accent.

"If only. That would sure help me pass my tests." I saluted her with my sandwich and took a bite.

"Tell me about it." She winked, picked up the plastic spoon and dug in. I didn't mind her moaning because I was very near to asking my chicken sandwich to marry me.

By the time she had plowed about one-third of the way through her swirler, I had inhaled most of my sandwich and my first plate of salad.

"So, where were you when I came in?" She put aside her ice cream long enough to gather up her trash and put it on the end of the table.

"You're not going to believe this."

"Sister-mine, after the summer I had, I could believe almost anything. Even if you tell me Elvis is teaching first semester." Tonia couldn't stand Elvis. Something to do with capes and rhinestones, and the fact that even though the guy was dead, he kept coming out with new albums.

Chapter 2

I told Tonia about running into Andy at the Student Center and having lunch.

"So that was yesterday. What about today?" She spooned up a big blob of her swirler and paused, with brown drips plopping down into her cup. "Don't tell me. He suckered you into helping him answer questions?"

So I told her the highlights -- or lowlights -- of the day with the team.

"Lizabeth and Marcy are both nice," she said, "once you get to know them. Unless they think you're after Andy."

I had to laugh. Once Andy didn't need my help, he wouldn't even know who I was. I told Tonia that.

"A guy who's so involved in missions and the Chapel Team might not be that shallow. Did you ever think of that?"

"Ever hear of legalists trying to earn their way to Heaven?"

"You are such a pessimist."

"Nope, just burned too many times to go anywhere without an asbestos suit."

Tonia had witnessed several bad situations courtesy of self-appointed Saint Bill. He leap-frogged from one church to another every time his feelings got hurt and he didn't get the authority or adoration he thought he deserved. Every time his new church family gave him a list of sure-fire requirements to get into heaven, he threatened my parents and me with hellfire if we didn't conform. Being away at college hadn't protected me. Not even from lecturing phone calls at midnight.

"Hey, that stuff is dangerous. Keep away from me." She leaned back in her chair and made a cross with her fingers.

We laughed. The world was finally how I expected for the start of the school year. Tonia was there, I still glowed from a great summer, I had a job for next summer, and I was just tired enough to decide if I never saw Andy Carleone again, it wouldn't matter.

That satisfied, warm haze stayed with me even when we got back to the dorm and two notes hung on the door. Tonia snatched them both up and read them to me as we stepped into our room. Andy had called, apologizing for not waiting for me for dinner. The other note asked me to meet for breakfast, to do some last-minute work on the chapel service.

"Evie's got a da-aa-ate," Tonia sang.

"With the Chapel Team?"

"Oh, fudgicles." Her smirk died, and she dropped down onto her bed.

*****

Tricia came to get me the next morning on the way to breakfast. That just proved I was valued for what I could contribute to the team and had nothing to do with Andy. We talked about the skit as we walked across campus to the cafeteria. Lizabeth and Marcy caught up with us, coming from the eight-plex where they shared a bare-bones apartment with two other girls.

I sat at the far end of the table from Andy at breakfast. He thanked me for all the work I did the day before, which was nice. But *noticing* Eve Miller, the nearly-invisible-girl? Nope.

The skit was a success during chapel. Marcy insisted I had to join the team. She was a drama major, and according to her, the backstage people were just as important as the ones with lines. That glow from feeling wanted and appreciated lasted me the entire day.

Lizabeth flagged me down at lunchtime and asked me to sit with her. Along with the dates and times for the Chapel Team meetings for the entire semester, she gave me the scoop on World History 201. Specifically, Dr. Throckmorton's pop quizzes and where to go in the library for the scavenger hunts he sprang on students to destroy their weekends. She also warned me that Throckmorton awarded points or took them away for attendance. What college teacher actually took *attendance*?

So, with very little fanfare and nothing officially said, I joined the Chapel Team.

*****

Just three weeks into the school year, catastrophe struck. The speaker for first semester Spiritual Emphasis Week had to cancel. All the arrangements made last year were trashed, and SEW was only two weeks away. Chaplain Nate called the team together to brainstorm.

Andy and Chaplain Nate both told me they were glad I was on the team. My experience organizing Bible camps and fixing last-minute catastrophes and failures might just come in handy. So we got to work, full steam ahead. It felt good being part of the team, and needed.

I thought I was *just* part of the team, until something weird happened just four days later.

Andy met up with me in front of the cafeteria, on the way to breakfast. We slid through the line, talking about the progress of SEW. I thought we were headed for the table where the team usually sat, but Andy led me into the overflow annex instead. We talked about SEW during breakfast, which was hurried because we had errands to run. On the way out the door, I looked at our usual table.

Most of the team was there, with open notebooks and Ken taking notes. Their trays had dirty dishes, meaning they had been there, eating and working, for a while.

Why did Andy hide from the team?

Thanks to years of Bill's taunting, my first reaction was to assume

Andy didn't want anyone to see him come in with me.

I always hated those novels where the girl suffered through half the book and then found out the problem between her and the hero was all a misunderstanding. She should have just *asked* the guy in chapter two what was going on.

So after trying *not* to stew about that mystery all day, I ran into Andy in the cafeteria line at dinner. I figured, get it over with quickly. After all, it wasn't like we were *together* in any way, shape or form.

When I asked him if he went into the annex to avoid everybody else, Andy gave me a crooked grin, like a bad little boy caught making a mess. A bad little boy who knew he would be forgiven because he was so cute.

For about two seconds, I wanted to punch his lights out.

"If you didn't want to be seen with me, you could have just let me sit down first, and then sat somewhere else at the table." I turned to walk away. No way did I want him to see me cry. Not that I was about to cry. But why risk it?

Andy stepped in front of me to stop me. "What makes you think I don't want to be seen with you?"

"We could have sat with the team and got some work done."

"Yeah, but don't you get sick of living and breathing and eating Spiritual Emphasis Week?"

"It's fun."

"For you, maybe. Sometimes I just want it to be us having breakfast. Got me?"

The *Hallelujah Chorus* went off in my head, but I had enough self-control to keep my face calm and say I was sorry. We got into line for dinner. I knew something good had happened, but the breeze from something passing right over my head was strong enough to be felt.

"Hey, Eve." He leaned in so close I caught a whiff of his spicy aftershave. He grinned. "Rewind the tape. What'd I just say?"

"You need a break from working on Spiritual Emphasis Week." All I could do was mirror his grin as we moved up in line.

Andy wanted to be with me.

We ate dinner with Mike, Tyrone and Amira. It was nice, once I remembered to breathe. Just a bunch of college kids. Mike had work-study at the Playhouse fall semester, and he had been helping me collect all the props for SEW. Tyrone was this unwashed art geek who hung out with the theater students. He did most of the talking because nobody could stop Tyrone talking. We sort of slipped comments about SEW in among his rambling discourse. Amira was there because she was in love with Mike. He didn't know it, because he only saw her as a friend. At least he was nice to her. When I was relatively sane, I knew that was all I had with Andy.

*****

15

Sunday, the team went to Andy's church in a college van. The plan was to ask his pastor to speak at the big wrap-up for SEW. Andy and those who had visited his church before insisted his pastor was perfect for the wrap-up. After listening to his sermon that morning, I agreed. He had a good sense of humor. He spoke about Solomon, and what a mess he made of his life. Kind of like all the pretty people in high school who rested on their successes and didn't do anything with their lives once they got out into the real world.

After the sermon, we hung around near the front of the sanctuary while Pastor Hellingar greeted people and answered questions. It was a nice little church. Clean and modern inside, with a decent sound system. The pews weren't packed, but full, with room for growth. Pastor was a big man with an uneven tan, making me think he was part-time pastor and part-time farmer.

When Andy presented his request, he demonstrated a great talent as a used car salesman. He sounded like he was doing his pastor a favor by asking him to speak to us. Pastor Hellingar said he'd need to look at the themes of each day and the scripts, but he was sure he could rearrange his schedule to help with the wrap-up.

"It'll be good to see you in action," he added, and slung a big arm around Andy's shoulders. "I'll bet your mom is proud." He looked around the sanctuary, which was empty of everyone but us. "She didn't make it today?"

"She called last night and said she was having one of her spells, so I didn't swing by to pick her up this morning." Andy shrugged.

Andy picked up his mother for church? His town was forty minutes from Blue Bell City. That was a lot of traveling.

We took a detour through a KFC and got enough food for an army. Then we went to Andy's house. His mother was waiting on the porch in a wheelchair, wrapped in a quilt. This was a warm afternoon. She knew everybody on the team, and asked about their classes and what they did over the summer.

"Chapel Team is all juniors and seniors," Mrs. Carleone said, when Andy introduced me. Why did he have to tell her I was a sophomore?

"Chaplain Nate approves, Mom," Andy said. "We wouldn't be halfway as far along in all this if it wasn't for Eve."

"That's an ill-luck name if I ever heard it," she muttered. Then she forced a creaky little laugh. "Oh, I'm sorry. I didn't mean it the way it sounded." She patted my hand. Hers felt cold and clammy. I wanted to wipe my hand on my skirt. "My medication. I have this awful tendency to say almost anything that comes into my head, whether I mean to say it or not. You'll forgive me?"

I nodded and smiled and went to help Ken and Marcy set up lunch. What was I supposed to do? Tell her she was just using her medication as an excuse to be a witch?

We had people like her at my home church, and I've met more like them everywhere I've gone. Disabled people who thought the world owed them, and they didn't have to be nice to anyone. Even knowing such an attitude wasn't Christian, I let her tick me off.

"What possessed your parents to name you Eve?" she asked me after we sat down to eat. Talk about judgmental.

"I'm the first girl in Dad's family in three generations." I shrugged, like it meant nothing. If she offered me an apple, I'd sock her one.

"How charming." She smiled like a normal, nice person, and left me alone during the meal. God's mercy.

Then she seasoned the meal with random, critical comments about people at church and in the neighborhood. I couldn't figure out why she needed to say those things when nobody on the team knew any of the people she was talking about. Would she blame this on her medication, too?

Lizabeth and Marcy gave me the lowdown on the way back to campus. According to them, Mrs. Carleone liked me. If she didn't, I would have received a lecture on how Andy was going to be a traveling minister. Any girl who wanted to join her life to his had to give up everything and everyone.

What made them think I was interested in Andy in a dating-and-hogtie-him-into-marriage kind of way?

They went on with their warning. With Andy ministering on the road, his wife would get to stay home to take care of Mommy-in-law.

I thought I knew them well enough to believe they weren't teasing me. It was a real warning, self-defense mode. I thought about all the nasty, petty complaints I had heard over lunch. My years of working for AMEA had already exposed me to people like her who suffered physical problems as a result of their bitter spirits. If Andy's mother would just give up complaining about other people, would she feel better?

I kept my thoughts to myself and was a little relieved when Andy didn't show up for breakfast Monday. The entire team met for breakfast and lunch almost every day that week. We had a lot of revising to do. Either the administration vetoed our plans, or we couldn't get the props we needed. Not encouraging.

Andy missed breakfast and chapel on Thursday, and the hurt feeling surprised me. What was wrong with me?

When I got back to my room after my afternoon class, there was a note from Andy to meet at dinner.

I waited nearly half an hour in the lobby of the cafeteria, but he never showed up. Ten minutes before the food line closed, Tonia and a couple girls from our floor walked in, so I went to dinner with them. Another note waited, taped to our door, when we got back from dinner. Tonia got to it first and just shook her head as she looked it over.

"You know, Evie, God made men first to give them a head start because He knew they'd be late for everything." She handed me the note, then grinned.

The note said Andy would call at 7. Tonia and I sat in our room with the door open, listening for the phone to ring while we studied the newspaper for the movie listings. The phone didn't make a sound. Karla and Natalie came up from first floor at 7:30, to see if we were going to the movie we talked about during dinner.

Why should I sit around waiting on him? ran through my head as we walked down the stairs and out the side door to go get Karla's car in the parking lot. There was no message from Andy when we got back.

I deliberately went to breakfast twenty minutes earlier than usual the next morning to sit alone. Just my luck, I ran into Andy in the breakfast line. He didn't even have the guts to say anything about yesterday. He just talked about the improvements in the week's skit. If he showed up early to miss me, he didn't look irritated. He probably didn't even notice.

Liberal applications of chocolate and popcorn Friday night didn't help. Neither did walking downtown to spend Saturday morning bowling with our brother floor in Willis Hall. I still gnawed on my irritation with Andy. A waste of time and energy. I knew it, but I couldn't help myself. There was enough snarling in my heart that when Andy called to tell me he was picking me up for church the next morning, I nearly said not to bother. The Chapel Team could do their work without me

I reasoned that if I changed my mind, I could tell one of the other girls on the team that I wasn't going, and they could tell Andy.

The only problem with my plan was that the team didn't go to church with Andy that Sunday. It was just Andy and me.

And his mother.

Shakespeare wrote a play called *A Comedy of Errors*. I could never figure out why all that misconnection and miscommunication was supposed to be funny. The day was a mess.

Andy drove his own car, but didn't bother telling me that. I sat in the lounge, waiting, wondering why the other girls were late. I really hoped everyone had left already. To compound the problem, Andy just sat and waited for me. After ten minutes, he could have at least got out of the car and waved to get my attention. Or even come up to the door. Why did he expect me to know what his car looked like?

At fifteen minutes, I stepped outside, thinking maybe the van was parked out of sight. As soon as I came out the door, Andy opened the door of his olive green VW minibus and waved. Finally.

"What happened to the van?" I asked as I got in the front seat.

"This is my car." He gave me a funny look, part amusement, and a little part of dawning suspicion that maybe he had messed up. This was the first time he wore that look in relation to me, and it took a few (dozen) repeated exposures before I interpreted it. At the time, I thought I had done something wrong. That was the way I was trained to think, after all.

A tiny curl of apprehension settled in my gut. Why, I had no idea. I hadn't yet learned to trust that warning sensation when it contradicted what people told me. People lied, but my inner warning system never did. If I had listened that morning, I never would have got in the van with him.

At least, I hope that was what I would have done. Who really knows? Hindsight is a whole lot clearer than how we see when we're in the middle of the mess.

"Nobody else is waiting," I said, as he started the engine.

"Nobody else is coming." He flashed that crooked grin that jumbled my brain. Then he dove into talking about all the work the team had to do this week. That saved me from asking dumb questions. Talking about SEW covered the entire drive to Andy's house.

His mother waited, in her wheelchair, out at the end of the asphalt driveway.

I choked when she pushed on the armrests of the wheelchair, stood up, and walked five wobbly steps to the front passenger door. That shot of adrenaline cleared my head. I figured out she intended to sit in the front seat. I hopped out, tried to smile, and stepped out of the way while Andy folded up the wheelchair to put it in the back.

"She wasn't ready on time?" was all his mother said, once we were on our way again.

"Eve was ready." Andy glanced over his shoulder at me and winked. "I just forgot to tell her what my car looked like."

That confession, even if it was to his mother rather than to me, was about the best part of the day.

Pastor Hellingar was a little flat that week. Maybe it was me. It wasn't much fun sitting in the front row, even if Andy did sit between me and his mother. That was where she wanted to sit, but I was raised strict Back-Row Baptist.

We went out to dinner with Pastor Tom and Ginger, the youth minister and his wife. Back home, "youth minister" meant senior high and college. In Andy's church, it meant from nursery through Singles. All Singles. No matter how gray and toothless they got.

At lunch, Mrs. Carleone made me wonder if I had met her twin sister the week before. Or maybe the sermon affected her. She smiled so much during lunch she reminded me of Jack Nicholson as the Joker.

"Evie is quite an accomplished organizer," she said, when Pastor Tom asked about SEW. "I don't know how Andy and the team managed without her before this."

I had a panic attack. Had Mrs. Carleone decided I would be the perfect, slavish pastor's wife, always in the shadows?

"Ginger, dear, I can't remember. What was your major in college?" Mrs. Carleone's eyes were bright, like this was the most important thing in her life to know.

"Accounting." Ginger laughed. "I was going to be a high-power CPA and make partner in Dad's firm before I hit thirty."

"Yes, we all have such big dreams when we're young and thinking only about what we want in life."

"I see nothing wrong with following our dreams and talents." Ginger looked at her cup of tea, not Mrs. Carleone. "How can we figure out what God wants us to do with our lives if we don't strike out and explore?"

"Yes, but as a minister's wife, your first priority is taking care of the home and your children."

I already had some ideas of what to say in defense against this line of attack. Some of the old biddies back home were already hitting me with the "college is a waste if you're going to be a wife" hammer. Problem: None of the snark I had come up with was appropriate for the moment. Pastor Tom broke in before my nerves snapped like guitar strings and I said something stupid.

"Ginger is a perfect example of what she just said." He winked -- at Ginger and me, with his head turned so Mrs. Carleone didn't see.

I loved that man, even though I had just met him.

"Ginger uses her training to benefit the church as our part-time treasurer. She brings in extra income during tax season and teaches business math at the high school." Pastor Tom smiled and stared down Mrs. Carleone. "And it doesn't interfere with her very vital role as my wife and the mother of our children."

"We tell our youth that if they put pleasing God first, then the desires of their hearts will lead them in directions that will please Him," Ginger added. That little smile she and Pastor Tom exchanged made my heart thump.

Now, that was partnership. And communication. Like they could read each other's minds.

"What do you do, Eve? What's your major?" Pastor Tom asked.

"She's only a sophomore. She's still too busy getting her requirements out of the way," Mrs. Carleone said, with a little laugh, as if Pastor Tom had wasted his breath asking.

"Eve is majoring in administration," Andy said. "She's been doing summer camps and kids' crusades and snow camps for Allen Michaels since -- what? -- middle school?"

That grin on his face made me think he was proud of me. The next astonishing deduction was that to be proud of me, he had to feel...possessive?

Tonia and I later discussed the whole weird day. She theorized Mrs. Carleone was either trying to condition me to brainless slavery or scare me away. Why would she try to scare me away when I wasn't interested in Andy, and he certainly hadn't expressed that kind of long-term interest in me?

Back to lunch: Ginger said it sounded like I had a full-time ministry waiting for me when I graduated. Mrs. Carleone countered with the old "Not if she gets married" line. So dummy me, I had to blurt that I had no boyfriend, no plans for marriage, and all signs indicated God wanted me to stay single.

"I've never had a date in my whole life," I added.

"What do you call this?" Pastor Tom gestured at Andy and me on one side of the table.

"Church isn't a date. And I thought the whole team was coming today."

Andy snorted. His face got red. "My fault," he said, when his mother demanded an explanation. "You should have seen the look on Eve's face when she came out to my car and saw we were all alone. Sorry -- guess I forgot to tell you it was just going to be us."

"I think that's charming." Mrs. Carleone smiled, her first genuine, warm expression all day. Probably because she realized I had no plans to drag Andy to the altar.

At that point, all I wanted was a silent ride back to school. The day couldn't get any worse.

I was wrong.

When we took her home, Mrs. Carleone insisted we come in and have some tea. Andy agreed. If I knew the way back to college, I probably would have walked. But since childhood, I was trained to endure lots of unpleasant things for the sake of peace. I was my father's daughter. So I said tea sounded nice, and sat down where she pointed. Mrs. Carleone smiled and rolled her wheelchair into the kitchen to make the tea.

Andy rummaged through a low bookshelf that ran the full length of the room and went right under the picture window. He said he was looking for a volume of sermons Ken wanted to borrow for class. When I commented on how many books they had in the house, Mrs. Carleone proudly told me she had been building Andy's library since he decided he was going into the ministry. In ninth grade. Half the books in the house were biblical research.

It frightened me, how much she had invested in him being a preacher. I should have stayed frightened and got away before things got serious.

Mrs. Carleone didn't put out cream or sugar with the tea. There was all sorts of debris floating in it because she didn't use a bag or infuser. I could only be grateful the spout strained out the bigger clumps. I had been raised rather sheltered. Tea came in bags and was black or orange pekoe. Period. This tea smelled spicy, was kind of a greenish-amber, and the last cup poured seemed syrupy. I prayed Andy would give me the first cup.

He did. My hero.

It tasted okay but still needed sugar. Then Andy asked his mother about the book he was looking for, and she told him it was probably in the attic bookshelves. Worse than the crazy image of someone putting bookshelves in an attic was the realization that I was going to be *alone* with her.

"You really ought to prepare yourself to consider what your husband wants," Mrs. Carleone said, the moment Andy disappeared up a flight of stairs hidden inside a closet in the living room.

"What husband?" I honestly had no idea what she was getting at.

"You'll marry eventually. You appear to be the kind of girl every mother wants her son to find. Capable. Sensible. Modest. Spiritually inclined. I'm not sure about your maturity yet." She tipped her head to one side and looked me over, head to toe.

"I'm not even dating. If I ever fall in love and decide to get married, that's when I'll consider how to change my life. Why ruin my life by limiting what I'm learning and doing right now on the off chance some guy will be desperate enough to want me?"

"Desperate? My, you do have a bad self-image, don't you?"

"Criticism from people who don't know me doesn't help."

Maybe that was a little too strong. She deserved it.

She just smiled a little wider. Kind of like a shark.

"A Christian wife puts her husband's ministry ahead of her life, her dreams, everything she's ever done until that time."

If she had a pulpit, she would have been banging it.

"Shouldn't *my* ministry, the talents that God gave me, be considered? Why would God give me work to do just to chuck it all for a diamond ring?"

"Marriage is a partnership, Mom," Andy said.

I was so glad to see her jump and spill a little tea on her lap. She even looked guilty -- for about half a second.

"Anybody who knows what Eve can do, and demands that she give up everything to stay home and cook, is an idiot. And you've got no business hitting her with questions like that, Mom." His shoulders were hunched and his voice was really tight. I had never seen Andy mad before, and it scared me.

Fortunately, he had found the book he was after. We left about ten seconds later.

Andy and I were both quiet until we got through all three stop lights in town and reached the county road.

"Sorry. Kind of a rough day for you, huh?" he said.

"Starting when you picked me up this morning. I wish you had warned me."

"Why wouldn't I take you to church, just the two of us?"

"It's not like we're dating."

"Do you want to?"

"Guys like you don't date girls like me."

Ever since I could remember, my mother's friends would say, "Sure, guys date girls like *her*. But they marry girls like *you*." That never helped. How could that guy know he wanted to marry me if he didn't want to date me?

"Okay, I'm confused. What kind of guy am I?"

"Smart and popular, and you can play all those instruments. I can't even get hold of a guitar, much less get lessons. And you always seem to know what to do and say. You always look good, no matter how tired you are and..." I shrugged.

"That sounds good. Why wouldn't I want to date a girl like you?" He laughed. It had to be his nervous, maybe irritated laugh, because he didn't snort, and it didn't last long.

"We're completely different."

"Okay. Blonde and brunette. Senior and sophomore. I'm from close by and you're three states away. Male and female. What's the big deal?"

"I never know what to say, and I'm clumsy and fat and I don't dress right and -- look, doesn't the fact that I *don't* date make you wonder what's wrong with me?"

"You're not fat, and talking isn't everything. Maybe there's something wrong with the guys you grew up with. City living, y'know. Clouds the brain."

I had to laugh. I finally dared to look at him. He was smiling at me.

Then I looked around at the intersection where we stopped.

"This isn't the way back to school."

"I know. Want to hit a movie?"

"Why?"

"Hanging around together at school isn't dating. So, let's make it official, okay?"

Andy didn't try to kiss me when he dropped me off at my dorm, but it was an official date. He also offered to teach me to play guitar, which meant he had actually *listened* to my gush of words.

Tonia and I talked for about an hour after I got back to our room, analyzing the whole weird day, and then I had to go to bed. The next morning was the first day of Spiritual Emphasis Week. I had no time to get used to the idea that Andy and I were dating. No time or energy to think about it.

Maybe if I had the time to think things through, I might have decided to walk away.

Chapter 3

"There she is!" Ken called, when I reached the team table for breakfast Monday morning. "Hey, Eve, we were taking bets that you'd finally had enough and jumped ship." He grinned at someone over my shoulder -- who turned out to be Andy, coming up behind me. "I know this guy is a slave driver, but don't let him scare you away. We've all decided, even if you can't stand Andy, you have to stay on the team with us."

The rest of the team laughed and took turns begging me to stay for the sake of their sanity. Marcy reminded me of some of the horror stories they had told me, big mistakes Andy made when he was in charge of things last year. I put my tray down. Jake slid his tray over to take over the empty seat next to me. Andy slammed his tray down, blocking the move, and slid into the seat next to me.

"Don't let these idiots scare you off," he said. "I like you for more than how you keep me in line."

"Like what?" I challenged. Andy's mouth moved a few times, but no sound came out. "So you only keep me around for my notebook?"

Andy winked at me and leaned closer, lowering his voice, but not enough to keep it just between us. "Even if you were nasty and had bad breath, I'd keep you around. You're kind of useful."

What made him think that was flattering?

*****

How come when a sign says "Keep Out," or the equivalent, everybody and his dog wants to get in? I spent more time Monday playing gatekeeper backstage than cueing people. Why did everyone want to get backstage when they should have been attending chapel?

Coach Wagner offered a couple of his linebackers to stand guard the rest of the week. The football players were more than willing to help. They got chapel credit and didn't have to go inside if they didn't want to.

Tuesday, however, we learned that it was useless to worry about the doors. Someone should have guarded the ceiling!

In a word: Paratroopers.

Gerbils, with parachutes made of green plastic garbage bags and harnesses made from dental floss. Dropped down through holes in the ceiling where the basketball backstops used to hang when the chapel doubled as the gym. Right on the stage. During the opening skit.

Spot-on timing. Andy came out dressed as Death with a black robe and skull mask. He got the first gerbil right on top of his head. A perfect four-point landing. I stood in the wings and had a front row view of all the action when the garbage bag flopped down over his face.

Greg shrieked and danced around with a bag hanging down his back. He had been kneeling when a gerbil hit his neck and went into the gap of his collar.

Five gerbils in all invaded the skit. It took ten minutes to catch them, despite those garbage bags dragging like chutes on Indy cars.

Chaplain Nate revised his lesson to take in the invasion, and chapel only let out ten minutes behind schedule. He had to fight not to laugh when some of his comments got snickers and whispers from the audience. There was some whispering behind stage that made me think I had been left out of an inside joke. What were the chances someone on our team had been involved in the miniature paratrooper stunt? It gave me an odd, betrayed sensation to suspect I was on the outside looking in. I had really thought I was part of the "gang" now.

I didn't have time to brood over the state of my social life. I flew through classes and scrambled to get last-minute changes smoothed over for SEW. When I dropped into bed each night, I wondered where the energy came from.

Thursday, I found out how Andy looked and sounded when he got righteous, wrath-of-God *angry.*

Somebody stole all the chairs from the chapel. Nine hundred chairs. Thirty rows of fifteen chairs on each side of the central aisle.

At least the chair-nappers hadn't taken the chairs from the cafeteria. We could hold chapel with everyone standing. Not all that comfortable for forty-five minutes, but it could be done. Eating meals standing up would have been a little harder.

Andy went quiet when he got mad. He talked slowly, clenched his fists and jammed them in his pockets, and glared at the floor. It struck me that he seemed paralyzed for the first few minutes of shock, rather than galvanized by his anger, like some people.

While the rest of us stood around with no idea what to do, twenty minutes until the doors opened for chapel, Andy stomped out through the side door by the stage. Something clattered and banged, sounding like metal crashing against the cinderblock wall.

"I think he found a chair," Ken said.

I looked. He was right. One folding chair had been left leaning against the wall. Andy had tripped over it.

His face was still red when he came back two minutes later with Chaplain Nate. And a ransom note, with the stereotypical letters cut from the newspaper and glued onto a page.

And just what did they demand, to return the chairs?

Pizza for dinner. "Real pizza. Preferably Godfather's. Or the Grease Pit."

The thieves had a point. The soggy cardboard, wax cheese and red watercolor that passed for pizza in the cafeteria certainly wasn't worthy of the name.

Coach Wagner and the day's volunteer guards showed up about then. He took the note from Chaplain Nate, read it, then laughed and pointed at the doors.

"Hit the mats, boys."

Specifically, wrestling and gymnastics mats. We got them lugged over from the gym and spread out just before the doors opened.

Despite having no time to review the skit and schedule, and only enough time for a quick prayer along the lines of, "Lord, help us!" chapel went well. Lots of energy.

The chair-nappers were sloppy. They left a trail of chairs all the way to the hiding place. By the time chapel finished, the maintenance staff had retrieved the long carts full of chairs, ready to put them back in place once the chapel had emptied out.

Getting the chairs back meant no pizza ransom.

We wouldn't have minded some real pizza. Especially after all the work of dragging those heavy, smelly wrestling mats back and forth.

Somehow, we got through to the big wrap-up Saturday afternoon without any more immature tricks or a dozen possible disasters. I should have been celebrating my freedom to go back to my normal schedule. Instead, the celebration dinner just added to the weird quotient.

We went to the Gondola, a pseudo-Italian restaurant about a mile down the highway from campus. Pastor Hellingar sat at one end of the long table. Chaplain Nate sat at the other. We ended up with mostly the girls on one side and the guys on the other. Somebody made a joke about old-fashioned church seating. Andy ended up opposite me, by Pastor.

Conversation was loud with a lot of laughter, basically rehashing every glitch and glory moment through the whole week. When the waiter brought our entrees, conversations broke into small, separate knots.

Pastor leaned closer. "So, how are things going with you and Andy? According to his mother, you two are a couple."

"A couple?" I glanced at Andy. He was talking to Buckley. "She thinks every girl wants to marry him."

"Hmm, maybe. She's justifiably concerned about his dedication. There are a lot of temptations in this world, especially for a young man with so much talent."

"She thinks I'll lead him away from the pulpit?" That fit the message she had slapped me with the week before.

"No. Just the opposite." Pastor Hellingar shook his head. An adorable, crooked grin brightened his chunky farmer's face. "She thinks you're a good choice as a helpmate. If you can keep from being discouraged."

"*She* was trying to scare me away."

"She wants someone who will make it easier for Andy to devote himself full-time to service."

"Barefoot, pregnant and in the kitchen."

"Excuse me?" From the sparkles in his eyes, I knew he understood exactly what I meant.

"Last year, I was warned to stay away from the pre-sem students. Especially Dr. Rittsmer's devotees. They all believe a pastor's wife should never work outside the home -- *after* she spends years working to put him through seminary. If she has an education, she has to give it up. She's nothing but his shadow, there to sit in the front row and make dinner for visiting ministers."

"Does that sound like any pastor's wife you've ever seen?" He laughed loudly enough to get Andy's attention.

"No." I avoided Andy's gaze and wished he'd go back to talking to Buckley.

"Do any of those pre-seminary students have girlfriends?"

"From what I've heard, they mostly get freshmen. They claim they want a girl who hasn't chosen a field of study. So she won't have wasted her time and money on school."

"You're talking about the pre-sem monks?" Andy said. "Did you hear about Sledewski's paper for Rittsmer?" He waited. Pastor Hellingar and I both shook our heads. "He got his new girlfriend to type it for him. She got as far as 'barefoot, pregnant and obedient,' and tore the paper to shreds. Then she went out and enrolled in the business club."

I had heard about Randall Sledewski. He was a senior, heading for some big, ultra-conservative seminary that required jackets and ties to attend class. Rumor said he was panicking because that seminary only admitted married students. The premise was that both partners in the team got necessary training, but how could a wife get that training if she was working to put her husband through seminary? Sledewski hadn't lied last year when he was accepted. He had been about to propose to an education major. He applied for a couple jobs for her *before* he asked her to marry him. I was there when she came back to our dormitory the night he made his lame excuse for a marriage proposal and heard her side of the story.

Sledewski's first mistake was to tell her she'd have to wait for her diamond ring until after he got out of seminary. Then he declared it was God's will for them to get married. When she said God hadn't told *her* to marry him, he responded that she should get used to it. Once they were married, she had to accept God speaking solely through him, because married women were just extensions of their husbands.

His mouth was faster than his reflexes. She popped him one and he never saw it coming. She pitched in a summer softball league back home.

"You believe a minister's wife should have a life and interests of her own, don't you, Andy?" Pastor Hellingar said.

"Absolutely." Andy toyed with his glass, drawing in the condensation on the wooden tabletop. "If she's interesting enough to fall in love with, he should want her to stay interesting. Not be a Stepford wife."

"You two are a good team. You like each other. You're both devoted to the Lord's work." Pastor nodded. "Many people have started with a lot less and made good marriages."

"We only had one date," I blurted. "I'm not looking at rings and invitations any time soon, thanks!"

Andy laughed at that, too. I felt relieved, but kind of sick, too. That made no sense.

Pastor glanced back and forth between us. "Andy, you're a good son. You stay close to look after your mother, when you would thrive at a bigger school. Your short-term missions and service trips can't last forever. You're heading to seminary next winter."

"Next winter? What about next fall?" I had to ask.

"I'm technically a senior," Andy said with a shrug. He didn't look me in the eye. "I won't be graduating until the end of fall semester next year. It's just the way the classes are scheduled around here. The ones I need for graduation are only offered every other year, and I didn't take them last year, so..." He offered a lopsided smile. "Lucky me. I get to do Chapel Team one more year."

"And it allows more time for your mother to get her full strength back," Pastor Hellingar said.

"Yeah, well..."

"Your mother thinks Eve would make a good pastor's wife for a big, busy congregation."

"I'm going to be a youth minister." His usual grin was back. "I plan on traveling, doing youth camps, seminars and revivals. I couldn't tie myself to one pulpit. It's not me."

"I'm afraid your mother is trying to convince you to do just that."

He forced a chuckle, and that fake, vicious grin returned. "Sorry, Eve. I really like you, but I can't get tied to one place. I have to ditch you and find some bimbo to ruin my life."

"Thanks for the warning." I managed to laugh, and from the way he relaxed, I was pretty sure I put on a good performance.

*****

October rolled in. I only saw Andy at Chapel Team breakfast meetings. That just backed up what I had suspected: he was only interested in what I could do to help him. Those guitar lessons, "As soon as SEW is over and we have free time," never materialized. I wasn't surprised.

I had my first fibroid attack of the school year, probably brought on by all the stress of SEW. I was in pity party mode, so Tonia and I hit the grocery store Friday night for provisions to have breakfast in bed

Saturday. We stayed in our pajamas until ten and read for fun instead of studying. It was pure bliss, until Andy called, wanting to know why I didn't show up for breakfast. He sounded irritated. I didn't show up when he expected me, so I was in the wrong?

That probably wasn't the situation, but that was how I saw it. How was I supposed to know how to act with a guy who *might* be my first boyfriend?

I was trying to figure out what to say without whining when he asked me to meet him for lunch. I didn't think, I just agreed.

"Girl, I think you're making a mistake. The guy is Houdini for days, and you just come running when he whistles?" Tonia said, when I got back to our room and told her about the call.

"I thought you liked Andy."

"He could be a Nobel Prize winner, but he just broke the first rule of a good relationship: expecting you to read his teeny tiny mind and show up when he wants you. Call and tell him you got a better offer. Then you and me, we'll go to the Pit."

That sounded like something Natalie down the hall would do. Sure, she had two guys fighting for her attention, but she always struck me as selfish. Besides, who had time for *two* guys in her life? I couldn't figure myself out at that stage, let alone try to understand a male mind.

Before I left for lunch, Tonia said, "If Andy doesn't make some kind of commitment, even if it's just breakfast every day, he isn't interested enough. Let him go. Other guys will be interested. Especially if they know you dumped him."

"Guys aren't worth the headaches."

She laughed. I gnawed on what she said on my walk to the cafeteria. So when Andy asked how come I missed breakfast and didn't tell him I wasn't coming, I spoke my mind.

"I honestly didn't think it was set in stone."

"Set in stone?" Andy snorted. I recognized that sound now. It translated as *you're being ridiculous.*

"You've got a lot of nerve, expecting me to show up for breakfast when you feel like showing up." Tonia was right. I should have bailed on him.

"So a guy can't be worried when you're not there like you always are?"

"How do you know? You only show up for breakfast when it's a Chapel Team meeting."

"Hah! So it *is* about me missing breakfast."

"No, it's you expecting a commitment from me, when I can't depend on you."

"O … kay …" For some reason, that got through to him. "So it's time for the commitment talk?

"Hardly!"

"So you're getting ready to dump me before we even get started?" Laughter touched his eyes.

I wanted to punch the arrogant jerk. I focused on my toasted cheese and salad and hoped he would vanish while I wasn't looking at him.

After about five mouthfuls, I couldn't choke down any more. Tonia was right. I should have gone to the Pit with her. I stood up to leave and he caught my wrist when I reached to pick up my tray.

"What's your hurry?" he said.

"I have things to do."

"What about me?"

"You can do whatever you want."

"Eve, what's really wrong?"

"You're a thoughtless, oblivious jerk." I tugged hard enough to free my wrist. "You're no different from all the guys in my church."

The really sad part? Andy had been touching me, and I didn't get any tingles.

"Let me prove I *am* different."

"How?"

Yes, I know, that was the wrong response. It implied I was interested, if not desperate.

"Let's just goof around this weekend." Andy's smile relaxed. "We'll go to a movie tonight, okay? The last Concert on the Square is tomorrow afternoon. We'll go after church."

I froze. Inside and out. No way was I ever going near his home church or his mother. Ever again. Not after the Mama Jekyl and Mrs. Hyde routine.

"You're doing it again. Assuming I agreed to something when I didn't. Meeting for breakfast. Going to church with you."

"What's wrong with my church?" He had a little ripple in his voice, like he wanted to laugh but couldn't figure out if he should.

"I don't want to go anywhere near your mother."

"Mom's just...careful. She's trying to protect me."

"What happens when she isn't around to nag you to stay on the straight and narrow?"

"It's not like that." Andy's voice could have turned lava to ice cubes in about ten seconds flat.

"I don't think she's protecting you. She wants to make sure you stay close to her."

"What's wrong with that?"

"Ask Oedipus."

His mouth dropped open. He stared at me for about ten, fifteen seconds. I knew because my heart was thudding loud enough and fast enough to keep accurate time.

Andy leaned back in his chair and laughed. I grabbed my purse to run. He snagged my sleeve when I reached to pick up my lunch tray for the second time.

He snickered once more. "I think I'm going to be flattered you're so upset."

"I don't care toad squat, you know that? You're just like every other guy in this college."

"Mom likes you."

"Your mom thinks I'm chasing you. I'm not. I refuse to chase any guy."

"Gee, I kind of like being chased. Good for my ego."

Long before I met Andy, I had deciphered some basic rules in dating: Guys who get chased keep running. If you catch them, they feel trapped. They only value what they have to work for. If they think they've been caught or trapped, they run. If a guy chases a girl, he'll always wonder if he's really got her, and he keeps working to make sure nobody has her. He's too busy to get into trouble. Everybody's happy.

I couldn't tell Andy that. It would probably scare him away. Tonia told me later that he was probably scared already. She believed guys didn't have any idea how girls saw the whole dating and mating routine. If they did, it'd scare them and the Human race would be doomed.

When I tugged my arm free, he let me go. My stomach felt so hollow, it hurt. It made me mad. No stupid guy was ever going to make me feel that way. I grabbed my tray and my purse and stomped up to the dish line.

I had no idea if Andy was still sitting there when I went out the side door. I refused to turn and look. Letting him know I cared enough to look would only feed an ego big enough to swallow New York and Tokyo and still have room to take on Chicago for dessert.

That afternoon, after Tonia gave me a lot of good advice and interpreted the whole stupid argument, we agreed on one thing: The only reason the Human race had a chance to continue was because so many jerks were either cute or charming, and so many girls were either desperate or stupid or both.

*****

I didn't see Andy for a whole week outside of Chapel Team meetings. We didn't talk. Nobody seemed to notice.

Chaplain Nate asked me to work on the Thanksgiving mission trip. This year, it was a youth program in Nebraska, to keep high school kids busy over the holiday weekend. I refused. Not because I wanted to go home for Thanksgiving. Who would want to endure another pilgrimage to Uncle Lawrence's house, for indigestion and lectures about how every part of my life was a mistake?

I planned to stay on campus even before I was asked to work the mission trip. Lots of students at SCC didn't go home for Thanksgiving because it was such a long trip for such a short time home. I told Chaplain Nate I already had plans. I planned to sleep in late and relax and read.

I was a coward, and I knew it. The idea of being in close quarters with Andy for five days straight gave me a headache. I kept telling myself I was better off without him. St. Paul said being single was better if we really wanted to focus on serving God, right?

Then the fall rains hit. People told me the fall rains were worse than they had been in twenty years. I wasn't around for the last flood, so I had to take their word for it.

Flooding and a couple direct hits with lightning knocked out power through the whole town. It was pretty awesome to walk through Blue Bell City and see nothing but flashlights, candles, and lanterns. Then some idiot in a pickup without headlights decided he didn't have to stop at an intersection and wait his turn when the traffic lights died. He hit a tank truck -- full of chlorine.

Most of the campus on that side of town got evacuated to the Student Center. Chaplain Nate asked me to help pass out supplies to those who were stranded overnight. Sandwiches, blankets, flashlights. Fortunately, my dorm was on the far side of town from the accident, so we didn't have to move.

I ran into Andy when I was helping unload one of the trucks bringing food from the cafeteria. Literally. I turned around with a crate of sandwiches and he backed into me as he maneuvered a stadium-sized dispenser of milk. He started to smile, then froze. Like maybe he expected me to hit him?

About five feet away, rain pounded down in a solid curtain off the overhang, so hard I expected to see an ark pull up. Loud. And cold. Everyone else had taken loads inside, so it was just us in the doorway.

"Kind of wet, huh?" He set down the dispenser.

Andy's comment was so lame and so not him, I had to laugh. He grinned. "Ready for midterms?"

"Is anyone ever ready?"

"Nope."

We traded grins. There was nothing more to say.

"Been keeping busy?" Andy slammed the gate on the truck.

I should have said something neutral and got out of there. "Always busy."

"Wish you were helping with the Thanksgiving trip."

"I am." That came out a little stronger than I meant it.

"Yeah. Prep work. But you won't be with the team." He gave me his sad puppy look.

"I'd like to go home for Thanksgiving." Yes, I lied, but he was trying to make me feel guilty. "Not like I can go home every weekend if I want."

He frowned at me. Okay, it was a low blow, but I was cold and Andy made me nervous. I missed that extra oxygen feeling I got when he smiled at me.

"I know Mom can be a little pushy. But she does like you."

"She wants to guilt-trip me into being her nursemaid."

"What?" He shook his head, like that would help him hear better.

We weren't together anymore, so why hold back? I told him what Lizabeth and Marcy told me about his mother. Andy frowned deeper, but it wasn't like he was mad. More like confused.

"You know, a live-in nurse is a whole lot cheaper than marriage."

"Oh, that makes me feel better."

Andy laughed. Standing there, looking into his eyes, everything seemed all right again, despite the damp, cold, and rampant flooding.

"You know, we've both been really stupid," he said so softly, I almost couldn't hear him over the rain. "Mom doesn't need a nurse, anyway."

"She doesn't really need that wheelchair, does she?" I adjusted my grip on the crate and turned to leave. There were some things better left unsaid.

"You think it's all in her head?"

"Maybe not her head, but her heart."

"That's a new one." He didn't sound or look angry. He finally hefted the dispenser up onto the cart to push it into the gym.

"There was this guy in my church. His wife left him. Just drove away with her boyfriend. And their little girl ran after the car. Screaming for her to come back. Within a few months, he was crippled by arthritis. The doctors couldn't do anything for him. When he let go of his bitterness and forgave his wife, he improved."

"Mom's not--" He sighed and nodded for me to go through the door ahead of him. He didn't look angry, so I took the chance and kept talking.

"That's why she scares me, I think. She's so critical. That first visit, all she did was criticize people in church and in town. People none of us even knew. I'm no doctor or psychologist or whatever, but I've seen some really weird things, working for the Allen Michaels people. Our heads can make a big difference. I'm not saying she'll get healed if she's nicer, and thinks about other people, but it might help her to help other people, instead of griping all the time."

"Yeah, I can just see Mom wheeling around town, delivering flowers and meals for the shut-ins."

He laughed with that snort I had come to really -- well, not love, but I missed it. We reached the gym and put our loads down on the table where the food was being set up.

"Want to head into Davenport for a movie, maybe that video game place Troy was so hot about?"

That question caught me off guard. Enough that I didn't say the first thing that popped into my head. Namely, that he'd do all the playing, and I'd watch.

"Uh...I guess. When?"

"Well, if all the bridges haven't been washed out, tomorrow afternoon?" His grin just about took my balance. I certainly didn't feel cold or wet or tired anymore.

"Sounds good. That'll give us time to sleep in and study."

"That's what I missed. You always remember the important things. I'd be a mess without you."

That wasn't the best thing to say. It meant he hadn't really been listening because hadn't I just said I didn't want to be somebody's caretaker? But dummy me, feeling that hollow sensation again and missing it so desperately, I didn't realize what I had just learned: Andy was looking for a babysitter.

The next day, I had an impromptu lesson on how God makes us eat our words.

Chapter 4

The whole mess started with...a mess. A bunch of idiots (seniors) decided the lake that had taken over the Commons would make a perfect football field. Mud football is *the* sport for real men, supposedly.

Real men didn't believe in avoiding hundred-year-old trees.

I was heading to the cafeteria for lunch with Tonia and Lynn and a couple girls from the basement. We heard the shouting and stopped to watch the battle of mudmen. I didn't even know Andy was playing. Any sensible person would have been catching the last half hour of lunch and maybe studying.

Then again, these were senior boys. Proof that testosterone caused brain damage.

I heard my name. Honestly, even in a Christian college, how many Eves could there be? I turned, and there was this muddy figure waving at me and jumping up and down, holding the ball. At least, I assumed that dripping glob in his hands was the ball.

Tonia laughed. "That can't be Andy!"

I had my doubts, until he pulled off his stocking cap, revealing semi-clean blond hair. He waved the hat, spattering mud in every direction, and shouted for me to stay and watch.

"No way," one of the basement girls said. "There's Tim McCarr!" She shrieked and ran. We all ran.

Tim McCarr made the Incredible Hulk look like a featherweight. Plowing through mud and water, he churned up a wake the Loch Ness Monster would have envied. Waves swamped the sidewalk as McCarr headed straight for us.

Some guys shouted for him to leave us alone. Andy led the charge of five guys headed on a collision course to stop McCarr. When they hit him en masse, they changed his direction and went rolling and sliding through the mud and water.

The whole ugly, tumbling knot of them hit probably the biggest tree in the entire county, sitting in the corner of the crisscross of sidewalks through the Commons. Naturally, Andy was the point of impact.

He only broke one bone in his forearm. It could have been his head or his back or his legs or both arms or a combination of all of the above.

We spent the afternoon in the emergency room instead of going to Davenport.

To make a miserable situation worse, Drake, Andy's idiot roommate had some Tylenol with codeine, left over from getting his wisdom teeth pulled. Did that explain why he was such an idiot? He gave Andy two before they put him into a hot shower to wash the mud off so they could assess the damage. Then someone else saw the container and gave Andy two more, and he was in too much shock to refuse to swallow.

At the hospital, Andy huddled on an ugly pea green vinyl two-seater couch in the waiting room, trying not to fall asleep, while Drake and I tried to talk the nurse into putting him ahead of everyone. We couldn't even get a doctor to talk to us long enough to tell him about the codeine, much less look at Andy's arm. He just sat there, curled up around his arm and the makeshift splint, whimpering every once in a while. Then he looked ashamed for making each sound. Like he wasn't allowed to feel pain? Andy wouldn't say, or maybe he couldn't say, if something else got whacked against the tree. We had to wait for x-rays, or at least for the daze from the codeine to wear off, so he could think clearly.

Drake went to find the cafeteria. I was relieved, because he was driving me crazy, rocking back and forth and cracking his knuckles. Some people were just nervous in hospitals, even when they weren't the patients. How did Andy ever get stuck with him? I asked, and Andy said they'd been friends since freshman year. Well, no accounting for taste. I laughed when I thought that.

"What's so funny?"

"Nothing." I didn't want to start a fight with him while he was miserable.

"Please. Distract me." He sounded half-asleep, but there was this cracking at the back of the droopy sound, the pain of his arm cutting through the codeine fog. He laughed when I told him about "no accounting for taste."

"You've got a pretty low opinion of me, huh?"

"Well, look at who you've been reduced to hanging around with." I hooked my thumb at my chest.

"Come on. You're lots of fun." He levered himself upright. "You know, I can't believe I'm the first guy to date you."

"It's true. You're either desperate or blind."

He laughed. "Not blind. You're cute. You're smart. You're fun. Name one other girl in the whole school who'd sit in the emergency room with me on a Saturday afternoon."

"Lots of girls."

"Yeah, but I don't see 'em. I only see you. My Eve. Pretty, smart Eve's gonna take care of me. Those other guys must have been stupid not to see you before."

"Yeah, well, the fatter you are, the harder it is for people to see you."

"Huh?"

"I was fat, okay? Over the summer, I lost about thirty pounds. I still have about forty to go, but I look a whole lot better than I used to."

"You look great. Anybody tells you you're fat, I'll punch 'em." His eyes drooped closed, and he had a dopey smile on his face. How could a girl not love a guy like that? Andy slid over sideways a little bit. "Even if you were fat, but you're not -- even if you were fat, you'd be cute. Chubby and cute."

Andy told me I was cute, but it didn't count, because he was flying on codeine.

Which just showed how shallow I was, to be upset about something so stupid while he was in such misery.

*****

As Andy's official nursemaid and go-fer, I spent the entire day Sunday in the boys' dorm. God must have been watching out for me because I didn't go insane from the smell or the mess.

Andy honestly needed me. Thanks to all that codeine, he didn't realize his ankle also was messed up until we left the hospital Saturday night. Instead of going back to the emergency room, we turned to ice packs and Ace bandages wrapped around Andy's ankle until he could hobble around on both feet.

I discovered the guys in the dorm were nice, actually human, once they were separated from an environment that turned them into testosterone-impaired morons. Such as muddy fields. They even cleaned up the floor lounge for us. I found some dirty socks among the couch cushions, but I didn't say anything, considering how much a slob's den the place must have been before that.

Being the only girl there, I expected the guys to treat me like an alien, but guys who hadn't talked to me since orientation last year acted like we were old friends. Maybe the easy atmosphere came from the fact that, all of a sudden, I was officially Andy's girl, announced for the entire floor to hear. Some sleepy goof wandered into the lounge to get a Coke from the machine, wearing nothing but boxer shorts. Four guys yelled almost in chorus: Girl on the floor!

While the poor guy peeled himself off the ceiling, someone else yelled, "Don't go scaring off Andy's girl."

I realized the guys were so comfortable with me because I was considered safe. I wasn't on the hunt. They could treat me like their sister.

Guys are so weird. Why do girls put up with them?

We had our own church service in the lounge. About a dozen of us. Andy couldn't play his guitar, so someone else led singing. He promised he'd teach me to play guitar when his arm was better, but I decided not to hold my breath.

I fetched lunch for us from the cafeteria. Thanks to the pass from Andy's RD, I got in before the cafeteria opened. After lunch, we watched some TV and did a lot of studying. Andy took a couple of naps.

Then our own version of *Invasion of the Body Snatchers* hit.

I went to get our dinner, and when I got back, Andy's mother was there. No wheelchair. And she wore pants, not her usual ankle-length sack dress. She was quiet, which was totally not her. She stood over the couch while Andy struggled to sit up, and looked like she might cry.

It struck me right then -- for the first time, duh! -- she loved him.

"Hey, there you are." Andy smiled like he had been worried about me. I wondered what his mother had said to him before I got there. "See, Mom? I'm fine. Eve's taking good care of me. We've got the whole schedule worked out. Between her and Drake, I won't have any trouble. Somebody'll carry my books to class and get me settled, and my friends will share their notes with me until I can write again. No problem."

Amazingly, we didn't have to convince Mrs. Carleone that her baby boy didn't have one foot in the grave and the other on a banana peel. She didn't whine and whimper and blame everybody from the college president to the maintenance guy at the hospital. She asked a lot of intelligent questions, like where the hospital papers were, so her insurance could take care of the bills, and did Andy need money, and did he want her to take his dirty laundry home so he didn't have to worry about it?

I wondered if she really was twins, because she should have made some pointed remark about it being my duty as Andy's girlfriend to do his laundry for him.

There was nothing more disgusting, in my imagination, than having to deal with the dirty underwear of a man who wasn't a blood relative. Two girls on my floor almost broke off their engagements because once the ring went on, the guys expected them to do their laundry. Reason enough to encourage all Christian girls in college to consider celibacy as a life choice.

We survived Mrs. Carleone's visit, once she made sure Andy wasn't wasting away in his room, suffering silently in pain. She even smiled at me. Plus, she left soon enough our dinner was still warm.

"Kind of freaked you out, huh?" Andy said a little while later.

"What?"

We weren't alone. There was a football game on the TV at one end of the lounge, and a *National Geographic* special playing on the TV at the other end. Behind the sofa, five guys sat on the floor playing *Risk* at the top of their lungs. Four guys sat at our study table, speculating on whether their French teacher was going to give them a test in the morning.

With all that noise, we didn't have to be quiet to have a private conversation.

"Seeing Mom on her feet. She hardly needed that cane."

"She looked good," I offered.

"You were right, you know. About Mom feeling better if she thinks about others." He put his plastic spoon back into the cardboard tub and shoved the remains of his chili toward the center of the table.

"She's worried about you. Adrenaline does wonders."

"Don't be so generous." He drew pictures in the puddle of creamy veggie dip. "I keep thinking about your story, about the guy who didn't heal until he gave up his bitterness."

My chili turned to lead in my stomach. I pushed away the remains and contemplated running. Did I really want this?

"My dad had a second family." He shrugged and took a sideways glance at me, probably gauging my reaction. "He married Mom, but he had a -- what do you call it? A common law wife. They had three kids. Dad decided he liked his other wife and his other kids better than us. When I was about eight. Mom had a lot of headaches right after he left. She made me pray every morning and every night that God would zap Dad and make him come back to us."

"He didn't come back, did he?"

"God zapped him." He hunched his shoulders, and there was this look in his eye. I caught only a glimpse of it. I couldn't figure out what it was, but it scared me. "He was in an accident. And he was in the hospital for months before he died."

"No. That's not right."

"Oh, yeah, he died."

"I mean about God zapping him. I can't believe -- God doesn't work that way." I felt cold, all of a sudden. And very small. "Does He?"

"No. But it's a pretty hard thing to hit you when you're eight. Mom took it bad. Like she had never realized the power that goes into praying for something every day." He took a long, deep breath and looked at the guys on the other side of the table. They were still arguing about their French test. "Mom was glad. And then she felt guilty. She knew it was wrong to want him dead just because he didn't love us anymore. She lost a lot of weight, and she couldn't sleep. Things just kind of got bigger until," he made a sweeping motion with his good arm, "we're here."

He finally met my gaze. I didn't see any anger. Just some confusion, some hurt, a lot of...resignation, maybe?

I stayed until closed dorms at ten. The football game turned into a black-and-white movie, and everybody drifted down to that end of the room to watch, leaving Andy and me alone.

"You know what I just realized?" he said, when I had my coat on and I was ready to go out the door.

"You forgot about a class?"

"I spend a lot of time trying to make God like me."

"But God loves you. He loves everybody, even when we don't deserve it."

That sounded pretty lame coming out of my mouth, which was kind of sad because it was true.

"I know. But when you're scared you're going to get zapped the first time you step out of line, you kind of forget about the love. Y'know?" He gave me a pitiful little smile.

"So, I'll make a note to remind you about that, too."

His smile got closer to normal, and that was all I wanted. "Don't ever leave me, Eve. I don't know how I'll get along without you."

"You got along fine all these years until we met. I'm sure you'll manage." I stuck my tongue out at him -- so mature! -- and got the laughter I wanted.

Thanks to helping Andy get around and studying for and then taking mid-terms, I was wiped out by the time we reached the end of the week. That didn't stop me from going to a movie at the Playhouse with Andy on Friday night to celebrate surviving mid-terms and his regained ability to walk. I missed the last half of the movie. I think I fell asleep or went into a coma. I didn't drool or snore, fortunately, and the closing music was loud enough to bring me back to life.

Andy put his good arm around me on the way back to the dorm when I started weaving.

That alone should have told me I was sick. Andy put his arm around me, and I couldn't even enjoy it. He took one look at me when we got inside the lobby and sucked in his breath. He got this angry-sad look and shook me a little.

"What are you doing, running around sick?"

"Not sick." My mouth tasted awful, and it wasn't from the greasy butter substitute on the popcorn. Which I didn't eat much of, anyway. I hissed when he touched my face with his icy hand.

"Then you're an alien, and your normal temperature is one-twenty. Get on upstairs and go to bed, you hear me?"

"Thank you, warden."

He pulled the door open and held it for me. "You're not too sick to be sarcastic. Stay in bed tomorrow. I'll bring you breakfast."

"Dorms don't open until after lunch."

He growled, shoved me inside, and pushed the door closed.

Tonia had some herbal tea in her hot pot. She made me drink it and gave me some cold medicine. I went straight to bed and kind of died until Sunday evening.

Andy brought breakfast on Saturday. I didn't remember any of it. Tonia said I tried to eat, but then I had to run for the bathroom. I learned then that God looked after sick girls and the girls who had to live with them, because I didn't heave all over the floor. Any of the three times I did the twenty-yard dash.

When the dorms opened and the opposite sex could visit, Andy came upstairs with orange juice, but Tonia wouldn't let him in. He brought more cold medicine and pizza for dinner. I couldn't eat it, of course, but the thought counted for something.

Monday morning, Andy insisted on driving me to breakfast because it was pouring icy rain. I really liked the offer -- until he ruined it by saying he owed me for looking after him when he was hurt.

I wished he had kept his mouth shut.

There was no use explaining to him the difference between him taking care of me because he *wanted* to take care of me, and doing it because of some stupid sense of obligation.

Then I had bigger problems to worry about: Andy's mother wanted me to stay with her over Thanksgiving if I didn't go home. I considered staging a fight with Andy so we could break up. Naturally, I let everyone assume I was going home.

*****

Andy was with me when I checked my mail that mid-November lunchtime, and he saw the big packet of material AMEA sent me about my summer camp job. Most of our lunch conversation was about AMEA, my future with them, my scholarship, all the work I had done, and all my good experiences. He mentioned that the missions group he planned to work with over the summer hadn't contacted him yet. They were supposed to put the leadership teams together in October. I suggested he look into working with AMEA instead. He got a cold, distant look in his eyes for about two seconds. Just long enough to notice. Then he laughed. His face lit up with that alive, eager look that made me think sometimes I would follow him anywhere.

"Hey, that's the answer. Talk about God having to hit you between the eyes with a two-by-four." Andy picked up his glass of Sprite and saluted me with it. "We're meant to work together. Get me some info? If I don't hear from Gabe by Christmas, that's it. They've left me dangling too many times. I'm really tired of scrambling to fill in for them and make things work. Maybe it's time for me to switch over to a winning team."

"You want to work for AMEA? With me?" I had to ask, just to make sure I heard right.

My brain kind of stalled out for a few seconds. Suddenly it occurred to me that I really hadn't planned on any kind of future with Andy. I was pretty much just enjoying the novel experience of having a boyfriend. I didn't expect Andy to wait for me over the summer. I was ready to come back in the fall and find him with a new Gal Friday. Someone four sizes thinner than me, who could sing and already knew how to play the guitar -- which he still hadn't started teaching me to play. I thought I was okay with the scenario.

Now, though, the idea of Andy considering a future in ministry ... with me ...

Okay, I liked it a lot. More than I should have.

If Andy worked at the camp that coming summer, we could see how we would work together in a lifetime of ministry. It was perfect.

43

"On the other hand," he continued after a few minutes of eating and letting the babble of the lunchroom wash over us, "what if your plans fall through? What if something happens and you don't work there? That has to mean God has other plans for your summer, right?"

"I don't think God would make me spend another summer running six VBS programs in a row. That's like Protestant Purgatory. I know God isn't that cruel." I started to laugh, but there was something in Andy's eyes I couldn't read. It stopped the sound right there in my throat.

"There're lots of other things you could do." He concentrated on the crust of his sandwich. "You could travel with my team."

"Maybe."

The thought of spending my summer on the road made me queasy. That *ick* sort of feeling I got when I walked into a public bathroom at a campground, smelled that pine disinfectant, looked at the wet cement floor, and wondered what sort of bugs crawled over it at night.

"I'll get you that info from my contact at AMEA," I said instead. "I know there'll be a spot for you. We need musicians."

"Spend my summer playing for chapel every night and sunbathe all day? Sounds like a great time." He slouched in his chair and shoved cheese twisties into his mouth like he thought they'd run away.

"Actually, there are five chapels every day, different age groups, plus youth and adult orchestras to direct. You'd be working your tail off. Just like I will."

"You're going to be the big boss's right hand. That means telling everybody else what to do."

"Including you? Is that what's giving you second thoughts?"

"You know," he said, when I expected him to make a joke, "they could really use someone with your skills on the music tour."

"I have to get to class."

Fortunately, that was the truth, but I was glad to have the excuse to run before Andy could turn on the charm.

The info packet from AMEA came in record time, and Andy just shrugged when I gave it to him.

*****

I learned an important lesson that Saturday before Thanksgiving. When Mrs. Carleone started a conversation with "Eve, dear," that was my cue to run for the hills.

She called to find out when my plane was leaving. I figured since I was at school and not sitting in her living room, I was safe. Wrong!

"I'm staying at school," I said, without even stopping to phrase my answer. I couldn't even blame being half-asleep, because Tonia and I had been up for an hour already pretending to study.

"Andy told you I wanted you to stay here, didn't he?" Her voice got really quiet.

Since Andy got quiet when he was angry, chances were good she was preparing to take my head off.

"I have work to do, long distance calls to make to get ready for my summer job."

"You should be on that trip if you're not going home. And since you're not going home, your place is with me."

"How do you figure that?"

"Oh, come on now, Eve. Common sense will tell you where this college romance will end up. I have a responsibility to look after you, if not offer you guidance. Of course you're staying with me."

She was trying to put a guilt trip on me. Nobody had the right to do that but my own mother.

"Andy and I are nowhere near serious enough to make plans for the future. Besides, you make me uncomfortable." I really expected her to start shrieking, but all I heard was silence. "I know you don't like me. *Stay* with you when Andy isn't around to referee? No way."

"But suppose you marry Andy?" She lost that quiet, cold tone. I had no idea how to take it.

Maybe I had earned some respect from her?

"Why would I? Why should I? You aren't listening. I've been preparing my whole life for ministry. And besides, you have made it very clear that you don't like me, you don't think I'm good enough for Andy. I've watched my mother suffer with--" I stopped before I said some things I would regret for the rest of my life. Even if I didn't see Mrs. Carleone ever again. "Like you said, it's just a stupid college romance. It won't last once we split for the summer."

"Are you so sure of yourself? Or should I say, so sure of Andy?"

"I'm not sure of anything. I have work to do. Good-bye."

I waited a few seconds, but she didn't say anything, so I very carefully, quietly hung up the phone.

Andy was waiting, pacing in front of the dorm steps outside when Tonia and I came down for lunch three hours later. We didn't have plans to eat lunch together, so chances were good something irked him.

"Do I get to tell you my side before you lecture me on what I've done wrong?" I said, while he was still taking a deep breath.

That stopped him. He nodded, crossed his arms, and took up a "prove it" stance that made me want to punch him. Tonia muttered something I didn't catch, then patted my shoulder and scurried away down the steps.

Andy wasn't too happy to know I basically lied about my Thanksgiving plans, but he gave me a crooked smile when I finished. So I knew he didn't hate me.

"If you didn't want to stay with Mom, you could have just said so."

"And you wouldn't have argued with me?"

"I guess." He sighed. He just looked tired, instead of that cold, quiet anger. "So she really makes you uncomfortable?"

"Big time."

"Big enough to be a problem?" He tried to smile, like it was a joke. Yeah, some joke.

"We're not serious enough for it to be a problem. I'm happy the way things are."

"Just how serious does it have to get before we have a problem?" His smile looked a little more normal.

"I have no idea."

*****

There were no classes on Wednesday. The dorm was deathly quiet by Tuesday afternoon. Gloria arranged a group dinner for those of us who were staying in the dorm. We couldn't all fit in her little apartment on the first floor, of course, so we had a picnic in the lounge and watched movies. Andy didn't call before the mission trip bus took off, and I tried not to think about it or make excuses for either of us. I kept busy while he was gone, studying and making long-distance phone calls, either having my interviews with the administration at AMEA or talking with Mrs. Zeminski.

The cafeteria workers who stayed over Thanksgiving break put everything out on the tables, buffet-style, so they didn't have to serve. It was nice, even better than last year's Thanksgiving. The biggest thank-you on my list was that I didn't have to spend time with Mrs. Carleone. Tonia agreed with me that it might be smart to let the argument with Andy be our break-up, so I wouldn't have to face future holidays with his mother.

Maybe I should have told him that was the plan?

He called Sunday afternoon before his team hit the road. He didn't say anything about wishing I'd been on the trip with him. He just said he missed *me*. So like a dummy, I agreed to meet him at the Grease Pit when he got back to school.

*****

Andy was standing inside the big recessed doorway in front of the Grease Pit when I got there. He put his hands on my shoulders and pulled me close.

Miss Most-Likely-to-become-a-Nun had no idea what was going on. My first clear thought was that Andy was going to hug me. The next thing I knew, I had a close-up of his nose. I closed my eyes, mostly startled, and he kissed me.

For first kisses...it was okay. I guess. I smelled spearmint from his gum, and he didn't have any beard stubble to scratch my face.

Where was the big spark, the zing, the trumpets or chimes or violins or whatever you're supposed to hear on the first kiss?

When he pulled back, Andy's grin was a clue he enjoyed the kiss. So he didn't know I was a total newbie at kissing. I let him wrap his arm around my shoulders and lead me to a back booth. There were maybe a dozen people in the Pit, and they barely glanced at us as we went by.

Stupid, paranoid me wondered if he kissed me outside so no one would see. Still, Andy had said he missed *me*, not my organizational skills. Then he walked through a restaurant where everyone could see he had his arm around me.

We didn't talk about what I did over Thanksgiving break. What was there to talk about? I slept in late, avoided going out in the rotten Iowa weather, studied, and worked on camp preparations. We talked about his trip. It was such a big success, the church that organized the youth weekend wanted SCC's team to do it next year. Everyone involved planned to go back. He wanted me to come with them.

Which meant he expected us to be together in another year. That was good, right?

Andy kissed me again after he walked me back to the dorm. It was barely ten, but he had to get back to his room and call his mother to let her know he got in all right. I felt kind of giddy, knowing he skipped that highly important phone call to meet me for supper. Maybe that was what made the kiss so much nicer. Or maybe it was because the second time, I was prepared. It still wasn't anything to get excited about, but I did like how Andy wrapped his arms around my waist and held me close. I could get used to that.

Chapter 5

The next few weeks were nice. Andy got all gung-ho on taking long walks in the snow after dinner. We always had slow, gentle kisses for dessert just before I went into the dorm. I could have worried about the fact that he kissed me outside in the semi-darkness so no one could see us, but my brain was occupied with a puzzle: How come kissing seemed kind of blah? After two weeks, shouldn't I have gotten better at it?

Two Sundays into December, Andy drove us to Davenport after church. We hit the Greek restaurant in the mall and made pigs of ourselves on olives and gyros, and baklava. Then we walked around. There was something very satisfying, secure, about walking around in a crowd of Christmas shoppers with my boyfriend's arm around me. Especially knowing everyone who saw us knew we were together. It didn't matter that no one knew us. They just saw a couple.

We came to a huge bank of coin-op machines stacked three high and ten wide, front and back, in the middle of the walkway. Andy said we had to stop and try our luck. We had our choice of glitter-filled rubber balls, plastic snakes, temporary tattoos, key chains, and all sorts of stuff about two steps up from Cracker Jack prizes. He had a pocketful of quarters.

Andy spent about three dollars' worth on a machine that gave him opaque plastic bubbles, while I was still trying to decide if it was worth trying a machine that offered a miniature pack of cards or a ball and jacks set -- or a dozen other cheapo prizes they couldn't display on the front of the machine.

The bubbles all held costume jewelry rings. Andy emptied them out into his hand and asked me which one I liked. One looked like a cloudy tiger's eye opal and would have been pretty, but the silver paint was already peeling off the band. Another one had a glass diamond the size of my thumb. One had a thick band and a snake wrapped around a poison-green stone that certainly looked real. I picked an icy blue, square-cut piece of glass.

Andy jammed the other rings into his pocket and his smile went crooked. He caught hold of my hand and turned it over -- and slipped the ring on my finger. "We'll make do with this until I can get you a real engagement ring."

"A real--"

I had never in my life fainted, but the floor started to get kind of rubbery under my feet for a few seconds. My hand got huge, filling my whole field of vision.

Andy stood there, holding my hand, his smile shrinking a notch or two, waiting.

"I didn't think--" My throat closed up like I was about to heave. "I mean -- I know you like me -- and we're good friends -- and we work really well together -- but--" I curled my fingers, making it impossible for him to take the ring off my finger without a fight. "Even if you change your mind, I'm keeping this, you know."

Andy burst out laughing. He wrapped his arms around me and kissed me hard, right there in front of hundreds of strangers.

"You can't say it, can you?" He shook me a little. "Why is it so hard for you to ask if I love you or not?"

"Guys like you don't fall in love with girls like me?"

"Wrong! You are so wrong!" And he kissed me again.

Finally, I got tingles. Or that could have been because I held my breath while he kissed me.

Later, I realized what should have been a warning sign. Andy hadn't *asked* me to marry him. He just assumed. And dummy me, I didn't hold out for a real, official, legitimate will-you-marry-me question.

Andy had it all figured out, and it sounded good. I guess I was in enough shock not to be thinking clearly. I just agreed with him. We would have a simple wedding, get married in the fall, and live in the campus apartments while Andy finished his final semester of his senior year. If we stayed to finish out my junior year or moved right away would depend on when Andy managed to get into seminary.

He decided we had to sign up for our campus apartment right away. So at six that evening, we stood outside the manager's apartment, asking if there were any openings or if there was a waiting list.

The manager wasn't all that nice until Andy said we were getting married in the fall. Then he was all smiles when he took our names and current housing information, and put us on the waiting list.

"You know what he was thinking, don't you?" Andy led me up the steps to the second floor instead of outside. I just shook my head and gave him a dumb look. Still in shock. "He thought we wanted an apartment now because we *have to* get married."

For about five seconds more, I still had no idea what he was talking about. Such things honestly hadn't occurred to me. Despite Andy kissing me every day, I hadn't let my mind move in that direction. I never expected to go there, personally. I still expected to break up when we split up for the summer.

Sex and babies. We hadn't talked that far. Did we want kids? Did Andy like kids? How long should we wait? Whose ministry career had precedence when it came time to rearrange our lives to take care of those kids? Mine, with everything lined up and a place guaranteed for me with AMEA -- or Andy's vague dreams of working with youth?

Then there was the whole might-never-happen issue with my fibroids. They were small and went through cycles of growing and shrinking. The doctor never discussed with me the chances for or against getting pregnant because I didn't *need* to think about it. Until that Sunday afternoon, I had never considered whether not having children would bother me. I never had a potential daddy for those theoretical children.

When should I tell Andy about my whole reproductive lottery problem? The thought of having that talk with him kind of made me queasy again. I wasn't paying attention to where we were going until the door on the second floor opened, and Andy landed us in the middle of a bunch of his married friends. Friends I'd never met until that moment.

All of a sudden, we had to change the people we hung around with. That gumball machine ring on my finger meant we were officially part of the pre-married group, so we had to hang around with other pre-marrieds and marrieds, and listen to all sorts of advice and disillusioning talk. Within an hour of walking into Dale and Rita's apartment, Andy and I got separated. He sat in one corner with the guys, and I was in the kitchen with the girls, getting the lowdown on the unglamorous parts of marriage. Morning breath. Sharing a bathroom with a man. How to get him to help with the chores -- more than killing bugs and emptying the trash. Doing the disgusting man-generated laundry. Getting him to do the laundry. Preferred methods of birth control. Deciding which parents to visit on what holidays. I got advice on how to get a weekend job to save money for the big move after graduation. How to set up a separate account Andy couldn't get at, so we would have money for emergencies.

Hide money from my husband? Why?

All the wives basically agreed that college student husbands didn't know diddly or squat about handling finances, and it was up to their wives to save them from themselves.

It didn't occur to me until after everybody gushed over my ring and how romantic it was that I hadn't told Andy I *loved* him. He didn't ask. Kind of pathetic.

Andy never once said those eight important words:

Eve. I. Love. You. Will. You. Marry. Me?

On the short ride back to my dorm, we talked about things Andy obviously considered much more important -- I would call my parents to tell them, and Andy would tell his mother. I did not look forward to the call she would make to me.

No way did I want that kind of downer at the end of what should have been one of the happiest days of my life.

Knowing all the misery my own mother had suffered at the hands of in-laws, why did I want to walk into a similar situation?

That just showed what a rotten self-image I had, thanks to Bill and Dad. I was desperate for some confirmation that yes, I was worthwhile enough for a man to marry.

When I called, nobody was home. I had to leave a message. Getting engaged was not news to leave in a message on an answering machine. I asked if my plane tickets to come home at Christmas had been ordered yet, or if I should still try to get a ride with someone. Then I asked them to call me right back, and promised I would be up late. My mistake was mentioning that I had some really important news to tell them.

Twenty minutes later, I was making some hot chocolate in my room. I heard Tonia's voice as she stepped out of the stairwell, coming back to the floor. I stepped out into the hall, preparing to do my first official ring-flash-in-the-face move. The phone rang. Nancy was closest to the phone nook, and she answered it.

"Eve, it's your brother," she said, holding the receiver out.

For about five seconds, I just stood there, expecting someone else to take the phone. Then my brain shifted gears from Andy and my ring. Talk about deflating fast. Tonia was halfway to our room, and she snickered.

"I don't have a brother," I said, loud enough for Bill to hear me. "Just hang up on the lying jerk."

Bill obviously heard me because he shouted something unintelligible that made Nancy's eyes get wide. She continued holding out the receiver to me. No way was I taking it now. Tonia gestured for Nancy to hang up. That cut off whatever poison was coming out. I wished I could cut Bill out of my life that easily.

Tonia saw my ring. Her shriek brought more than half the floor running. Funny, but I didn't mind telling the story over and over again, each time someone else got to the floor and came to get the details first-hand. It was kind of fun being the center of attention. I got more excited about the whole scenario from their reactions.

With all the squealing and giggling and congratulations, I stayed up past eleven, Iowa time, which was midnight Ohio time. My parents didn't call. I was tempted to call, but I knew they didn't stay up that late. Besides, Bill's presence in the house when my parents weren't there meant he had moved back in. He would play his "concerned big brother" game and dominate the conversation. He only worked in two modes: criticism, or turning the situation to his benefit.

I called home the next morning and prayed Bill would still be in bed. The last I knew, he was still working midnight shifts at a gas station.

I was wrong.

Bill's voice was in the background through the whole conversation, which my parents put on speakerphone so they both could hear. When I asked why they hadn't returned my call from last night, he claimed the answering machine must have malfunctioned. Bottom line: Bill had erased my message. He got even louder after Mom and Dad's stunned and eventually excited response to my news. He kept shouting questions, so I had to repeat five times that Andy was going into the ministry. Dad repeated the news for Bill just as many times. Then his voice got louder, meaning he was coming up to the speakerphone. I took the prudent (cowardly) way out and told my folks I had to head off to breakfast, I loved them, and I would call back in the evening when the phone rates went down. I hung up, so Bill only managed to say, "Eve, you have to give me--"

I found out later from Mom that Bill wanted Andy's phone number, address, and the name of his church. It was easy to guess Bill wanted to put Andy through an inquisition. He always excused his interference in my life as his "duty" to look after me, since my father was ineffectual (according to the rest of the family) and my mother couldn't be trusted.

It occurred to me that when I married Andy, I wouldn't have to spend any more vacations at home enduring Bill's continued efforts to brainwash me through torture.

*****

My ring hadn't been on my finger for more than three days when the gloss started to wear off. Not just the fake silver coating on the plastic, but the giddy planning-for-the-future feelings. I had to keep reminding myself that Mrs. Carleone hadn't called, so that was a good thing.

I now had to get by on maybe five hours of sleep per night. That was the only way I could get all my studying in, do my work-study, and spend time with Andy.

The most important things in my life were getting through finals and discussing our future, near and distant.

I had to regularly remind Andy I was booked for the summer. He kept saying things like, "Gee, you'd be such a great part of my team," or "Are you sure you have to go to Colorado?" He knew I had signed a contract to work at the camp. He promised to send his application in to AMEA. If he wanted to work at the camp, I couldn't understand why he kept hinting for me to break my promise to AMEA and come with him.

Besides, there was a lot of work to do that summer if we planned to get married in the fall. With Andy on the road, I had most of the responsibility for organizing things.

According to my new married friends, I should have been happy to escape arguing with Andy about the details. Even though Andy and I agreed things would be simple, I was pretty sure Mom wouldn't let me leave it at shoestring budget, college-style simple.

Then things got more complicated. On our first week anniversary of being engaged, Andy stuck his tongue in my mouth when we were kissing goodnight.

My first reaction was a totally blank brain. I just stood there and held my breath, and then it was over. Andy smiled, so I guessed I did all right.

The whole long walk up the stairs to my room, I wracked my brains:

Was I supposed to *like* that? Do good Christian girls let a guy do that before marriage?

I finally worked up the courage to ask Tonia if it was supposed to be fun. She gave me a look that clearly said I was hopeless.

I had never paid attention to the makeup discussions and that period in youth group when we talked about dating rules and tricky situations. I thought I'd never be in "that" kind of situation. So I was totally unprepared for Andy to take the physical part another level higher.

I had been doing a lot of panic prayers in the last week. No time for the "Blessed Lord, I thank Thee..." King James Bible prayers. Lately, they consisted of mostly, "God, help!" Which wasn't really so bad. God wanted honesty, right? So as I lay in bed in the dark and stared at the light from the street on the ceiling, I prayed silently, *Okay, God, I really need some help with this. Where do I put on the brakes and where do I start demanding that I have some fun, and he can't have fun unless I do?*

A few days later, I learned I had to be more careful about what I prayed for.

I went to Nick and Paula's to study since I was now part of that "gang," and she was in my Victorian poetry class. Studying quickly devolved into looking through bridal magazines. Paula showed me a couple flower designs she thought would be pretty -- whenever we nailed down a date for the wedding. In just a week, the sensible fall wedding had come untied and became like the debate on Pre-, Mid- or Post-Trib Rapture. Should we get married before Andy's final semester, after, or when he found a place to live?

"Were you ready?" sort of slipped out while we were looking at a ten-page spread on what passed for nightgowns.

Paula laughed. "Ready and then some. Let me guess. Sex ed class was all technical and different versions of 'don't let this happen to you'?"

"Basically."

"It's fun."

"Duh. I already guessed that. But how can it be fun if I don't know what to do?"

"Learning is fun, too."

"Yeah, but..." My face got hot enough to heat the room. "I like kissing. And that took a while. What if he wants more than that? Is it okay... beforehand, because we're getting married?"

"My Dad's a youth minister, and he gave me a really good way of judging how far we could go even with the excuse that we were engaged." Paula waited until I could look her in the eye again. "Ask yourself, if Jesus walked in on you two, would you be embarrassed by what He'd see?"

I thought about that for a while, and Paula kept flipping through the magazine. "So, it worked?"

"Until we started rationalizing things. We figured as long as we stayed in dark places and kept our clothes on, we were safe. There are an awful lot of stupid things you can do to each other's body with all your clothes on."

That wasn't what I wanted to hear.

"Eve." Paula scared me, putting her hands on top of mine on the table. "God made us to enjoy sex, okay? Why do you think He had the people who compiled the Bible put the Song of Solomon in there? If God gave us sex only to have babies, men would only be interested when we're ovulating. And they'd leave us alone the rest of the month."

"Maybe that's why God created football season," I offered.

She laughed. I laughed too, feeling a little better. It occurred to me, after a few more talks along those lines, maybe God created sex as a gift to make up for the misery of in-laws.

The Friday before I headed home for Christmas break, Andy and I had to go to dinner with his mother. It went better than I expected. Maybe I had some respect from her at long last?

She oohed and aahed over the book I bought her and thanked me for the chocolate fruit. She didn't go on and on about how I shouldn't have. I learned a long time ago that meant the person getting the gift really didn't want it. She bought me a devotional book for engaged couples, which was nice. I was pretty sure it would focus on what the wife had to give up, sacrifice, and compromise on. Still, the index had nice, encouraging words like *partnership* and *mutual compromise* and *listening*. There was even a chapter titled, "Husbands Will Make Mistakes: Learn to Apologize. Wives Will Be Right More Often Than They Know: Learn to Forgive."

I still hadn't told Andy about my fibroids problem. Why worry about that until we sat down and had the talk about birth control and how many children we wanted to have, if any?

In a lot of ways, it was a Christmas postcard kind of evening. Carols on the stereo. A little tree covered in twinkle lights and silver tinsel sitting on the coffee table. Pine air freshener.

I scored points when I ate two slices of fruitcake. I have always liked fruitcake. I learned to eat it when I was little because Bill hated fruitcake and always gobbled the Christmas treats I liked. Andy hated fruitcake. He actually pushed the plate away to the other side of the table, and I had to ask for it to be passed to me. Mrs. Carleone gave me a real smile when I asked where she got it because it really was good. She made it. That was one of the things she did to make her living -- custom baking, tailoring, and teaching piano, violin and guitar.

Amazingly, we forged one pleasant bridge between us. The question was whether a foundation of fruitcake could turn into something more solid.

She gave me two fruitcakes to take home for my folks. I was feeling pretty good until I saw the note tucked in between the fruitcakes, asking

Mom to call Mrs. Carleone so they could discuss the wedding arrangements. Ugh -- the last thing I needed was that woman trying to influence my mother.

Cramps struck hard that night on the ride back to college. I had a vision of creeping through the airport on my toes and fingertips, twisted into a knot.

I was so miserable the next day, Andy actually noticed when he drove me to the airport. We finally had that talk. I tried to soften it as much as I could with as few details as possible. Despite being kind of buzzed on painkillers, I knew better than to use the really lame line of, "We can always adopt." No guy likes to hear that -- or so I've been told. Andy was really quiet. I couldn't decide if that was thoughtful quiet, concerned-for-Eve quiet, or that angry, seething-under-the-ice quiet that he and his mother did so well. Part of that was because we still hadn't talked about whether we wanted kids or not. How could I know if he was stunned or disappointed or relieved?

*****

Mom took one look at me when they picked me up at the airport and knew what had happened. She got me an appointment with our gynecologist as soon as we got home.

On top of the fibroids, I now had endometriosis, aggravated by stress. Gee, what kind of stress could I have been facing?

I needed to pay better attention to my diet and activities so I could learn what brought on the attacks and what eased them. Oh, joy, as if I needed more things to think about.

One form of anticipated stress didn't materialize. Bill's new church didn't believe in celebrating Christmas in December because Jesus wasn't born in the winter. Well, duh, my pastor had been saying that for years. So Bill refused to participate in any Christmas activities. He spent a lot of time studying the "true" doctrine he had been "denied" all his growing-up years. His new tangent meant spending all his time with his new church family, so he wasn't in the house very much.

For which I thanked God repeatedly.

As usual, Dad had me come into the office to handle last-minute gifts for the employees in his accounting firm. Translation: take him shopping for Mom's presents. He hadn't gone yet. Despite constant reminders and lists of gift ideas. Even with Mom's wish list, he hadn't gone shopping yet. It was the same story, year after year. Even Mom knew I wasn't office shopping. Talk about stress.

Andy didn't call Saturday. Didn't call Sunday. Didn't call Monday. Which kind of made a lie of, "I'm going to miss you so much. Do you have to go home for Christmas?"

My first thought was that my news had prompted him to break up with me. Starting with a silent treatment.

Or Andy got in an accident on one of those unplowed farm roads on his way home. He might have been lying in ICU in a coma.

So I finally got up the guts and called his mother's house. The phone rang and rang, and nobody picked up. Not even an answering machine.

Christmas Eve was the requisite visit to the Miller side of the family. Dinner was usually pleasant. My grandmother and uncles saved their complaints about Mom, Dad, and me until after my uncles had had a couple glasses of wine. The first toast celebrated my engagement. I learned then Bill had them convinced I was a lesbian and wouldn't date a "real man" to save my life. Mom got the usual thinly veiled complaints that she hadn't produced a son to carry on the Miller family name. They always conveniently forgot that none of my uncles could hold onto a wife long enough to produce children, other than Bill.

Sometimes I was surprised Mom had stayed with Dad all those years. Somewhere amid all the neglect and obliviousness, he must have proved to her that he did love her. Somehow. She must have loved him.

For once, the holiday stress was a blessing. I had an attack of cramps while I was helping clear the table to bring in coffee, cookies and nuts. Dad noticed and insisted we go home. No one argued. I found out later, thanks to Bill's exaggerated reports, everyone expected me to collapse, bleeding from every orifice. Of course, they blamed Mom for my "poor constitution," but didn't get time to say much because we left that quickly.

We made plans all the way home for how we would spend the rest of Christmas Eve, with music and table games and fruitcake. It was picture-perfect, other than the prospect of Bill lying in wait to lecture us on how unbiblical our celebration was.

He wasn't there. Neither was a message on the answering machine. Andy should have called me on Christmas Eve, right? With Iowa an hour behind us in Ohio, I knew it would be all right to call him to wish him a merry Christmas, even at the risk of talking to his mother. I called and let the phone ring, and no one answered. I called an hour later -- still no one answered. I contemplated staying up until midnight to call once more. But didn't.

When Mom announced we would spend a day visiting bridal shops, I nearly told her to forget it. I was still a little ticked with Andy over our one and only discussion about wedding clothes. He *claimed* he didn't care about style or design. We were going for a simple wedding, and he trusted me to pick out the perfect dress. Paula and Tonia agreed the translation from "guy speak" was: *Don't spend a lot of money, don't get fancy, don't expect me to care.*

Even worse, Andy was right. What did I need an $800 dress for when I would wear it maybe three hours for a very simple wedding? If Mom wanted to spend gobs of money on me, I should ask for sensible things like pots and pans, dishes, and linens.

But of course, I gave in to bride fever. At the third shop we went into, I found the perfect wedding dress. It made me look thinner and taller, and it was on sale!

It had a shallow scooped neckline and tiny, iridescent beads sewn into the shape of roses around the neck. The skirt was simple, light material in tiny pleats. That's all. No fancy train, no pearls and glitter and lace. Simple. Just like our wedding would be.

Mom put a deposit down on the dress, and I had until the following week to decide. We would lose the deposit if I changed my mind, but that was better than being stuck with a dress we couldn't return.

We were almost to the door out of the mall when I considered going back and canceling the deal. It was only ten minutes after putting the deposit down, so we could get it back, couldn't we? I would spend the money on a guitar instead of a dress. Did I need a *wedding* dress? Couldn't I get by with just a pretty white dress that I could wear for special occasions later?

What if Andy never followed through, and he didn't teach me to play guitar? I would be stuck with a guitar that would be just as useless as the wedding dress.

I was so busy with that thought, we were out to the car and out of the mall parking lot before I got back to the original thought of forgetting the dress altogether. So I kept my mouth shut.

Andy finally called, three days after Christmas. He didn't apologize for never being home or for not calling until then. He wasn't happy to hear about the dress. Even when I told him it was a simple style, like we agreed.

"When I said simple, I meant, you know -- a suit and a tie for me, and you'd wear a church dress. Not a wedding dress. I'm going to look really stupid in my brown suit if you're wearing a fancy wedding dress."

He didn't think our wedding was important enough to dress up a little? I said so, and he got huffy. I had a headache, and I wasn't going to let him make me a villain. He was being a brat.

"It doesn't have to be a tux. But black would be nicer than brown. You need a black suit, don't you?" He agreed. Not too happy about it. "You can take your time looking for a suit that you really like, and you can get it on sale after Prom."

"Yeah, maybe." He sighed. "Mom wants to reserve the date for the church."

"Shouldn't my Mom take care of that?"

"Why?"

"Well, it's tradition. The bride's family handles the wedding. The groom's family handles the rehearsal dinner."

"Yeah, okay, but why make your mom do all that long-distance work?"

I couldn't talk for a minute. It hit me like the roof slammed down on me. Andy -- and his mother -- planned on us getting married in *his* church. Even though we had pretty much given up on having the wedding in the fall before school started.

"Andy, tradition--"

"How are all our friends going to attend if the wedding is in Ohio? How is my Mom going to get all the way out there?"

"The same way all my relatives would get out to Iowa. Plane. Car. Train. Bus. Whatever."

Instead of the wedding *after* he graduated, now he was back to getting married in the fall. All our friends could come up to school a couple days early, and they wouldn't have to worry about where to stay.

I decided one thing, and I told him so: I was not giving up my pretty wedding dress. Yes, we were going to have a simple wedding, but I was determined to look like a bride, not someone who hurried up and ran to the judge because she *had to* get married.

*****

Andy didn't call again until the Friday before I headed back to school. I wished he hadn't called at all. He was back to trying to get me to change my summer plans. No more hinting. He had committed to the touring music team and practically promised to bring me along as the coordinator and troubleshooter. I reminded him that I had signed a contract. He said he had to go to a meeting and hung up. No "I miss you," and certainly no, "I love you."

Mom came home from shopping just in time to see me slam the phone down and then curl up, fists digging into my abdomen, and topple sideways on the sofa. She didn't even have to ask what was wrong, just wrapped her arms around me and let me spill everything.

I told her I would pay her back for the deposit on the wedding dress. The disappointed, sheepish look on her face told me what she had done before she said so. She had picked up and paid for my dress without telling me. She thought it would be a nice surprise. Now we were stuck.

My flight back to Iowa included two layovers that were longer than the time spent in the air. That gave me a lot of time to think. My first plan was melodramatic, based in my pity party over the last few days. I imagined how good it would feel to walk up to Andy and throw my engagement ring in his face, in a nicely crowded place with lots of witnesses.

By the time I landed, however, I had talked myself into buckling down and praying and trying to work things out. What was I going to do? Run away from it all? Chuck school and go home to hide until it was time to go to Colorado? Andy and I needed to talk and pray hard, and depend on God to sort things out.

Chapter 6

Instead of going off somewhere to talk and get some things ironed out, Andy spent our first evening back together going through second-hand furniture stores. Everything he considered inexpensive and perfect for our school apartment was *junk*. Beat up and wobbly. Who was going to fix it so we wouldn't be ashamed to have people visit? Andy just laughed every time I pointed out the problems. By the time we hit campus, I was ready to just run upstairs. No goodnight kiss. Ever again.

"You know I love you, Eve, don't you?" he said, before he pulled into the parking spot in front of the dorm. I didn't say anything, because the automatic answer sounded a lot like *No*. "Let's take a walk."

I shouldn't have let him take my hand and lead me away. We walked in silence, past the center of town with all the dark and closed stores, to the park by the river on the other side of town. There was a little three-sided shelter. Andy led me into a dark corner, and he kissed me. Full body press, tongue nearly touching my tonsils, one hand squeezing my butt and holding me against him, kissing. When the shock wore off, I decided-- guessed, hoped-- I kind of liked it. I could hardly breathe, and my heart was banging in my ears loud enough I couldn't hear anything except Andy's heavy breathing.

On the walk back to the dorm, I was wobbly. I had this funny, heavy feeling deep in my stomach, and my mouth was sore. Andy kept his arm tight around me. We didn't talk. I couldn't clear out my thoughts enough to say anything. Every once in a while, he'd brush a kiss against my cheek or nuzzle my ear or something. I'd stumble, and he'd laugh. Well, I guess it was good for a guy's ego to know he could affect a girl that way.

It wasn't until I got up to my room that I realized we hadn't settled *any* of those disagreements we really needed to talk about.

That became a habit.

We decided to get married after I finished my junior year, once Andy settled somewhere and decided what he wanted to do. I should have caught it a lot earlier and asked some questions, but he no longer talked about where he wanted to work for AMEA, the ministry work we would share.

Not getting married for an entire year? A reprieve and a gift from God. Another school year with Tonia as my roommate. Time to lose those last forty pounds and look really good in my dress and put things together nicely for our wedding. A chance to get my health problems under control. A year to de-stress.

Would waiting reduce the pressure coming from Andy's mother's direction? Maybe I didn't pray hard enough about that problem.

*****

Early in February, we had lunch after church with Andy's mother and Pastor and Mrs. Hellingar. I thought their presence would guarantee a pleasant meal. Before we finished our salads, Mrs. Carleone was grilling me about not going on the spring break mission trip.

"I can't cancel my plans now." I concentrated on my lunch so my eyes wouldn't betray the fury burning in my gut. Just fury. The one time I needed an attack, maybe bad enough to faint, and my body didn't cooperate. "My ticket is already paid for."

I didn't feel like it was anybody's business that AMEA paid for the ticket, and I wasn't going home but to Colorado for training.

"Did you consult with Andy before you made your plans?" Her voice could have frozen boiling water, yet she still sounded pleasant. I needed to learn that trick to deal with hundreds of camp parents and their sunburned, sandy brats. "All the work he's done, and now you're backing out on him at the last moment. Pastor, tell me, is that the action of a loving fiancée?"

Andy concentrated on cutting up his steak instead of helping me out.

"I think there's some mistake," Mrs. Hellingar said. I did like her, but her approach to being a minister's wife was to be vague about everything. Nobody could pin her down, so nobody could really get angry with her. "Eve's name was never on the list of participants."

"That's a mistake. I know Andy was planning on Eve's help this spring."

Andy knew last fall I had other plans and couldn't participate, and I said so before she could go into "your duty," round two. Ad nauseum.

Even when Andy admitted I was right, his mother went on about how I should have canceled all my plans the minute we got engaged. It took all my self-control not to point out that engagements could be broken.

Andy knew I was peeved with him for not setting his mother straight. When we got back to the dorm, he apologized. We must have sat on the couch in the corner of the lounge for an hour, sneaking kisses, ignoring the movie and the other people in the room. I had learned to like kissing.

When I went up to my room later that night, I had a scary vision: That day's events could be the pattern for our lives. His mother trying to control us. Andy only defending me when he had to, and making up with kissing instead of talking. Was that how it had been for my parents? Scary thought.

*****

On Valentine's Day, Andy missed breakfast, and didn't show up for lunch. I waited for half an hour, then called his dorm. He wasn't around. I didn't go in to eat. How could I, on Valentine's Day, with all our married and engaged and dating friends sitting under paper hearts hanging from the ceiling?

I got a burrito and a bag of barbecue chips from the Quick-Snack to eat in my room.

I called his dorm between his last class and dinner, and left a message for him to call me before he went to dinner. I wasn't going to eat alone on Valentine's Day.

Our first Valentine's Day together, and we weren't *together*.

No card. No candy. Not even one of those carnations they were selling in the Student Center for fifty cents.

Every time the phone rang out in the hall, I stopped and listened. I couldn't decide if I wanted the caller to be him or not.

The really embarrassing part? What I did.

I had prepared for Valentine's Day, with Andy's favorite chocolate bars and a funny card, because I knew he wouldn't go for romantic. I broke the bars and tore up his card and put them in campus mail to him the next morning. After he didn't show up for breakfast. Again. When I went to lunch, I swore that if he wasn't waiting for me, I didn't want to see him for the rest of the year.

He wasn't waiting. I waited ten minutes, and then I got into the line. When I got through the cafeteria line, I saw Andy sitting at our usual table, laughing with his buddies. I was *five* minutes late. The jerk couldn't be bothered to wait for me, after all the times he had made me wait for him.

I took a table in the corner, where I could see him but he couldn't see me. I was almost late for class because I couldn't leave until he left. I didn't eat a thing.

Not once did he look around like he was waiting for me to show up.

When I checked my mailbox, I found a white rose. No note. How was I supposed to take it? An apology? Why couldn't he have given me a red rose, for love? He probably waited until the last minute to get me something, and they were all out of red roses. Or white roses were cheaper.

When Tonia came into our room and saw the rose on my desk, she pretended to have a heart attack that Andy had actually come through. Then I told her about the lack of note or phone call. She swore she'd make Andy sing soprano if he didn't straighten out. My stomach chose that moment to growl. We started to laugh, then everything got mixed up and I cried.

We made plans to go to the Grease Pit for dinner because she refused to let me go to the cafeteria and risk running into Andy.

I spent the rest of that Friday afternoon lying on my bed with the heating pad. I tried to study to take my mind off the big question: How could I be so stupid as to let a guy be so important to me? I had been ready and content to spend the rest of my life single, in ministry. How could I be so pathetic that I repeated my mother's mistakes? Much as I loved my Dad, I refused to let a man treat me the way he treated my mother through sheer neglect and obliviousness.

I decided to put my ring in campus mail to send back to Andy in the morning.

I went to the Student Center before breakfast. Andy followed me to the mailroom, but I didn't see him until I took off my ring and put it in an envelope with his mailbox number on it. Then he grabbed me and dragged me outside to the Alumni Gardens. It never occurred to me to scream. Mostly because I had been trained all my life not to make a scene, not to embarrass other people, no matter what they were doing to me. And I was scared. Andy was icy quiet furious.

We were all alone, nothing but snow and benches and an empty goldfish pond. He shook the envelope so the ring went flying. All that red left his face when he snatched the ring out of the snow. A stupid gumball machine ring.

"What is wrong with you?" He growled low and soft, like he fought not to shout.

"Oh, nothing. But the jerk I'm supposed to marry avoids me on Valentine's Day, and I can't find him anywhere. He can't wait five stupid minutes for me at lunch when he makes me wait for him all the time. I figure, you don't want to be with me, fine. Just giving your stupid cheap ring back so you can catch the next gullible idiot with it."

I turned to stomp away and Andy ruined it. He grabbed my arm and turned me around so I fell right into him. What I did next surprised even me. I punched him. Not really hard. I barely got a grunt out of him when my fist hit his gut, but by the look in his eyes, it surprised him too. He pushed me down on a bench all covered with snow, but I was too angry to feel anything.

"You know how long I waited for you yesterday? Two hours! Don't tell me I never wait for you."

"You don't. I was late five minutes, and you were already in there and you never saw me come in."

"Well -- you saw me. Why didn't you come sit with me?"

"Because there was no room at the table? Because you didn't save a seat for me? You sure looked like you were having too good a time with your friends. Probably laughing with them about how you ditched me on Valentine's Day." I stood up. He reached to grab my arm again and I slipped, trying to get away from him. I fell down on the bench again.

Andy sighed, turned as if he would walk away -- I wouldn't have been surprised -- then turned back to me.

"I didn't ditch you."

"You didn't call. You didn't leave any messages. You didn't return my messages. If you think one stupid white rose is going to make up for being a jerk, forget it."

"I had more than a white rose for you, which you'd know if you bothered showing up."

"Show up where? I don't read minds!"

"At the Playhouse. Like I told you."

"You never told me."

"On the card with the rose."

"There was no card."

He opened his mouth to argue with me -- I could see it in his eyes. Then he got that uncomfortable look, which I was learning meant he was unwilling to admit he was wrong. Andy dragged me back to the mailroom and told me to open my mailbox. His weird look deepened when he saw my box, above eye-level. I reached in and felt around. Nothing. Andy nudged me out of the way and looked in. He was a good three inches taller than me. He reached in, going past his elbow.

He pulled out a plain white index card with some torn tape on it, a greenish-brown smear, and the words, "If you want the rest of the roses, meet me at the Playhouse at six." All the red was gone from his face.

"It was at the end of the box, jammed in the seam." He shrugged, tried to smile. "No way you could know it was there."

"What is so hard about using the phone? When I didn't show up, why didn't you look for me?"

He shrugged. Andy shrugged to avoid explaining things. Just like we seemed to do a lot of kissing to avoid talking.

"So you got me roses. Big deal. You didn't say you were sorry." I tossed the card in the trash as I turned to leave.

"Eve, come on! You broke my candy bars and tore up the Valentine's card you got for me."

"Did you buy the roses *before* Valentine's Day, or did you forget and get them the day after?"

He looked away instead of answering. That was my answer. I tried to take a step, and he grabbed hold of my arm again. I considered kicking him. It didn't matter where, just as long as he shrieked like a little girl.

"We're both being stupid."

"What's stupid is letting you *keep* hurting me." Then I did kick him. In the shin. That was enough He let go of me and hopped backwards, and I stomped out of there. He caught up with me on the sidewalk.

"I put together this big picnic." He hooked his arm through mine.

"Not hungry." My stomach hurt enough to feel like a hole in my middle. Fortunately, just my stomach.

"Last night. At the Playhouse. Paula helped me. She said even though I had a good reason, I handled everything wrong, and I had to make it up to you big time."

"So Paula knows you ditched me. On Valentine's Day. Great." I kept walking. If he wanted to hang on and go wherever I was going, I didn't care.

"Not on purpose! Mom was working at church, and she fell. I had to take her to the emergency room."

"It took all day?"

"Most of the day."

"You couldn't be bothered to call when you got back? Or the next day?"

"Sorry," he muttered.

Now he said he was sorry. What good was an apology I had to beat out of him? My head hurt. My stomach hurt. Even worse, I had thrown out the rose he gave me the day before. It was a good bet I wouldn't get the other roses, and I missed out on a picnic, just the two of us in the Playhouse.

Probably the only romantic picnic I would ever have in my life.

"Why didn't you call? It was open dorms last night. Why didn't you come looking for me?" I sniffled big time, to keep from crying.

"I thought you were avoiding me."

"Do you blame me?" I didn't fight him when he pulled me into his arms in front of the library.

"Please don't hate me, Eve. Kick me a couple more times, but don't hate me."

I started to laugh, but I lost control of my tear ducts. While I got myself under control, he held me, rubbing my back. It would have been comforting -- if I hadn't felt like such an idiot.

We went to breakfast and sat with the married gang. Andy made himself the slapstick villain, telling how he goofed up our first Valentine's Day together. That felt kind of good because the guys told him he was an idiot, and the girls all sided with me. When we left the cafeteria, Andy made me promise I'd go out with him for lunch, and we'd talk and fix things. Then I went back to my room to study.

He called half an hour later to cancel our plans. The fall his mother took did more damage than they thought. She had hit her head, and now she was complaining about feeling dizzy. By that time, Tonia was gone on an all-day outing with her study group, so I spent the rest of Saturday alone.

In the silence, I realized this had become too strong a pattern in our relationship. I really wished I hadn't let Andy put that ring back on my finger.

Spring break didn't come soon enough for me.

*****

I loved Colorado. It was like coming home, in a way home never was, but should have been. If that makes any sense. I rode the horses without a time limit. A dozen other people weren't waiting to ride, and I didn't have to run somewhere to attend to another emergency. Best of all, I didn't have a single cramp the entire time I was there. Something in the air? Or just total reduction of stress? Or just the atmosphere Mrs. Zeminski seemed to carry with her?

Every morning, I visited the waterfall to have my devotions. It was hidden in a canyon at the far end of the campgrounds, and fed a long stream perfect for wading, full of fish and frogs. I played with ideas for the summer as I walked the long meadow big enough to play baseball, volleyball and tug-of-war simultaneously.

Mrs. Z was the greatest. She was little and looked like somebody's favorite cookie-baking granny -- if that granny was dressed in workout clothes in neon colors, moving at the speed of light.

We spent our afternoons hiking everywhere, making notes, inspecting everything, and making sure the campground would be in tip-top shape when the first campers arrived. We spent our evenings in the big old cabin we'd be sharing with four other women staffers, talking in front of the fire. Mrs. Z was like a second mother and best gal friend. It only made sense to tell her about Andy, all the problems we'd been having, and my hopes that things would be improved when we were both working for AMEA.

"Honey, what if he doesn't get hired?" Mrs. Z said after a long time looking into the fire. "I pulled those strings like you asked me, but nobody has seen his application yet. It could all fall apart."

How could she say that? Andy had to get hired because this was where I belonged. He had asked for the application materials so we could serve together. How could God not bless that? She must have seen the answer on my face. She gave me the saddest, sweetest smile, and reached across the gap between our old-fashioned easy chairs and patted my hand.

"Put it in God's hands, Honey. Put it in God's hands." Her violet gaze sharpened, and she tipped her head to the side. "You have, haven't you?"

"I guess so."

"Make sure of that before you go to bed. Hear me?"

When Mrs. Z spoke, we had to listen. She didn't yell, didn't threaten, didn't use guilt trips. She just said what was and what needed to be, so sweetly. A honey-coated, steel-plated brick wall. She was one of those saintly grannies who prayed about everything, who wouldn't shut up until Heaven gave up. Anybody standing against them might as well give up, too, and save themselves a whole lot of slamming against that wall.

I tried to give Andy and all our questions about the future into God's hands. Starting right then. However, to paraphrase Yoda, trying was not exactly doing.

*****

I came back to school from spring break revved up despite all the work we did. Six weeks until school was out, then two weeks at home before I left for Colorado and a week of preparation until our first camping group came in. At the end of the summer I would help close down the campground, giving me a week of downtime to go home and collapse before I headed back to school.

Despite the tight schedule, I couldn't wait. I was so excited. I should have gotten right to work on my homework as soon as I returned, but Andy was nowhere to be found. I left messages for him, but he didn't respond. So I looked for other members of the spring break missions team.

The missions team was due at noon, and dragged in just before seven on Sunday night, filthy and sunburned. They ran into bad weather coming back and got stranded by a washed-out bridge. The flood had rerouted traffic for miles in every direction. The cafeteria stayed open an hour later than usual, to let them unpack and wash up before they ate. Everybody on the team had a boyfriend or girlfriend who came to dinner with them, so there were four tables full of people.

The talk all through dinner was about the trip. The living conditions of the people the team ministered to. They built four cinderblock houses to hold two families each, dug a well, and set up a water purification system. I couldn't quite comprehend the idea that less than fifty miles south of the border of Texas there were people living without electricity, sewers or running water.

That evening, I learned how the wives felt when soldiers got together to reminisce. They could hear the war stories and get an idea of what it was like, but they would always feel like outsiders. I wondered if anybody else felt left out. All of us who didn't go on the trip couldn't add to the memories, just listen.

I didn't like feeling left out of a part of Andy's life. How would I feel when he came back from a summer traveling with a music team? How would he feel, not being a part of my work? Granted, he could call me, but I couldn't call him because he would be at a different location every night. Yes, cell phones were around, "back then," but still too expensive for college students relying mostly on scholarships. A whole summer spent apart from Andy. A week hadn't been so bad, but I had been too busy to really feel lonely for him. What would a whole summer feel like?

Like Mrs. Z said, I had to leave it in God's hands.

Andy gave me a really weird look when I told him about it, on the walk to my dorm.

"What's that look for?" I forced a laugh, mostly to fight the churny feeling in my stomach that had nothing to do with the mislabeled lasagna they fed us for dinner.

"Haven't you put it in God's hands before this?"

"I don't remember getting down on my knees in the mall when you gave me my ring, and asking God if it was right. Did you pray about it?"

"You're kidding, right?" Then he kissed me before I could say anything.

Was there something wrong with me, that the kiss seemed rather...blah?

I put that into God's hands, too.

Too many things made me so afraid I would end up like my mother: Andy missing meals and forgetting to call me. His mother's little digs about how I had to abandon everything I *knew* God wanted me to do, in favor of Andy's nebulous future. Andy expecting me to know when he needed to be reminded about things -- without asking me to remind him. Every time he did something that upset me, his answer was to get off somewhere dark and private and kiss until my brain turned to jelly and I forgot what bothered me.

Life would have been so much simpler if I had let myself fear a little more, get angry a little more, and stop trying to be such a good, patient, mature Christian. The problem came from my doubts, just as much as from Satan's attacks. And convincing myself we were being attacked because there was a grand and glorious future in ministry for us as a team.

Funny, I thought I had chosen God over everything because I wanted to, not because God was the only one who wanted me. Hindsight is so clear. And humiliating.

It's easy now to say I should have given the ring back during those last, hectic weeks before we split for the summer. Then again, I would have missed that totally epic dinner discussion that solidified a lot of things and helped me settle my priorities.

Andy and I arrived after a discussion had started among a bunch of guys who were on the fringe of Dr. Rittsmer's devotees. They made the mistake of talking really loud as the cafeteria started to empty out, so our gang of married and engaged students overheard and joined in. The argument was whether a wife should allow her entire mind and spirit to be absorbed into her husband's ministry, until she had no thought of her own that didn't mirror his. Was that the highest spiritual goal or just plain creepy and cultish? A few protested that she had a responsibility to God first, to evaluate everything, and not just accept her husband's thoughts and decisions as gospel. What if he veered away from biblical truth?

The jerks argued it was the woman's fault if her husband abandoned his calling in God's service. While she should never argue with him or question him and always support his every decision, it was still *her* fault if he made the wrong choices. Nobody could explain how that could happen if *he* did all the thinking for both of them.

One bozo added that if a man fell away from God's will, it was as a punishment for his wife's sins. Not his own sins or his own bad choices. When challenged by some of the pre-sem married guys, they either wouldn't or couldn't explain where that reasoning came from.

Then Paula spoke up, and I wanted to cheer.

"What if God clearly speaks and gives the woman a ministry? Clear signs of His blessing on what she's doing, making a big impact on the world, providing vital services. What happens if all the guidance is for the use of the woman's gifts and talents, and the man's talents are for support, so his wife is on the stage, speaking and leading, and he best serves as her support?"

Some of the more reasonable of arguers looked a little confused. The biggest mouth of the extremist element turned bright red.

"God would never do anything like that! Any woman who gets on up stage and speaks to men is living in sin. She is shaming her husband! Their pastor should drive both of them out of the church until she repents and he learns to stand up and become a leader." He slammed his fist down on the cafeteria table, making several trays with plates and glasses jump.

"What about Deborah, who was a judge in Israel?" one of the guys asked.

That started a fifteen-minute argument, calling up all sorts of writings that most of the guys on both sides of the issue disagreed with. One taught that Deborah was a widow. She was allowed to serve God because she didn't have a husband to humiliate by her actions. Another offered that Deborah didn't have children, so she had time to devote to service. I wanted so much to counter that scripture clearly called her a "mother in Israel." Someone else offered it, and that quieted a few. Until the loudmouth shouted that most of the stories in the book of Judges were just fables, and they hadn't really happened.

That got a ringing silence. A few of his cronies moved away from him, like his apostasy was a communicable disease. They didn't move far, but enough to notice.

"So Anne Graham Lotz is living in sin?" Paula said, after the echoes from his voice died away.

He opened his mouth with his clear answer of "yes" on his face. Then he paused.

"Doesn't make sense to me that if she was sinning by taking a position of leadership in ministry, her own father and brother wouldn't have noticed years ago and said something to her about it," she added.

"What if the woman God is calling to ministry isn't married?" I had to say.

"Well...that's a different story altogether," he said. Didn't he notice all the faces wearing *give him enough rope to hang himself* expressions? "There's the whole teaching from Paul about unmarried people being able to serve God better. That's the entire justification for a woman giving up her entire life once she's married, to support her husband. That's how she serves God once her husband absorbs her into his life." He grinned at me, like the big arrogant booby thought I was agreeing with him.

Absorbs her? Like the Blob?

"Then anyone who wants to serve God should never get married. So Christian who have children instead of going into ministry are living outside of God's will. Is that what you're saying?" I had to ask.

Andy gave me a weird look, like he couldn't decide if he wanted to laugh and agree with me or argue. Paula got up and picked up her tray to leave. I decided that was a good time for me to make my exit. Andy didn't come with me, and I didn't even look back. I didn't need to see him lean in to continue the conversation.

That whole weird incident gave me something to think about. Maybe despite what he said, Andy did lean toward what his mother had been saying. Maybe he expected me, even if only subconsciously, to drop everything to support him. All my plans. All the work I had done, rising through the ranks. All my training. All the commitments I had made.

Would it be so bad, so arrogant and sinful on my part, to expect him to use his talents to support what God was telling *me* to do?

My only excuse for holding on was that glorious dream of Andy getting his first assignment to work for AMEA, and the two of us starting a long life of ministry working together. Maybe if I had been a little more selfish and focused on being happy with Andy, rather than some totally naïve, hyper-spiritual hope that putting ministry first would guarantee marital bliss, we would have had that knock-down fight we so desperately needed. I confess: I was a wimp. A dreamer. Rolling over for the sake of peace. I was my father's daughter.

*****

On my last day of school, I was helping Andy pack up his room to either haul it home or put it in storage in the dorm basement before he left for training camp. I found the info packet from AMEA under his bed. Covered in dust. Months' worth.

Still sealed.

He never opened it after I gave it to him. He lied when he said he mailed the application. So many other times he broke promises, didn't show up when he said he would, didn't follow through, flashed through my mind. Like those guitar lessons.

I handed the packet to him, and all he said was, "So?"

"You didn't even give it a chance."

"I've been busy." He picked up a box and heaved it up onto his shoulder to take down the stairs.

"Don't you care about your future?" I followed him to the door and raised my voice to travel down the stairs. "About something long-term? We have to think about some security once we're married, you know."

A few seconds later, I heard the fire door at the bottom slam open. I tossed the envelope in the trash. I finished emptying his clothes into his laundry basket. I didn't care if dirty laundry mixed with clean. After all, I wasn't his wife yet.

"It's just not something I want to get involved in," Andy said when he came back to the room.

"You *asked* me to get the application. You were so excited about working together. Remember?"

"That big organization isn't the route I want to take." He turned his back on me to fill another box.

"Why? Do you know specifically where God wants you to go? Maybe you just don't want to do it because it's what *I* want? Heaven forbid you should let your wife lead in anything."

"Leave my mother out of this."

"I wasn't even thinking of her."

"Liar."

I stared at his back for ten of the longest seconds in my life. Then I headed for the door.

"Have a nice summer, Andy. You have the number and the address of where I'll be."

He didn't say anything.

He didn't call before my ride picked me up for the long drive home. He didn't call until the next Sunday morning while we were at church. He didn't ask how I was doing. All he could talk about was what a great time he was having in training and what a great summer he was going to have.

My folks didn't hear the message, but Bill did. He spent the next week saying "I told you so," and claiming he had been sure all along that Andy was wrong for me. My foolish choices gave him more ammunition to insist I change my plans for the summer, and my life, and join his church. I took courage through that week of misery by starting each day looking at my wedding dress. Soon, I would be free.

Andy called the next Sunday. Again, while we were at church. He said he would try to call before his team headed out the next weekend. If he didn't get hold of me, he would call me at the camp. I held onto that hope.

Chapter 7

That summer changed my life. After Mrs. Z, my word was law. Most of the staff knew how I had worked my way up through the ranks, proving myself. We got along like family, for the most part. The good kind of family.

I had devotions every morning looking at a mountain, listening to birds singing. I needed the quiet, the sense of something enormous and joyful, poised to break over me like a wave, to handle each day. I was dealing with sixty-plus families and at least 200 youth in residence, for two-and-a-half months.

Mrs. Z decreed Saturday mornings were my time. Nobody was allowed to approach me with questions or emergencies unless it involved blood or fire. I needed that quiet, self-indulgent time. Even if all I did was sit on a mountainside and let my brain shift into neutral. The rest of the week, I was crazy-busy. Rounding up the rug rats, lawn lizards and drape apes. Getting them to the craft counselors and riding instructors and swimming guides and hiking leaders.

I loved the kids. Even when some acted up just to hear me blow my whistle. Each person on staff had a unique whistle sound. Mrs. Z gave me a wooden train whistle. It hung around my neck on a chain of metallic rainbow beads. She said she gave it to me because I didn't make a big noise or steamroller anyone, and I needed to get everyone's attention.

The whistle was mine to take home at the end of the summer, and I contemplated using the whistle to get Andy's attention in the next school year. I prayed for him every day, and that niggling little voice at the back of my head got louder, asking: *Does he pray for me? Or does he just pray for me to change to suit him?*

The kids were salve to my soul. I loved them. They made me want children of my own. I had at least a dozen hanging all over me at each closing campfire. They were all my darlings -- though I usually considered each one a monster at least once during the week.

The third week of camp, Nebby and Sasha got in a fight on Wednesday in the craft cabin. Both boys declared that when they grew up, they were going to marry Miss Evie.

At the final campfire, Nebby brought me a ring he bought when his dad took him to town to cool off. A gumball machine ring. Blue glass. Not quite my engagement ring, which I had left at home, but close enough to make me cry.

I guess that was proof I did love Andy. It wouldn't have hurt so much if I didn't love him, right? I even felt like crying when one of the mothers offered to teach me guitar, which just brought back memories of all those broken promises.

Just about that time, my prayers over Andy changed. *Please, God, fix this?* changed to: *Please, God, if it never was Your will for us to be together, give me a clear, unmistakable sign? If You've been sending me signals, I missed them.*

I got some good advice from Mrs. Z, when I took my doubts to her. She said I could only control my own reactions, feelings and thoughts -- I couldn't control anyone else. So I had to change myself and let everyone else be responsible for themselves. I had the choice of giving Andy control over my life or taking back that control.

Gee, I thought *God* was in control. Maybe that substitution was the problem?

It was a good thing she had that talk with me, and I got a few things calmed down and settled in my brain, because the second week in July, disaster came down on us. Proof that God did listen and answer prayers.

Something to keep in mind: Be ready for God's answer to be something you won't like. *No* is just as legitimate an answer as *Yes.*

Andy's tour bus broke down a few miles from the camp. The bass guitarist in the group, Lacy, was the daughter of Rick and Morgan Irish, who ran our stables. Lacy called them for help. We had to do a little rearranging, splitting up some of the married staff and putting them with the singles so we could temporarily house the band while their bus was getting fixed.

Andy knew I was there, but I didn't know the stranded musicians were his until I walked into the dining hall and saw him with Mrs. Z. She had recognized him and corralled him until I got there.

No apologies from that rat fink. He didn't notice -- or if he did, he didn't say anything -- that I wasn't wearing my engagement ring.

That night, three teenage girls went missing right after chapel. We found them in the hayloft with Andy's boys. The girls knew the rules. The boys claimed they didn't know the rules. The people settling the traveling band had given Andy the rules packet, and he was supposed to pass the information on to his kids.

Andy didn't even apologize. He muttered something about, "Well, I guess you don't want to go for a walk later on," and walked away with his juvenile delinquents.

I knew exactly what Andy had planned for that walk: his favorite tactic for avoiding serious discussions.

We ran ourselves ragged for the next thirty-eight hours and forty-two minutes -- yes, I counted -- keeping the band's boys away from our girls, until the bus was repaired. Andy didn't even try to talk to me. When they were loading up the bus to leave, I finally confronted him about not calling me.

He claimed he lost my number.

An angel must have warned me he'd have that answer. I gave him a notepad -- not a piece of paper, but an entire notepad -- with my phone number, the camp number, my home phone and the dates I'd be home before school started, all written on the cardboard cover of the notepad.

Andy didn't kiss me goodbye. Mrs. Z stood with me and watched until the dust from the bus leaving finally settled.

"You've made up your mind, haven't you, Honey?"

That was all she had to say.

As if God's answer to all my prayers and doubts wasn't clear, an attack of cramps put me out of commission the rest of the day.

*****

Chris Hawkes was head of security for Dr. Allen Michaels, with a sideline in screening personnel. He hijacked his sister and her kids and pretended to be a family, so he could see how the camp was being run, first-hand. He just happened to come the same week Andy and his musicians invaded. A week after the invasion, Chris came to talk about his report. I could actually laugh with him over some of the glitches and minor catastrophes that kept body-slamming us while he was at the camp. It helped that he took me and Mrs. Z out for lunch at the best rib joint in the entire Rockies. Who wouldn't be in a good mood when they're up to their earlobes in the most incredible barbecue sauce ever made?

"I would have worried if you didn't lose your temper a few times," he told me. "When you were out of line or you found out you accused the wrong person, you were mature and humble enough to admit it and apologize. That's important in our ministry."

"In front of witnesses, too," Mrs. Z added with a chuckle. "I have a hard time doing that myself."

"I guess all my problems with Andy have taught me a lot in that aspect, at least," I admitted.

"That's your fiancé?" He frowned for the first time since we sat down in the big corner booth. My stomach did a drop to my knees. Was he going to hold me responsible because I was stupid enough to trust Andy's judgment? "I hope he won't be a problem."

"We complained to the band's parent organization," I hurried to say. "Did the girls' parents put up a fuss?"

Suddenly, I knew exactly why he was there: because my fiancé couldn't control the juvenile delinquents under his authority, my future with AMEA had been cancelled. This incredible lunch date was a treat, a consolation prize. And, because Chris Hawkes was Dr. Michaels' eyes and ears, the big boss knew how I messed up, too. Just one step down from God. Yeah, I knew God knew what was going on, but it hurt more that Dr. Allen Michaels was disappointed in me.

Epiphany: I had finally figured out what mattered. Catering to Andy

Carleone's short-term dreams at the expense of my future and my talents and training and hard work wasn't even on the list.

"Don't worry about that." Chris winked, like we were buddies. My heart resumed beating. "I saw a lot more than you might guess. We're familiar with the band's parent organization. They want to be affiliated with us, but if they can't control their representatives, they won't get our support. The important thing is that you came through with flying colors." His smile widened. "We'd like to offer you a position, starting this fall."

Mrs. Z burst out in those wonderful soap-bubble giggles when my jaw nearly hit the table.

AMEA wanted me to be an administrative assistant in ministry development. They would pay for the rest of my college because all my courses would be for the sake of my job. I'd be a part-time student, so it would take me four years to finish my last two years of college, but I would already be full-time in ministry. That was what mattered.

I didn't wonder if Andy would walk my road with me. The question was whether I wanted him on the road God had given me to walk. Considering his actions and attitude when he was at the camp and the silent treatment all summer, I doubted he would support my heading off to AMEA and leaving him at college.

So I wrote Andy a long letter to tell him what happened. No ultimatum, just the options. I asked what he thought. Then I put it all in God's hands. Or at least I tried to.

For the rest of the summer, every time the phone rang in our cabin or the administrative office, my heart slammed. But Andy never called.

Mrs. Z brought up something interesting one night, when it was just the two of us, sitting on the porch of our cabin, looking up at the stars.

"Marriage isn't a fifty-fifty proposal," she said. "It's 100 percent from each side. The really wonderful part, which is the most painful part, too, is that God wants us to give 100 percent even when our partner isn't giving anything."

"Even if he's pulling a negative?"

"Especially then." She wrapped her arm around my shoulders. "Figure out if you're able or willing to give 100 percent before you get married. Now's the time for a strategic retreat. Before you make a promise to God that you'll come to resent later."

"What about what Andy's willing to give?" I nearly started crying. Stupid. I had resolved to stop crying and hurting because of him.

"You hit it on the head." She put her arm around me. "A lot of men are *willing* to give 100 percent, and that goes a long way to make up for not being *able*. A lot of men are able, but if they *aren't* willing, what's the use?"

That made a lot of sense. It hurt. It confirmed what I was slowly, reluctantly, realizing I had to do.

I couldn't give 100 percent to anyone just yet. It might take until I graduated, or until I hit fifty before I was strong enough and smart enough to give 100 percent to a husband. Even if he held back.

No matter how loving and noble it might sound, putting everything on hold for Andy's sake wouldn't be blessed by God. Mrs. Z said we had to climb together to have a successful marriage -- Andy couldn't stand on my shoulders, and I couldn't stand on his.

So even though I hadn't received any response from Andy, I made my decision.

I took the job offer and prepared to transfer to a college near AMEA headquarters. They had already arranged things for me, which proved how much they valued my contribution. All I had to do was accept. Then I arranged to go to SCC after camp to get my gear out of storage before I went home to pack for the move. I called Tonia. She was excited for me. She made plans to let everyone know it was Andy's fault we broke up.

It had to be his fault, right? After three weeks, he still hadn't responded to my letters. Even though my mind was pretty much made up, I still wanted and needed his input. Maybe this was a test just for me, but what if it was a test for him, too? What if I cut all ties just when he was about to have that big epiphany and pass the test?

I wrote to Chaplain Nate and told him what I was doing. His input mattered. I asked if we could meet for lunch, to talk, when I came for my gear.

One morning at devotions, Nancy suggested maybe I was using God as an excuse to run away from something I didn't even know I was afraid of. That got me thinking.

I didn't want God to be an excuse. I wanted Him to be the reason. The only reason. The best reason.

Maybe my school year with Andy had just been a detour or a test. Whatever it was, I was back on track.

*****

All my letters to Andy had to go to a central mailbox, then catch up with him on the road. So there was a chance some might never catch up with him. Some foolishly romantic -- or maybe pitiful -- part of me had copied every letter I wrote to him. I had some silly idea of filling in the holes in our summer narrative, when we got back together in the fall.

I put the copies of my letters in one big envelope, and sent them to Andy's school mailbox. What if he wrote to me, but I never got those letters? What if he never got my letters until he got back to school?

If he never got any of my original letters, I owed him an explanation. Even if that was true, he should have called me to find out why I didn't write. If he had just called me, once, we could have fixed this mess before it became a mess.

Mom sent me my engagement ring when she sent my birth certificate, checkbook and other important documents for the move. It broke in the

77

mail. I put the pieces with the letters.

Thanks to a moving allowance from AMEA, I flew to the Burlington airport and rented a car to drive to Blue Bell City. From there, I would drive home. I planned to pack up as quickly as I could and get out of town before Bill and his fiancée got to work trying to save my soul.

Yes, I said fiancée. I didn't even know she existed until I got a letter, my second-to-last day at camp, in her handwriting. If I recognized Bill's handwriting, I would have thrown out the letter unopened. When I realized who she was, I kept reading, the way people stop at horrific car accidents. They just can't help looking. Bill forbade me to drive cross-country. He forbade me to go to work for AMEA. According to Bill's new pastor -- the father of his fiancée -- Allen Michaels was a tool of some subversive Islamic cell slowly poisoning the church in America.

I could almost laugh, anticipating the problems Bill would face when he changed his mind, as he always did, and decided once again that working for AMEA was the only true road to heaven. He had used that tactic several times when he lost a job and decided that I owed him help in obtaining a good-paying job with lots of prestige. Then, he was proud of his "little sister" and her great connections.

Despite everything, it was a relief to get back to SCC. Blue Bell City was just the same. Sleepy quiet. A few tractors and other farming equipment trundled around in the distance. Sheep and dogs made a background hum. Hardly any cars were on the highway through town.

I took care of my withdrawal paperwork. Someone met me at the dorm to unlock the door and helped me haul my boxes up to load them into the trunk of my rental car. Then I hit the Student Center to check my mailbox for anything that might have come in during the summer (nothing), fill out the withdrawal form, and turn in my key.

My next stop was Chaplain Nate's office. We were to meet at his bungalow to go to lunch, but I was early, and I thought I'd save us both some steps.

I went up to the open door and knocked on the glass. Then I saw Andy standing in front of Chaplain Nate's desk.

I assumed all the papers spread out on the desk were my letters, because the broken pieces of my engagement ring sat on top of the pile. Chaplain Nate wasn't there.

I didn't have any idea what I should do -- go in and face him, finally get him to talk to me -- or run?

Then Andy turned around and looked at me, and it was too late to run. He didn't look surprised.

"You're early." If anything, Andy looked way too calm. Bad sign. "Afraid I'd be waiting, so you're just going to race through town and vanish?"

"Vanish?"

"You're running out on me."

"How can I run out on you when you dumped me? Not a single call all summer. You had my phone number. You knew where I was. Thanks for letting me know how you were doing and that you--" No way in the world was I going to say, "still loved me."

"That I wasn't fooling around behind your back?" He bared his teeth at me as if he wanted to laugh but couldn't. "Just because those morons tried to play Romeo doesn't mean everybody in the band was out to rape and pillage their way across the country."

"It certainly wasn't a good witness, was it?"

"That's what headquarters said. They cancelled our tour a week after I saw you."

"Just from one complaint?"

Andy's head bowed, and he shrugged. "No, there were other times. We didn't catch the guys, but parents complained."

"So, your tour was cancelled. How long have you been back in town? Did you get my mail?"

"All at once." He gestured at the envelope sitting on Chaplain Nate's desk. I wondered if they were in the middle of discussing what was wrong with me, how I had messed up.

"What about all the other letters I sent you?"

Another shrug. How was I supposed to interpret that?

"As far as I'm concerned, you dumped me at the beginning of the summer, but you didn't have the guts to tell me." I was so proud of myself. My voice didn't waver. Calm and cool. In direct contrast to the hot churning moving down from my throat, through my chest. When it hit my belly, I was probably going to fold up with the worst cramps ever.

"What does it matter?" He flicked the cracked glass square from my ring. "You've ended it."

"Are you willing to fight for me?"

"What?"

"Are you willing to work to keep us together? You said you loved me -- was that a lie? To get me to let you stick your tongue in my mouth? Which is pretty disgusting, by the way."

"Then why did you put up with it?" He grinned. Not his nasty grin. If I didn't know better, I would have said he felt sick.

"You're the first guy who made me feel like I was worth something, and I would have done anything to keep you."

"Guess you changed your mind." He took a step around me, heading for the door. I turned.

Chaplain Nate stood in the door, a full carafe of water for his coffeemaker in his hand. How long had he been listening to us?

"She grew up, Andy," he said. "I read those letters, too. Did you read the part where she said she was putting everything in God's hands? Did you hear what she said? She would have done anything to keep you. That's the wrong attitude for a Christian. Especially for one who's been preparing for ministry most of her life. Even when she's in love."

"That doesn't matter anymore, does it?"

"Then you're not willing to try to work this out, are you?" I asked.

I waited. Chaplain Nate waited. Andy just glared at me, until he couldn't look into my eyes any longer.

"I guess that's clear, huh?" I looked at Chaplain Nate and tried to smile. "Maybe we'd better cancel lunch."

"That's your answer for everything, isn't it?" Andy said with a thin chuckle. "Just cancel."

"Andrew." Chaplain Nate leaned into the doorframe, so there was no way anyone could get out without hitting him. "Eve presented her fears, her hurts, her questions quite clearly -- did you ever express your side to her? I understand where she's coming from, and I can see she's trying to leave a door open to fix this problem."

"Problem? The girl I wanted to marry is dumping me. She's going into ministry without asking what I want to do!"

"Do you have plans for after graduation? A ministry lined up? Applications anywhere?" He sighed when Andy only shook his head. "Eve has opened the door to wonderful opportunities."

"That's not how it works," he growled.

"The man leads, and the woman puts her brain on idle for the rest of her life. No thanks." I snorted. "Barefoot, pregnant and in the kitchen. I thought you agreed that wasn't going to happen to me."

"Mom warned me you were going to do this. You told her you'd never share me with anyone. That's the wrong attitude for a minister's wife."

"What?" I laughed, despite the feeling of being punched in the gut. Now was not the time for that to happen. "When did I tell her this? When she fell down and hit her head and she dreamed it?"

"Eve would never say anything like that." Chaplain Nate sounded angry.

"Only a really stupid girl would say something like that to her future mother-in-law." I wanted to pound Andy, but I just backed up until the doorknob ground into my hip. "Okay, so I was stupid enough to think we could be good together. But that's where it stopped."

"See?" Andy looked at Chaplain Nate, like I wasn't even there. "She'd never make it as a minister's wife."

"You can't call yourself a minister until you *have* a ministry!" Okay, so I shrieked. "I *have* a ministry. Maybe the problem here is that *you* can't stand the thought of sharing *me* with God."

"She won't listen. She has to have everything her way." He dropped into a chair and shrugged, wearing a brave little smile. Perfect mirror image of his mother's martyr act.

"Fine, blame me. I don't care anymore because you stopped caring a long time ago."

I stomped up to Chaplain Nate, and he actually moved aside and let me past.

Was I wrong, demanding equal partnership? I refused to believe God would expect me to abandon all the gifts, all the opportunities He put in my path, just to be a housekeeper and cheerleader for someone who hadn't grown up enough to keep promises or admit when he was wrong.

It was officially over. I thought I was prepared, but I wasn't.

I thought I didn't love Andy anymore, but something hurt so bad that day, I was in Illinois before I could breathe normally again.

Funny, but I didn't even realize the cramping had stopped until I was halfway to Indiana.

There are many different kinds of pain. Even healing hurts.

Part Two: Charles
Chapter 8

Near the end of my third year with AMEA, I joined a team to develop a new phase of children's ministry that tied into the crusade team's work. I had graduated from the dorm to share a three-bedroom apartment with three other girls. Jane had a night-shift job in the AMEA counseling center, so she and I shared the big bedroom with bunk beds. We would joke about her being a vampire because she was so pale and thin and only came out at night. She was great. We had the same taste in books; science fiction, adventure, and romance. She would read a book during one stint on the phones, come in from work while I was taking my shower in the morning, and leave the book on my bed. She'd usually be asleep by the time I got out of the shower and dressed for the day, so we'd talk books in the evening while I was eating supper and she was eating breakfast.

The other two girls in our apartment were Babby and Mini. I got along fine with Babby, despite her being so perky-cute. If she had been born twenty years earlier, she would have been a Mouseketeer, a dead-ringer for Tootie in *The Facts of Life*. Mini was the sour note. Actually, her name was Minerva. She must have thought she had to live up to the name, because she was a serial dieter and punished everyone for the torture she put herself through. Nervy would have been a better name for her, the stereotypical know-it-all who granted herself the right to criticize everyone around her.

I might have moved out after about six months of Saint Mini trying to reform me with the subtlety of a caveman's club. Just before I got to the point of "enough," I had a personal crisis, and she turned warm and supportive and knew all the right things to say. I had a few epiphanies during that awful period, and one was that Mini needed to be needed. She had a lot to give, and when she couldn't give, that cast doubts on her worth. So she got defensive. And we all know that the best defense is a good offense. To the max.

My crisis? Dad died. Maybe I shouldn't have been surprised. He was just a big, helpless baby with no common sense, when it came to his health. He caught a cold during tax season and didn't take care of himself. His usual bout of what he called accountant's exhaustion after tax season hit twice as hard that year. His stamina was shot, and his immune system crashed and burned. A simple cold turned into pneumonia and other complications. He spent a week sedated, on a ventilator, before he died.

All was quiet from his side of the family until someone got

information they had no legal right to, and discovered the size of Dad's estate. It was tied up nice and neat in several (healthy-sized) trusts that couldn't be dismantled, and Mom was in charge. We had to change the apartment phone number because the Miller clan called day and night. They wanted that money, Mom and Dad's house, and all the investments. When every lawyer they consulted told them there was no breaking the trusts in their favor, they turned to harassment. The Miller clan actually expected me to convince Mom to relinquish her authority and put everything into the hands of people who had mentally and emotionally abused her for decades. They spent big bucks in telegrams and certified letters to reach me once we got our apartment number unlisted. The switchboard at AMEA headquarters learned not to pass on any callers to me from numbers originating in Ohio. Bill came to see me twice, playing his "loving big brother trying to look out for my favorite little sister" card. After the third ambush on the way to work, I gave his picture to the security desk at headquarters, with instructions to stop him at the door.

That "unwarranted humiliation" was the last straw for the Miller clan. Those horrendous people actually thought they were hurting me when they cut all ties with me.

All that craziness was worth it, though. Mom and I had peace. We were no longer the Miller family "burden." My supervisors and co-workers were supportive and sympathetic and didn't blame me at all for the temporary ruckus. By this time, I knew the trouble from the Miller clan was the equivalent of mosquito bites, when measured against some truly vile abuse and attacks our organization had to endure. There was a reason why Chris Hawkes, former military and government intelligence officer, was head of security.

I was given a lot of traveling assignments to get me out and away, give me fresh air and new scenery. I can only imagine, looking back, how bad my stress-induced fibroid attacks would have been otherwise.

I spent time assisting the crusade advance team when they were working in southern Ohio, just because it was close to my old stomping grounds, just a few hours south. I worked with Kurt Green, one of my mentors when I first moved to headquarters. On my first trip, I met up with father and son, Royce and Nathan Hanson. Royce was a farmer, semi-retired. Nathan was a Marine, spending the last few years of his enlistment as a chaplain's assistant. Their family farm was semi-retired, too, until Nathan left the Corps and could come home to help his father. All his sisters were married and neither they nor their husbands were interested in working on the farm. Father and son came to help the support staff prepare for an Allen Michaels youth crusade.

By my second trip, in November, Nathan and his father had come to a decision. Nathan wanted to go to seminary once he was out of the Marines. He and Royce had to either hire people to run the farm for them, or divest themselves of their acreage. They preferred to see that land used for God's glory. Royce wanted to turn all that farmland into a training camp for summer missions work. The two weeks I was there, I spent most of it with the Hansons. We walked the property, taking pictures, studying the surrounding communities and the access roads, and getting information from all the people at headquarters who would be involved in a project that huge.

While it was a great idea, AMEA couldn't act on it right away. Another farmer in Georgia had already donated his family farm for the same purpose. This was a former cotton plantation with some very negative history. He wanted to make recompense for the suffering others had suffered to build his family's fortune.

About the time the Hansons made their proposal to headquarters, the first wave of landscaping had begun in Georgia. The camp would be used for summer labor team training. Crews of teens and college students and their adult supervisors would build homes and churches and orphanages, dig trenches, set up water filtration plants, and renovate homes. AMEA was creating the recruitment program for that summer missions effort. I had my name on the list for that team.

If AMEA accepted the gift of the Hanson acres in Coshocton, it would be years before they did anything with the property. If God blessed the campground project in Georgia, and recruitment multiplied every year, they might need a second training campground.

*****

By mid-December of that year of big changes, our apartment and my life finally had freedom and quiet, no more Miller clan harassment. Charles Lawson came into Mini's life. He was a law student clerking in a major business law firm. Nice looking. Spit and polish. Although, something about him made me think he'd never spit. Not even toothpaste.

He was definitely Mini's type. Well-dressed, well-groomed, well-spoken. Well...kind of stiff. Probably all that money in his back pocket made his back sore.

The first time he picked Mini up at our apartment, Babby just about had a seizure from holding back her laughter until Mini and Charles vanished down the sidewalk for their date.

"Did you see his eyes bug out when I walked out of the kitchen? Heaven save us, a black girl living with you poor, deceived white girls."

"He wasn't thinking that. He was shocked and disillusioned that an employee of my dignified organization wore sweatpants with holes in the knees." I stretched my legs out to demonstrate. Since it was Saturday, I was in full grunge mode. If I were a guy, I would have had a quarter inch of stubble on my face. Good thing Charles couldn't look at my legs!

The fact that I worked for AMEA impressed him. I did not fit his image of how an up-and-coming member of AMEA should act. I was sitting on the floor to watch TV. Horrors!

If he was hanging with Mini, Charles probably agreed with her opinion, which she inflicted on me regularly. Someone in my exalted and holy position was required to wear dresses below the knee, nylons (never pantyhose), shoes with heels no higher than two inches (but never flats), and perpetually flawless makeup and hair.

Babby and I agreed: the two of them deserved each other! Although, once we got over our giggles, we had to admit he was kind of nice. Babby wondered what he would look like if he let his hair get a little messed, and if he wore something besides a suit and tie. Mini glowed when he showed up, and he glowed back when he looked at her. Tastefully, of course. Babby and I were sure it was only a matter of time before a tasteful diamond appeared on her finger, and we could become three girls in a three-bedroom apartment.

Charles and Mini went out every Friday night, and met for lunch at least twice each week. We knew they did because she always reported to us every time Charles took her out. Maybe to rub it in that she had a serious boyfriend and none of us had had dates for months. This went on until March.

Then Mini's ex-boyfriend back in Buffalo launched a campaign to get her back. He obviously hadn't gotten the message that she had broken up with him when she moved away and stayed away.

Although, come to think of it, if my ex gave me his phone number when he moved to another town and kept in contact (I can vouch for this, because I overheard their phone calls at least once a month for the entire time Mini was living with us), wouldn't I consider it an invitation to *hope*?

Something was going on, something had changed between Mini and the ex, or maybe between her and Charles. Or maybe Mini herself was the one who had changed. Soon there was trouble in paradise. By the end of the first week of May, Mini had a big, socially prominent date with Mr. Soon-to-Pass-the-Bar Go-Straight-to-Partner, and she was not flying with delight. Babby and I agreed that all Mini's recent disdainful talk about her ex-boyfriend being a slob without ambition was just talk. The subtext was that she was trying to psych herself out of wanting him so bad.

It was kind of frightening to realize Mini and I had something in common. Me and Andy, Mini and Mr. Buffalo.

I hadn't really thought about Andy until recently. Mom had asked me to get the last of my things out of the house, so she could downsize to a condo. I took the time to look at my wedding dress in its long plastic bag when I loaded up my car. All the dreams and plans and misery came rolling over me like a really heavy, cold tidal wave -- full of sand and seaweed but with some pretty shells to pick up and keep once that first staggering cold shock had passed.

During that drive back to headquarters from Ohio, I did a lot of thinking and assessing of my life. Amazing how philosophical the sight of that unused, unneeded, and forgotten dress could make me. I realized I owed Andy something. I needed that ego boost that came with being "his girl" for a few months. I grew from thinking I wasn't worth a second look, to realizing that I deserved better than the stunted life he offered me. Along with blossoming once I got away from Bill's constant, critical, destructive input, Andy had a lot to do with my growth and confidence. I was actually mature enough to hope he had found someone he could make happy.

So as Mini slid into her campaign to give Charles the ladylike message that his company was no longer welcome, I felt kind of sorry for both of them. I hoped they had an easier breakup than Andy and I did.

Before the big "thanks, have a happy life" bomb dropped on him, Charles met "the family." He wanted Mini to go out to lunch with his friends the Sunday after their big date, and she told him she reserved Sundays to spend with her roommates.

Talk about oblivious! He completely missed the gradual brush-off job she was doing and decided she wanted *him* to spend the day with *us*. So he volunteered to drive all of us to church and said he wanted to spend the afternoon getting to know us.

When we got to church, Charles seemed surprised that adults had classes, including a class just for Singles. Yes, his church had a Singles Fellowship, but they didn't get together on Sunday morning. I guess Sunday school was only for children at his church, and once they reached high school, they were on their own. Jane had nursery duty that morning, and Babby was helping with the junior high class, so it was just Mini and me going to class together with Charles in tow.

Mr. Gruber, our teacher, was in rare form that morning, talking about his misbegotten youth as a drummer in a rock band. Considering that he sported a Friar Tuck haircut, it was hard to imagine Mr. G with long blond hair, a nose ring, and a tattoo across his chest. But he had shown us pictures of the "bad old days." Mr. G's point was that God could redeem anyone, and no matter how bad our foundation or how embarrassing our past, we could be steady and strong if we relied on God.

Mini usually had to be the answer girl, but that morning she just sat silent in class. She didn't even offer to share her Bible with Charles, who didn't bring one. That shocked me. Who went to church without a Bible? That was like going to school without textbooks.

When we went to the service, Charles used one of the spare Bibles in the sanctuary pews. He seemed to have a hard time finding the passages that Pastor Rodstandt quoted from. Again, Mini sat still, staring straight ahead, her eyes kind of glazed. No offers to help Charles stumble his way through the pages, no comments to illuminate what Pastor said. This silence and thoughtfulness was uncharacteristic. Weird.

I wondered if she was feeling sick. So when Charles left us on the sidewalk to go get his big, shiny black car, I asked if she was okay.

She blinked back tears and smiled. Very weird. "Tony called last night. He wants me to come home. He loves me."

I would have pointed out that she was dating someone else, but Charles pulled up to the sidewalk and Babby and Jane came running out the door. We all piled in and headed for home.

Mini was tense, fighting tears, but Charles seemed pretty comfortable. He loosened his tie and took off his suit coat at lunch, which we had at our apartment, instead of tormenting ourselves by going to a restaurant. Getting the four of us to agree on one restaurant could have led to World War III.

Jane made blueberry corn muffins. Babby opened up a bag of her designer coffee and whipped up a batch of her black bean and corn relish. I made three big oven omelets while Mini set the table and made a killer salad.

Charles was gracious and relaxed once the food hit the table. He had nice manners and was very complimentary of everyone's contribution. He also ate as much as Mini and Jane put together. I would have been more pleased if he hadn't seemed so surprised by my skill in the kitchen.

"Honestly, I didn't think you corporate types spent any time in the kitchen," he said, with a cute smile that made him seem about seventeen. I forgave him the "corporate types" remark because of that smile.

"Evie is just a regular Betty Crocker," Mini muttered. She could have zinged me good, so I knew something was wrong.

"Suzie Homemaker," Jane offered. She got up and made a beeline for the kitchen to start loading the washer. She was due to hit the sack in about half an hour, so she could get up at ten for the midnight shift at the counseling center.

"Martha Stewart," Babby said.

I made a cross sign with my forefingers, warding off the curse of those words, earning laughter from everyone. Even Charles.

It was a nice afternoon. Especially since Charles had the courtesy to leave about an hour after lunch.

If he could just relax a little more, I decided, he'd be a nice guy to hang around with. He liked movies and science fiction books, and we argued for a few minutes about what would happen if Weber wrote another Honor Harrington book. Then he ruined everything by giving me a blank look when I mentioned Discworld. So, he could relax enough to enjoy SF, but only military SF, and no fantasy?

Mini burst into tears the minute Charles vanished down the sidewalk, muttered something about Tony, and ran for her room.

By Friday, Mini was gone. She actually jumped in the car as I came in from work that night. She was on her way home to Buffalo. And Tony. She yelled something about Charles as she drove away, but I had no idea what she was talking about.

It was kind of encouraging to know that true love could win out over ambition and fashion, even with Mini.

Since Babby wasn't home yet, Jane was still in bed, and for some reason I had romance and true love on my mind, I pulled my wedding dress out of storage and tried it on. I had managed to lose twenty more pounds and keep them off since I bought it, so it looked good. I wondered if I would ever get a chance to wear it.

Would it be tacky to wear a dress to marry one guy, when I bought it to marry another?

Definitely a rhetorical question because I hadn't had a boyfriend since Andy. A few dates, sure. My average was about two dates per month for the last three or four years. New guys joined headquarters, we went out once or twice, but nothing sparked, nothing encouraged either of us to take the friendship higher.

Once burned, twice shy.

Saturday, I learned what Mini was talking about when she ran away. She and Charles had tickets for the afternoon matinee at the ballet. *Romeo and Juliet.*

He showed up two hours before the ballet to take Mini to a late lunch. I felt sorry for him, with his pink rose and a box of Godiva chocolates. I tried to soften it for him by saying her trip home was sudden -- and nothing about Tony. I had no idea if Mini had ever mentioned Tony to Charles. It couldn't be good for his ego to know Mini chose a mechanic over him. True, Tony was full partner in the family's chain of five garages spread throughout Buffalo, but Mini's complaints about him included the fact he was taking "forever" to get his college degree with evening classes, always had dirt under his fingernails, and thought pizza and wings made for gourmet eating.

Tony sounded like a great guy to me.

Discussing Mini's abrupt departure the night before, Babby brought up something that I hadn't heard before. Maybe because I had a tendency to tune out Mini when she got a little too my-soul-is-in-better-touch-with-God-than-yours. Part of Mini's problem with Tony was that she wanted to go into some kind of ministry and do something spiritually meaningful with her life. She had argued regularly with him about the level of commitment and involvement. He thought he could serve God just fine by working with the youth at church and writing checks for missionaries. Mini had somewhere gotten the idea that she wouldn't truly be serving God unless the man she married was involved in full-time ministry or a mover-and-shaker for reforming society. Okay, that kind of explained her attraction to Charles, who certainly had the moving-and-shaking qualification. I knew nothing about his spiritual life other than that he went to church and he didn't think Allen Michaels was the Anti-Christ.

That afternoon, though, I got a few clues that maybe Charles was a great guy, too. He didn't throw a snit when we gave him the news that Mini was gone. He didn't complain about how the tickets would go to waste and he couldn't get his money back. Charles had class.

"Would you help me by taking these off my hands?" He handed Babby the rose and box of chocolates.

Asking Babby if she'd take chocolate was like asking the Colonel if he cared to try a bite of chicken.

"Eve, do you enjoy the ballet?" He gave me a crooked smile that hinted at a nice guy trying to hide his hurt.

"Very much. What I've had time to see." I wasn't about to admit that I'd only seen video snippets, or *The Nutcracker Suite* at Christmas.

"I'd be grateful if you'd accompany me this afternoon." He gave my jeans and baggy sweater one glance and his smile widened a little. "I planned on lunch before the ballet, but I don't think we'll have time. Why don't we plan on dinner afterward?"

That was the nicest way anyone had ever asked me to dress up. How could I be insulted?

I wore my new midnight blue dress with a handkerchief hem and fitted sleeves, and silver jewelry. Charles's mouth actually dropped open when I came out of the bedroom in record time, decked out as if I had spent hours planning what to wear. Fortunately, my short hair looked good whether combed or not.

My only clear memory of that afternoon was that Charles made me laugh. It had been a long time between dates. It had been even longer (try never) since a guy opened the door for me and insisted on paying for everything. He even helped me with my coat and -- okay, I admit to vanity -- looked at my legs a few times.

Charles seemed to like having me with him at the ballet. He introduced me to people in fancy clothes as his "new friend, Miss Eve Miller." Made me sound important. Rather blue-blooded.

Despite my fantastic afternoon, Mini was the winner. She made the right choice. She gave up her job and fancy clothes for a future with a guy who ate pizza with dirty fingers -- but he loved her.

*****

Thursday of the next week, Charles called me at work and asked if I wanted to go to a movie preview. His roommate worked for a radio station and got the tickets for him. Believe it or not, Charles wanted to see the newest Marvel movie.

We sat in some coffee house afterward, talking until the staff threw us out. I didn't even like coffee unless it was all dressed up. What did we talk about? Anything. Everything. Charles was a well-rounded guy. A highly educated man who didn't try to impress me with his education. He was good with people, which would be useful once he got into the courtroom.

So why did he ask *me* when he could have asked a dozen other people?

Babby gave me her patented "Are you serious?" look, the first time I voiced my thoughts. I eventually convinced her there was no spark between us, and despite his good taste in fandom, Charles just wasn't my type. We did some deep thinking for a few days. Her theory: He was too proud to ask for news about Mini, but if he came by the apartment often enough, he would hear something.

I knew exactly how to scare him off: the spiritual maturity gambit. Babby and Jane used church to test how sincere guys were. Sitting through a few services with a pastor who really believed in and taught from the Bible always weeded out the creeps who saw "church chicks" as a challenge. Since Charles had already gone through one Sunday of class and worship service, it might take just one more dose. If he still hung on, the next step would be Singles Bible study. That was sure to scare away a guy who only went to church on Sunday to "get it over with."

Charles accepted the invitation. Babby was surprised, but I honestly felt sorry for the guy. His feelings for Mini weren't that obvious to me, but he had to feel something strong enough to stick around and hope for information. Or maybe he was just too proud to admit he was fishing.

He participated in class this time and seemed to enjoy it. At least until the questions in our monthly Bible quiz game went past the David-and-Goliath or Feeding-the-Five-Thousand level. When he consistently got them wrong, he didn't seem to have much fun. In the service, Charles didn't know the songs in the hymnal. It took once through the song before he picked up the melody and joined the singing. What was worship without music to get us into the right attitude?

*****

I was gone for two weeks, helping the team working on the Georgia boot camp. Kurt Green drove down from South Carolina where he was setting up for a youth crusade. I was surprised but glad to see him. He was like the big brother I never had -- we even looked something alike, with thick dark hair, red highlights, and dark eyes. He got a strange look on his face when I used those exact words. Instead of joining our meeting with the committee of local church leaders, he asked Howard, the team leader, if he could "borrow" me for a little while. There would be a recording because it was a video conference with offices in other states, so I wouldn't really miss anything. Kurt and I went for a walk.

"Funny you should say I'm the brother you never had." Kurt waited until we had put a wall of scrawny pine trees and a dip in the landscape between us and the church parking lot. "I remember you saying you were an only child. So I'm wondering what kind of trouble you're in when a guy who claims to be your brother--"

"Bill Miller is my cousin, not my brother. He only pulls the brother card when he wants something, or he's trying to run my life." I pressed both hands against my abdomen, anticipating a cramp.

At my last checkup, my fibroids had shrunk, and I hadn't had a flare-up since the whole ugly battle over Dad's estate.

"Uh huh." He squinted into the distance. "Can you fit the whole story into a walk, or do we need to go sit and pull out the big guns?"

"Chocolate peanut butter malts and onion rings?" He nodded, and I had to grin, despite that sinking feeling that Bill reappearing in my life always created. We had used junk food therapy a few times to work off stress of various projects. "No, I can give you the Reader's Digest condensed version by the time we circle the property."

I actually finished laying out the situation with the Miller clan in very little time. It summed up nicely in about ten sentences or so. I finished by relating how I had to give Bill's picture to building security, when he harassed me at work over Dad's estate.

"Hmm, interesting," Kurt said. "I don't suppose you have any pictures of your cousin available right now?"

"Why?" A flicker of ache touched my gut.

"Well, he showed me some pictures of the two of you together. I didn't get enough time for a good look, but I could swear he did a bad job of compiling a few photos together."

"That sounds like him."

"He knew details about you, where you went to school, how your father died, but the alarms went off when he asked me to keep your relationship quiet."

I nearly stumbled. "He's trying to get a job again, isn't he?"

"His line was something about not putting pressure on you to pull strings on his behalf, but now that your father was dead, he had an obligation to look after you."

"No, look after his own interests at my expense."

"He's moving into the area to look after you--"

"Spy on me."

"Probably." Kurt's grin released the pressure building up around me, threatening to steal the air. "He went on and on about how proud he was of you and how he didn't want you to risk your career to make sure he was given a good position to fit his talents."

"He has none, other than being selfish and a liar."

"The thing is…he was kind of right about you."

"Just kind of? In what way?" I grinned back at him. Oh, the glories of knowing I had someone on my side who hadn't fallen for Saint Bill's constant rewriting of reality.

"You'd risk your own career to help someone you cared about. You'd pull strings to help other people. And you're smart and a hard worker."

"I can't figure out how he thought he could get in the front door after the ruckus he raised last year."

"That's why I asked if you had any pictures of him. How does he look normally? What color is his hair? What is his build?"

Bill had put lots of effort into his latest con job. The guy Kurt described to me wasn't the egotist I had last seen putting on a performance at Dad's funeral. He had shaved off all his thinning, usually greasy, tangled hair; he had a gray-streaked beard; and he tried for the nerd look, with a pale blue button-down shirt, sweater vest, and beige slacks, over black penny loafers. Total change from the happy-to-work-a-gas-station-for-the-rest-of-my-life tee-shirt and jeans look. Also, now he had a huge stomach, meaning he had gained a lot of weight in the last year.

I couldn't stop Bill from moving to town. Kurt promised to do some digging when he got back to headquarters and take some preventative measures so no matter who Bill hoodwinked, he wouldn't get through the door. Not the front door, not a side door, and certainly not a back door.

I hated to do it, but I had to call Mom and fill her in on the latest maneuver. Just so she could be prepared for any fallout when Bill's plan failed spectacularly. Which I prayed it would.

*****

Thursday night when I got home, I found three messages from Charles on the answering machine. He wanted to get together.

What was I to think? We had a nice time at the movie and the ballet, but I honestly never expected him to call me again once he realized I was useless as a pipeline for Mini updates.

I called his apartment from work the next day and left a message, inviting him to Singles Bible study that night. I didn't think he would show.

Babby certainly didn't expect to see him. When we drove up to the church and saw him standing by the side door, she shrieked. I shrieked because she was driving and I thought she'd had a seizure.

The poor guy had a lot to learn about Bible study. He didn't know the order of the books, he didn't know the difference between OT and NT, and he didn't even know how to use the index. At least he tried.

At the end of the Bible study, the odd feeling I'd had when I heard Charles' messages got stronger. On our way out to the parking lot, he made plans to meet us at church on Sunday and go out for lunch with the gang from Bible study. I couldn't exactly tell him he couldn't come when everyone had been making plans right there in front of him. Not that I didn't want Charles to come to church and class and lunch with us, but *why* was he hanging around with us?

Babby changed her theory from trolling for news about Mini to Charles on the rebound. Not a comforting thought. I knew I had to send him away. Babby and I both agreed that missionary rebound dating was even worse than missionary dating. The problem was how to send him away. I had no experience in giving guys the brush-off because the "it's been fun, but this isn't going anywhere" had always been kind of mutual.

Besides, if Mini came back to town after deciding Tony wasn't Mr. Grubby-But-Wonderful after all, I didn't want her accusing me of trying to steal her guy while her back was turned. If my tactic of "just friends" didn't work, Charles had to get the message when I vanished for most of the summer on association business.

*****

Two weeks passed. Charles faithfully attended Bible study and church and class. No report came from HR about Bill trying to sneak into the building. Then some local trouble tried to blow up in our faces. I played with the idea that God had sent Charles to be a sort of white knight for AMEA, with me as the connection. If that was so, then he would soon ride off into the sunset to rescue someone else.

Channel 14 sent a video crew through headquarters that Thursday at the start of June, to talk to people, film candid shots of people at work, the daycare center, basically looking behind the scenes. Chris Hawkes played escort, a sign this was big and high-tension. There had been some complaints that AMEA never hired locally, that we brought people from other states to fill job openings. Essentially, we had to prove we had lots of local people on staff.

Local politics trying to make another faith-based organization look like hypocrites just made my day. I loved politics in any shape or form.

Yeah, and I also had plans to go whitewater rafting in Death Valley that summer. Without a raft.

Things were polite enough. Nobody tried to sneak off into areas they were told were not open to the public. We let them talk to anyone they wanted, with no guidance from the escorts. I was asked to join them about fifteen minutes into the tour, so I saw what went on. At my last tally, they nabbed about fifty percent local hires. Which was good for us.

Charles showed up halfway through the tour. He just waltzed right in and walked up to the assistant for the chief headhunter/newsperson and started talking like they were pals.

Actually, they were pals from high school. Every time a camera pointed anywhere near my direction, Charles tapped his buddy on the shoulder and said something, and suddenly I was out of the hot seat.

Of course, there was a price to pay. Charles took me and buddy Jason out to lunch. I had to answer a lot of questions, mostly about my training, all the jobs I had done for AMEA, and my take on future efforts.

"What do you think about today's invasion?" Charles grinned at Jason. For a few seconds, I thought I had been set up.

"I'm still trying to figure out the station's agenda," I said.

"Agenda?" Jason tried to put on an innocent expression. He failed miserably.

"I've witnessed enough interviews, I know no reporter worth his salt shows up at an interview without an idea of what he *wants* the story to say. It doesn't matter if the victim gives him what he wants or not, he'll just twist the truth and edit the quotes until the results agree with his preconceived notions. Considering the complaints that we don't hire enough locals, I have a good idea of your angle. Your boss already decided we were guilty."

"A little bit." Jason shrugged. "You folks are just a little too good to be true."

"The whole tolerance campaign in the country encompasses everybody but Evangelicals. It's open season on us, and the more damage the media can do, the happier everyone else is."

"Hey, that's not fair!" He grinned as he said it, as if he thought I'd made a joke. I hadn't.

"But it's the truth," Charles said. "Don't deny it."

"Yeah, well, it's so easy to find hypocrites. You religious folks have such high standards, but nobody lives up to them."

"So you ignore the ones who *try*, and you focus on the creeps who are into it for the power and money, not because they love God," I shot back.

"Okay, truce!" He laughed. "Where did you find her, Charlie? She's not your usual type."

"Yeah, I know." Charles looked at me with a little smile that made the shivers of warning crawl my back.

I had no idea what impression we left with Jason and what kind of story he took back to the station. I didn't want to watch when the story ran. My co-workers who did watch said it came off as more of a draw, and amazingly our detractors didn't seem upset that the allegations of unfair hiring practices were proven false.

I owed him, so I agreed when Charles asked me to help him with some tricky shopping. He was going to his sister's for Fourth of July weekend and wanted to take presents to his niece and nephews. I thought maybe he was one of those clueless uncles, but it turned out Charles didn't need my help. He knew exactly what each of the children would like and where to find it. Not like the men who could barely find a mall, let alone navigate inside one. Maybe he just wanted a female presence when he went into the Little Princess shop and bought a tea set, spangle jewelry, and a pair of fairy wings. In this day and age, a single man buying those things could be automatically considered a child molester buying bait -- no one would consider the explanation of a doting uncle until he was already under investigation.

Charles laughed when I said his sister's kids had him wrapped around their pinky fingers.

"I hope when I'm a father myself, I have better control. Over the children and myself. Can you imagine the junk my own kids would get just by looking up at me with big, pleading eyes?" He hefted the shopping bags from three stores as evidence.

"You'll need a mansion, at the very least."

"A really big house with a big backyard. Maybe a barn. For the dogs and at least one pony."

"Planning that far ahead? How many kids?"

"One of each. Two of each would be better, so they'll have playmates. If we live way out in the country."

His logic made sense, but it bothered me. What about what his wife wanted? Would he simply shop until he found a woman who had the same list? Or would he use his lawyer skills to persuade a woman who was almost perfect? Remake her, brainwash her, perhaps, until she toed the party line?

"How many kids would you like to have some day, Eve?"

That scared me, coming on the heels of my thoughts about the wife he'd choose.

"By the time I get married, I'll be too old to have any."

"You're not that old, are you?"

"Old enough to resent the question." I laughed.

"I'm serious." He caught hold of my arm to stop me.

"Why does it matter?" Suddenly I was scared. My roommates couldn't be right -- was Charles on the rebound?

"You don't look old enough to worry if you can be a mother or not." We started walking again.

"I'm not."

He could take that answer any way he wanted. I'd never confirmed with the doctor, but the chance I could never have children didn't bother me. It wasn't like guys were beating down the door to win my heart.

"I've pretty much resigned myself to spending my life as a single and spoiling my friends' kids when they have them."

"But you do want kids?"

"Inapplicable question." I suddenly wanted to pick a fight. "How old do you think I am?"

Being a lawyer and highly intelligent, he knew better than to even acknowledge the question.

Charles walked me to the door when we got back to the apartment. The phone rang when I had my key in the lock. I got the door open just as I heard the answering machine beep.

"Hey, where is everybody?" Mini cried in an obnoxiously cheerful voice. "Just want to let you know I'll be coming back to town on Monday, for a week or so. I have a bunch of loose ends to tie up, people I need to talk to. Tony and I are taking some time apart to get some really serious thinking done." She giggled, ending on a sigh.

I glanced over my shoulder. Charles had followed me inside. He didn't look me in the eye once Mini hung up. He thanked me for my help, apologized for taking up so much of my time, and left.

I was ready to drop to my knees and shout a prayer of thanks. When Mini returned, the rebound would end. Charles would shift into heavy duty win-my-girl-back mode and pull out all the stops to persuade her he was a much better choice than some mechanic in Buffalo. Maybe I could sell Mini my unused wedding dress?

I pulled my dress out of storage again and tried it on. Babby and Jane came back from grocery shopping while I was still standing in front of the full-length mirror in the hall. They both about dropped their teeth when they saw me there, all in white.

"Please, please tell us that suit didn't twist your brains around until you agreed to take him!" Babby almost shrieked.

I laughed, which went a long way toward convincing them that I was all right and no brainwashing had occurred. I assured them I already had the dress before Charles showed up, and then they demanded an explanation. They put away the groceries while I packed up the dress again. We settled in the living room with lemonade and popcorn, and I told them for the first time about Andy.

Babby shook her head. "Hold tight, girl. Don't let another self-important bozo suck all the oxygen away from your common sense cells!"

"I know our tactics haven't worked yet," Jane added. "We'll turn up the heat and make him run for it."

"Don't worry," I said.

"Girl, we'll do some heavy-duty praying. A slick lawyer-type on the rebound has to be a servant of Satan. We'll call on the Spirit to drive our enemy away," Babby insisted, slipping into a very fake Southern accent.

To stop their plotting, I went to the answering machine, pressed the playback button, and they heard Mini's message.

"She's coming back on Monday. So what?" Jane said.

"Charles heard the whole message when he brought me back after shopping."

"Shortest rebound in history." Babby nodded, grinning. "Lucky girl. But about this dress of yours--"

"I'm putting it up for sale if Mini doesn't need it," I said. "I'm never going to use it, so why have it taking up room? The money could go for something really useful."

"Like bongo drums," Jane said, and filled her mouth with popcorn. She was grinning so wide, trying not to laugh, she almost got popcorn up her nose.

We did an analysis we had put together in Bible study one night when it was completely girls. The guys had been at some he-man weekend retreat. This was a list of all the common sense things we had agreed a man needed to have or be before we could even seriously consider marriage. We applied the list to Charles, so we could give Mini advice, whether she wanted or needed it.

We had all seen enough friends struggling with their marriages. Love wasn't the most important element, but it was like salt. It absolutely had to be present.

Dependable -- Charles.

Good future -- Charles.

Good hygiene -- definitely Charles. He was always neat and clean and smelled good. He also didn't go overboard with the aftershave.

Polite -- most certainly. He used "please" and "thank you" when dealing with all waitresses and sales clerks

Good looking -- no-brainer.

Breaking point: less than the most rudimentary understanding of the Bible and Church history. He didn't understand Mid-Trib, Pre-Trib or Post-Trib, or the nuances that made Predestination such a hot topic. Granted, because a man wasn't into any of the big theological time-wasters didn't make him theologically handicapped. It was refreshing, in a way. Yet what if he didn't understand the *basics* either? What about being unequally yoked?

Then Babby brought up something we hadn't thought of: We didn't even know what church he went to because he never asked me to come to his church or hang around with his Singles group, and he never introduced me to his friends.

Chapter 9

That Sunday, Charles was waiting in the parking lot of our building, as if it had been planned, and drove us to church. In the bathroom at church, Babby, Jane, and I agreed to step up the pressure and conduct the test. It might drive Charles away, or it might prove he was good enough for Mini.

We played a low-key version of Twenty Questions on the way home from church. I asked Charles if he liked the sermon. Innocent and simple, right?

"Interesting. Food for thought." Charles glanced away from the road just enough to flash me his preoccupied smile.

"What do you think about the whole works versus grace argument?"

He didn't even look at me. Irritated or concerned about traffic? "There are just too many differing opinions and not enough evidence."

"Gee, you'd think one thousand pages of Bible would be enough argument for our side," Jane muttered.

"Look at all the denominations, all the in-fighting. Catholics killing Protestants and Protestants killing Catholics in Ireland. Muslims on a holy war against Christians, and Christians carrying bombs into Muslim shrines and refugee camps," he continued.

"Those people weren't *real* Christians. They weren't listening to what Jesus told them. They're listening to man-made dogma, fences put up to keep everyone separate and keep everyone who disagrees with them out of Heaven," Babby said from the back seat.

"Thank goodness God doesn't judge by all the stupid rules men have made up through the years," Jane said.

"Emphasis on men," Babby muttered. That got glares from me and Jane. We had to glare to keep from laughing because we knew Babby didn't mean it. At least, not entirely. Besides, what if Charles was watching us in the mirror?

"And how exactly are we supposed to know what rules God made? I don't think there are any." Charles came as close to heated as I'd ever heard him. "I honestly think that no one, anywhere, has a solid line on what God wants us to do, how He wants us to live. The best we can do is live moral lives and help the helpless."

"And live without hope."

Funny, how that came out of my lips as if someone else put the words there. Charles stared at me as if he couldn't decide if I was crazy or profound. It was a good thing we were at a stoplight.

Well, at least we had a good idea of his spiritual condition.

I was pretty sure Charles was irritated, because he didn't suggest a restaurant and didn't hint about being invited in for lunch. He just drove us straight home. It was a relief when his car vanished down the street. When we were alone in our apartment again, we agreed to start praying big-time Mini wouldn't reconnect with Charles.

Of course, God took care of the problem before we even got started.

Mini showed up Monday afternoon wearing blue jeans, not designer slacks. She hugged everybody, and she only had one small suitcase instead of a year's worth of luggage. I almost asked if there was a pod in the back seat of her car.

Then, when we had settled down for a gabfest, complete with pizza, the doorbell rang, and it was Charles. He never showed up without calling first. I froze. He could see past me where Mini, Jane and Babby sat on the living room floor around the pizza boxes.

"Sorry. I didn't realize you'd be busy." He had a sheepish smile that didn't convince me. "Could I drag you away for a movie tonight?"

He knew Mini was coming back tonight. I figured he was trying to make her jealous. Or maybe he hoped to catch her alone. I told him no, I was busy, thanks for asking. So he asked about lunch the next day.

I sensed the others staring at us, even though the chattering and giggling didn't stop. Fortunately, I didn't have to lie when I said thanks-but-no-thanks. My schedule was loaded with work.

He looked over my shoulder. Once. From the way he stared, I guessed he and Mini had locked glances. Charles finally left, after flashing that brilliant, yet no longer heart-swooning smile.

Then things got stranger: Mini *thanked* me for sending Charles away. Babby accused her of playing hard to get, and Mini just laughed and flashed her engagement ring at us.

We didn't see her engagement ring until then because the diamond was so tiny. She grinned like it was as big as a baseball.

Definite sign of true love.

Mini gushed about how great Tony was and how he had made all sorts of changes just to please her, and she realized that she needed to make changes for him because she really did love him.

Poor Charles, hanging out with me just so he could get a chance at Mini.

I offered Mini my wedding dress. Free. With all my prayers for happiness. It could be her something borrowed.

An even *stronger* sign that true love could work miracles? Mini thought my dress was gorgeous. None of that superior sneer she once used on people when she pretended to be nice, while very obviously pitying us lesser mortals.

"But it's too fancy. Tony and I are going for simple." Mini grinned and flopped down on the couch. "We're going on a camping trip for our honeymoon in the fall. I've never been canoeing, but Tony says I'll love it. We're going to Canada, where the water is so pure you can lean right out of the canoe and drink from the lake."

Babby and I exchanged stunned looks. Mini, rhapsodic over drinking from a lake instead of a designer water bottle?

This was a sure sign the Lord was returning at any moment because the world was about to implode.

*****

Mini was busy all week, tying up loose ends, selling her furniture so she didn't have to haul it back to Buffalo, donating most of her wardrobe she had left behind to the Salvation Army, meeting up with all her friends from work, and saying goodbye. We hardly saw her, so when she demanded that we meet for lunch on Friday, we all agreed.

Charles called as I was shutting down my computer. He wanted me to go to lunch with him and actually sounded angry when I said I had plans. No way was I going to mention Mini.

"Do I have to make an appointment all the time?" He had a forced laugh. "I suppose you want me to go to church with you on Sunday."

"That would be nice, but wouldn't you rather go to your home church?"

"It doesn't matter either way to me."

"Charles..." A shiver worked through me. "We don't have any kind of commitment to each other."

"Commitment?" His voice squeaked. "Why do you think that?"

"We've been hanging around together, but it's not serious. Dating on the rebound--"

"I'm not on the rebound!"

I couldn't decide if he sounded panicked or righteously angry.

"Whatever Mini has told you, she's wrong. I haven't talked to her since she ran out on me." He took a deep breath. "How about tonight?"

I reminded him that since it was Friday, it was Bible study. He changed it to Saturday. Did that mean he didn't plan on going to church with me? Was I finally getting him to walk away?

"Mini wants us to go shopping with her tomorrow morning." Then, I got mean. "She's shopping for bridesmaids dresses."

"Bridesmaids?" His voice squeaked.

"She's marrying the guy back home. I'm running late. See you Sunday?"

He mumbled something and hung up before I could.

I had really wanted to hang up on him.

Mini tried on my wedding dress before she left, just for fun. I was nastily relieved to see it was a little snug on her. Funny, but every time I looked at it, I remembered more of the good times with Andy and the dreams we had had, and less of the hurt and shattered dreams. Maybe God was healing me. I didn't know if I should have felt grateful or not.

Charles didn't show up at our apartment or meet us at church that Sunday. The sense of relief or reprieve was strong enough to scare me a little. Babby and Jane agreed with me: with no reason to hang around, we wouldn't see anything more of him.

The silence from Charles during the two weeks I was out of town confirmed our theory. I settled into my summer routine of providing support to all the AMEA on-the-road ministries. Translation: running all over the country like a headless chicken. I didn't think about him at all, so it was part-shock and part-creepy when I got home on Friday, tempted to skip Bible study, to find Charles waiting in the parking lot.

It wasn't entirely Charles' fault. Babby and Jane had let me know that we were getting a lot of hang-up phone calls. It got to the point that they decided not to answer the phone if they weren't expecting anyone and just let the answering machine handle the calls. Or maybe get rid of the answering machine altogether and rely totally on our own cell phones.

That sounded like a good idea until the day Babby let four calls in a row go to the answering machine. All hang-ups about half an hour apart. The day got late enough that when she took a study break to make dinner, she had to turn on some lights in the living room and kitchen. Just before she touched a light switch, she looked at the front window and saw a man standing outside, looking in through the venetian blinds, which were tilted at about a sixty-degree angle. She froze, staying in the shadows of the hallway, and watched him walk across the porch-like area in front of our apartment. We were on the ground floor and had an outside entrance. All she could make out was a fat guy wearing a dark hooded sweatshirt. He walked to the other front window, which looked into our little dining room and the kitchen. The blinds were closed tight, so all she got was a shadow cast by the big security light on the lawn. He left soon after that. She thought about running up to the front door and turning on the outside light to scare him, but what if he had a gun? What if he was somebody none of us wanted to see, and he came back and knocked, now that he had evidence someone was home?

Babby told Jane when she got home. They told the apartment complex manager. He promised to call the police so it was on record. Then they told me, while I was away. So I was a little nervous when I got home, running late and tired from traveling, and saw someone sitting in the car facing my usual parking spot. That person just stayed there while I struggled to get out of the car with my suitcase and computer case. I was ready to use my computer case as a weapon when that shadowy figure got out of the car and approached me. Charles was lucky -- and yeah, my nerves and my guts were lucky -- that he called my name just before he stepped into the parking lot lights.

The evening sort of went downhill from there. He was visibly irritated because I was late, and told me so. Late for what? We didn't have arrangements. When he announced that we didn't have time to go to dinner before Bible study, I compounded my sins by admitting I had had a fast-food burrito in the car on the way home. He had to settle for drive-thru food.

We hadn't talked for two weeks, so why did he assume we had arrangements?

On the drive to church, in between mouthfuls of burger, Charles told me all about his changing duties in the law firm. After my long day of driving, I just let him talk. Most of it passed over me. In one ear and out the other.

Charles *thanked* me for really listening and caring about what mattered to him.

That kind of guilt could make a girl stay wide awake at nearly midnight.

So I wasn't as alert as I should have been when I went grocery shopping the next morning. Charles really needed to learn not to look like a stalker. I let out a yelp and dropped a bunch of bananas when he stepped up behind me in the produce section and touched my arm. For some reason, he thought that was funny. He decided to help me with my grocery shopping, which meant advising me on everything I picked up. Then he followed me out to the parking lot and announced he was going to pick up sandwiches for us. I mentally fumbled because I wasn't planning on going straight home. I had other errands to run. Which was worse? Charles "helping" me with other errands, or eating lunch with him? I was pretty sure Babby would be home, and Jane would be out of bed. I told him the girls would be there and prayed he wouldn't decide to go out for lunch. He didn't, but he didn't cancel, either.

My relief didn't last long. On the drive home, I realized Charles didn't tell me where he was picking up the food, and he didn't ask me what I liked. If he intended to remake me by dominating my tastes, he had better think again.

My insides were giving me a few warning twinges. All I cared about was getting into the apartment with my groceries and having enough time to warn my roommates about the invasion before Charles showed up.

Just a few problems with that sensible plan. Maybe I didn't pray hard enough. More likely, this was one of those situations where God let us suffer a little for our greater good.

Charles must have called ahead to order the sandwiches because he pulled into the parking lot while I was still hauling the grocery bags out of the car. He walked up to the apartment door with me. Then he reached into my purse to find my keys. Creepy, anyone?

How could I tell a guy who was being nice that he was just

presuming too much on a relationship that didn't exist, except in his imagination?

Charles reached ahead of me and opened the door, then stepped back to let me go in ahead of him. I nearly lost my grip on one of the bags, so I was looking down as I hurried through the entryway, aiming for the kitchen off to the right. I saw these huge feet in muddy hiking boots, blocking the way into the kitchen. Those were not Babby's or Jane's feet.

"Oh, hey, how great! I was just getting ready to leave a note for you, and here you are!"

Bill lunged and hugged me, making me drop all the grocery bags. He pinned my arms to my side, so I couldn't take a swing at him.

The muffled crack-crinkle-shatter sound of a large jar of stuffed Spanish olives breaking on the tiles startled me, so I didn't shriek for Charles to call the police. I shoved free of Bill's arms and focused on the mini disaster, with the puddle of brine and pimentos spreading across the kitchen tiles. Bill laughed and stepped back and introduced himself to Charles while I went to my knees to pull the box of crackers and the net bag of grapes out of the puddle.

"No, he is not my brother," I shouted, paused in reaching for the roll of paper towels to blot up the puddle. "And he shouldn't even be in here. Charles, search him? Make sure he hasn't stolen anything? And then call the police."

"I am hurt." Bill pressed a hand over his heart and looked between me and Charles with tears in his eyes. "Where's all this Christian love you've been preaching all my life? I come here, trying to mend fences--"

"Fences are to keep thieves and liars out!"

"Okay, mend bridges, fix things between us. You and me, Eve, we were yanked around by the old farts in our family. They made us enemies, lying to both of us. It's us against them, don't you see? I just wanted to catch up with you and fix things, that's all."

"By breaking into my apartment?" I realized I had a handy weapon in the broken olives jar. I looked down at it, about two steps away from me. Could I get to it in time if I needed it?

Would Bill get nasty and take a swing at me as he had done when we were children? Of course, he only used violence when there were no witnesses around. There was Charles, looking at us with a growing frown of confusion.

"The manager let me in. I just explained that we're all the family either of us has left. Because it's true," he hurried on, when I opened my mouth to shout that he was a liar. Again. "I finally had it with Grandma and all our uncles feeding me lies right and left. And I'm here to tell you I'm sorry. That's the truth. Hey, me and Helen, we've got kids. You're the only aunt I can give them. My kids need someone to spoil them, you know? I want family. Helen would love to have a sister."

"You're the creep who's been looking in our windows the last couple weeks, aren't you?" I blurted. "The police know about you."

Bill went white under that beard. He took two steps back.

"If you were here for good reasons, you wouldn't keep looking in windows and waiting until everybody was gone. You would have knocked on the door. You would have called and asked if you could come over. Get out! Get out before I call the police." I tossed down the paper towels in the puddle and took my life in my hands by stomping past him, to the phone sitting on the end table in the living room. "Forget that. I'm calling them anyway."

"You really don't trust me, do you?" Bill's voice cracked. He turned his I'm-just-a-poor-misunderstood-soul look on Charles. "I don't blame her. Our relatives really did a number on us. But it's the honest truth. I'm here to fix things. Tell you what. I'll go away, and let you two -- do whatever. I'm guessing I interrupted something. And I'll come back tomorrow -- how about you come to church with me? You can meet Helen and our kids and have lunch with us. Okay? How does that sound?"

"Just go away!" I reached for the phone. Bill let out a sobbing sound and staggered to the door. I knew better than to trust him when he was working his traumatized, falsely accused routine.

He gave me the name of his pastor and the church, apologized to Charles (not to me, I noticed later) for "messing up good intentions," and finally stumbled out the door. I finished dialing, watching him as he retreated down the front sidewalk. His hunched shoulders straightened and his stumbling gait became a stiff-legged stomping before he'd taken ten steps. So much for being truly hurt. It was all a mask.

I didn't call the police. My first call was to the complex manager's office. He wasn't in, so I had to be satisfied with leaving a very detailed message, telling him what a colossal mistake he had made and instructing him to never, on pain of death and a lawsuit that would give me total ownership of every apartment complex the corporation owned, ever let anyone into my apartment just because he *claimed* to be a relative.

Then I thought of those cobbled together pictures Bill had showed Kurt when he was trying to get into AMEA. That was probably how the creep had fooled the manager, who I had thought was a smart guy. I called Kurt and had to leave a message on his office phone. Then I called the HR office at headquarters, again having to leave a message, and asked them to check with the security team for a copy of the picture of Bill. I added that he would be shaved bald, bearded, and fat. No matter what sort of story he told them, he wasn't to be allowed into the building.

I thought about calling the switchboard and the PR office to ask them to make sure no one would be given my contact information -- my desk phone, my email, my office address, any way of finding me. Then it occurred to me that I wouldn't be able to do my job if no one was allowed to contact me. Besides, it was probably too late to take that precaution. If Bill had my contact info, he would start in on a new harassment campaign. If he hadn't been able to get it, because Kurt's precautions had done the job, then...I wasn't sure what to think at that point.

When I finally hung up the phone and turned around, the door was closed. Charles had cleaned up the broken jar of olives and was putting groceries away. He rearranged the cupboards a little bit, I noticed later, when a few things weren't where they belonged.

He didn't say much, and I didn't know where to start to explain the background of the whole scene. Charles was a smart guy. He could probably read between the lines.

Then Babby came in with Jane. Some friends from church who lived at the other end of the complex had had an emergency and asked for their help. Someone had inherited canning equipment their grandmother had used, and decided to try to make jelly that morning. Jars had exploded all over the kitchen. In the middle of the laughter and trying to describe the enormous mess, Charles quietly announced that he could tell I was busy, and he would call later. He took the sandwiches. I couldn't blame him.

I wasn't hungry. In fact, I was so sick with an onset of stress-induced cramps and accompanying nausea, I spent the rest of the weekend on the couch or in my room.

Before that, though, and before I could tell my roommates what had happened, the manager showed up. Furious. Fortunately, he was furious with himself and apologized multiple times for falling for Bill's lies and letting him into the apartment. Babby and Jane freaked out a little bit, especially when he advised them to search the apartment to make sure nothing had been taken while Bill was alone there. Once we compared stories and details, we decided he had only been alone in the apartment maybe fifteen minutes. Certainly not enough time to do much searching and stealing. I had always known when Bill searched my room and took things he considered his right to "borrow" (permanently) when we were children, because he was such a messy thief.

Nothing was stolen, although it did look like Bill had dug in the drawers of the desk Jane and I shared in our room. I was almost disappointed. If something was missing, we could have filed a police report and pressed charges.

Filling my roommates in on the back story of Bill and his crimes turned into a gripe session that just aggravated the onset of a bad attack. I should have known better. I should have anticipated the physical effects of giving in to the fury and self-righteous hurt that I honestly thought I'd gotten over.

*****

Sunday, Babby and Jane came home from church with hot and sour soup, Szechwan dumplings, and news about Bill's church. I barely got down a cup of the soup and couldn't eat more than one dumpling. I had built a nest on the couch in front of the TV, to drowse the day away with the heating pad and my prescription painkillers for comfort.

Bill's church was real. Everyone Babby and Jane talked to warned them to avoid it. No surprise. Churches that ignored the Bible or rewrote it to suit their own ideals were the only kind Bill liked. I remembered that Bill's fiancée when I moved to headquarters was named Charlene. However, yesterday he said his wife was named Helen. I had a few pleasant moments, imagining Charlene coming to her senses and dumping Bill. Better yet, her father argued with Bill over their skewed revisions of theology and sent him packing. I should have said a prayer for Helen and their children.

The problem with Bill's new church was that appearances were deceiving. It was actually a very nice place with good people who were kind and had outreach ministries to the surrounding neighborhood. They adhered to the Bible. Most of it, anyway. That was where the problems started. Too many people got sucked in by the warm, loving, supportive atmosphere, so they ignored or shrugged off things that should have had them looking for the door.

Babby and Jane were directed to a number of people with stories about the one creepy aspect of that particular congregation. Their interpretation of "family-oriented." Everyone was *expected* to get married. Everyone was *expected* to have children. There were also stories of couples who had been driven out of the church because they didn't want to have children right away. The condition of their souls depended on being parents and having families. Big ones.

No one was allowed to date. The guy, preferably his father, went to the father of the girl and asked permission for a courtship period, carried out under close supervision. The guy had to prove himself worthy to the girl's parents, and she had to get the approval of his parents.

That made some sense -- until two people gave Babby and Jane the names of families who had left the church because the bride or groom was about to be forced into marriage. One or both sides decided they didn't like the other, but the church leaders didn't care. Entering into courtship was considered a commitment to marry and could not be broken.

According to church doctrine, an unmarried man was lost in his sins, his soul unredeemed, unless he had a wife to drag him into heaven. At least, that was the interpretation of the people Babby and Jane talked to.

Gee, what happened to that part where Jesus decides if someone is saved or not?

We laughed a little about the stories. Surely they had to be exaggerated. I was starting to feel better. Jane offered to heat up the soup, so I could try to eat a little more. That reprieve and improvement didn't last long.

Charles banged on the door. He never banged on the door or even knocked. He always used the doorbell.

Babby let him in and Jane leaned out of the kitchen doorway as Charles stomped up to my nest on the couch. He jammed his fists into his hips and glared at me. If looks could have killed, rigor mortis would have set in about ten minutes *before* he barged into our apartment.

"Let's get something straight, Eve. You are not converting me. You only want to see me if I go to church or Bible study with you, and you're punishing me because I won't be a religious fanatic. Like your brother."

"He's not my brother!" My head ached from my own volume.

"Fanatic?" Jane almost laughed, but she looked like she might be sick, too.

"Convert you?" Babby said at the same moment. "What makes you think we're trying to convert you?"

"This!" He dug in his coat pocket and brought out a folded sheaf of papers. When I looked at them later, it turned out to be ten pages of emails from Bill, starting about three hours after he left my apartment.

All we could figure out was that Bill had found Charles' email address in my desk. He must have done enough spying to know who Charles was and assume we were dating.

How could he decide that when I wasn't even sure about it?

The emails were full of questions and demands. Questions about Charles' spirituality. Demands that he change to become "good enough" for Bill's adored, precious, mentally and emotionally fragile little sister.

Me? "Adored" was definitely a lie. "Mentally and emotionally fragile" -- that fit Bill's justification for trying to run my life. I couldn't take care of myself, I needed protecting, and he was the one to do it.

Mixed in were diatribes against Catholics. That was when I learned Charles was Catholic. Followed by condemnation of lawyers based on Jesus' criticism of the teachers of the law. Then after that poison, Bill switched gears to begging and flattery, asking Charles to help him protect his adored baby sister.

The guy's grasp on reality was so greasy, it was a miracle he hadn't skidded completely off planet Earth years ago.

Bill assured Charles that I was in such an emotionally fragile state because I was terrified for his spiritual health. He couldn't let his precious sister marry a man who wasn't assured of a ticket to heaven. Then he insisted that Charles needed to come to his church that very morning and make a full confession of his sins and renounce all the false teachings he had grown up in. There was no time to waste. He could be killed in an accident at any time.

Charles could have used that email as an implied threat and pressed charges. I was highly disappointed in him that he hadn't.

When Charles didn't show up at Bill's church that morning, the lectures, accusations, and threats resumed. Bill sent emails to Charles all *during* the worship service. Either he had done it while sitting in the sanctuary or he hadn't gone to church. Or maybe the whole congregation was helping him with the email barrage?

Babby, Jane and I learned all this later, after we read the emails. At the moment, they were just a bunch of papers Charles flung down into my lap while he glared at me.

"This isn't going to work, Eve," Charles said, after a few heaving breaths that I could imagine him using for an Academy award-winning performance in the courtroom. "I can't have a wife who goes to one church while I attend another. I won't give up my church for you."

"You've been doing that all this time, haven't you?" I managed to say.

That got him to take about two steps back.

"Hey, yeah." Jane stepped up to Charles and poked him in the chest with her index finger. It was kind of funny to see -- along the order of a kitten fighting a dog that could double as a horse. "How come you go to our church if yours is so important to you? How come you never introduced Eve to your friends, or asked her to your church? We don't even know what church you go to."

"Maybe he's afraid she'd accuse him of trying to convert *her*," Babby snarled. She dropped down on the couch next to me. "He wants you to change before he introduces you to his friends. But you're not changing, so he's making up an argument to dump you."

"Making up an argument? Who has been under attack since I left yesterday?" He gestured at the papers that I hadn't even picked up yet.

"Right now, I am. Maybe you haven't noticed that I'm sick?" I mumbled.

That got a snort from Jane and a muffled chuckle from Babby. Charles sighed, loud and deep, and he turned back to the door.

"I can see this has been a waste of time. When I think of how you led me on--"

"Didn't I tell you we didn't have a commitment?"

Amazing. My brain finally kicked into gear, after most of the battle had been fought already.

"A man in my position needs a reliable wife who won't let religious fanaticism and petty inconveniences get in the way."

"Meaning you're not allowed to get sick. How long could she spend in the hospital when she has your kid? Two hours?" Babby said.

"Whoa. No way. No babies." I curled up on my side and closed my eyes as the cramps ripped through me. Definite proof my problems were solidly rooted in stress.

The door slammed.

Total silence in our apartment.

"Eve?" Jane whispered, and settled down at my feet. "You okay?"

"Did I just get dumped by a guy I didn't even know I was dating?"

Maybe when I was feeling better, I might feel something about Charles. Regret. Amusement. Relief?

This was the answer I had asked God for. I should have been grateful. I should have been relieved. All I could feel was tired.

Charles' ability to twist facts to suit him would guarantee him a great future in politics.

It didn't even hurt being rejected by someone I was trying to figure out how to politely dump. Maybe Bill had done me a favor?

I never heard from Charles again, and that was fine. I didn't hear from Bill, and HR assured me he never applied for a job at AMEA. Someone tried to break in when the three of us were out of town at Mini and Tony's wedding, but there were no witnesses, no security cameras to catch the creep in the act, and no evidence. Just a broken window and no entrance into the apartment. We didn't feel quite as comfortable there anymore, and Jane got the distinct vibe that the manager wasn't as friendly as he used to be. Who could really blame him when we seemed to attract trouble?

We had a deadline of November to either renew the lease or find a new place to live. We prayed hard about what to do, where to go, and for God to keep us safe. He answered, of course -- and of course, not at all in the way we were thinking.

Chapter 10

Jane got a promotion to head up a new counseling center -- on the west coast. Babby's long-time, on-again off-again boyfriend put their relationship in high gear and swept her off her feet. While she was still trying to catch her breath, he got a job transfer -- to Alaska -- and asked her to go with him. She was no dummy. She said yes.

I was made part of a new college outreach team headquartered in Philadelphia. That put me in semi-reasonable reach of the boot camp in Georgia, which would go into full operation that coming summer. During the school year, the team visited two colleges or high schools each week. In the summer, I helped with the boot camp, training teens and college students for summer mission work. We started in the US and Mexico, with plans to expand to overseas. When the students hit the road, I became nomadic, circling around to meet up with the different US teams, checking up on them, being available to troubleshoot.

Funny. That was the kind of work Andy had wanted me to do for his traveling music ministry, that summer before we broke up. The difference was not just in years, but in attitude. I loved what I was doing. It was no hardship to live in my car with most human contact being by phone or email.

Besides, the move took me completely out of reach of Bill and Charles, if either one tried for round two. Time to heal. Time to grow. Time to learn.

Then, just shy of eight years since I left Southeastern Christian College, I went back.

AMEA sent three construction teams from the Georgia boot camp to help rebuild two churches that had been demolished by tornados that spring. Both congregations were small, their buildings were old, and they didn't even have the budget for a full-time pastor, much less insurance. They sat almost equidistant from SCC, on the same highway, one to the east and one to the west. We provided the workers, the bricks and cement, paint, lumber, and tools. SCC provided lodging. There was plenty of room in the dorms since the student population dropped to about a third the normal size during summer session.

I reached Blue Bell City about five hours ahead of the busload of workers and the four trucks hauling trailers of supplies. My job was to make sure everything was ready for the workers. I would stay on campus for a week to get everyone settled, then head out to troubleshoot, and stop in every three weeks for updates. SCC hadn't changed much. New landscaping, the colors of paint on some outbuildings, another building added to the eight-plex complex on the far side of campus. I picked up the box of keys and keycards and dining hall passes from the administration building, and had to laugh. The girls were in my old dormitory. The laughter caught in my throat when I opened the box and found an envelope with my name on it, with the keycard, key, and dining hall pass assigned to me. Someone had assigned me my old dorm room.

That someone, I found out before I started to creep out, was Chaplain Nate. He was waiting on the steps outside the administration building when I came out. One of the women in the office called him as soon as I arrived to sign in the team. For a few seconds, I felt like the ground was going to slip out from underneath me. He was Chaplain Nate, and yet he wasn't. Small changes. A slightly receding hairline, a little gray at the temples, a hint of a belly. I swear, he was wearing the same blue plaid short-sleeve shirt he had been wearing the last time I saw him.

He spread his arms and grinned at me and we hugged. That weirdness just evaporated. I was home.

There was a new chapel on the other side of my old dorm. The old chapel was used mostly for the music students for performances and rehearsals and special meetings and presentations. Chaplain Nate got me settled in the dorm, let the Residence Director know I had arrived, then took me for a tour while we waited for the teams to arrive.

We walked around the chapel, with raked seating and built-in seats, and laughed as we remembered the chairs being held hostage. That particular escapade, and the gerbil paratroopers, were stories still told with fondness, sparking attempts at new heights of mostly harmless craziness. He suspected the new seating was permanent partly to prevent more incidents of furniture kidnapping. There were no holes in the ceiling to allow for other surprises to be dropped on guest speakers.

His new office was twice as big as his old one, with lots of built-in cabinets, and what he called the wall of memories. Prominent on that wall was a big, blow-up color photo from the victory party after we pulled off the Spiritual Emphasis Week "save." We laughed, reminiscing for a few minutes, as we settled down at his desk. No folding chairs this time. Nice cushions and wooden arms. He shook his head and said he was proud of what I'd done with my life and my ministry.

"You learned early that those in the background are just as valuable as those on the stage. God is blessing you because you let Him work through you." He sat back in his desk chair and his wonderful, warm grin faded a little. "I wish others had learned that lesson."

"We were all just kids," I said. Yeah, lame, but I had an awful feeling I knew what he was going to say next.

"Andy dropped out of the Chapel Team, that fall you left."

That wasn't what I expected him to say. I didn't interrupt as the words just spilled out. He needed to say it, and I needed to hear it, even though I didn't really want to.

Andy pulled back from everything and everyone that fall. Tonia never needed to go on the attack to punish him for hurting me. Andy cut his own throat, in some ways. He came across as a self-pitying brat. Tonia hadn't told me any of that. We lost touch during my first year at headquarters.

While he talked, words of defense and self-justification clogged in my throat. I didn't say any of them. What use was it to protest when my spiritual leader and adviser for two years just looked at me with those sad, loving, slightly disappointed eyes?

"I blame Andy -- mostly." He cracked a brief grin. "You contributed to it. If he had been more stable, emotionally and spiritually, losing you wouldn't have rocked him so badly."

"If he had been more stable, he might not have lost me." I choked on something that tried to be laughter. "If I'd been more confident, I never would have hooked up with him."

"Maybe. You two were good together. If you'd stayed together...who knows what God could have done through you as a team? You grew up that summer, Eve. You made the right choice, hard as it was. If you hadn't, Andy might have pulled you down with him. God's mercy, I suppose."

"Pulled me down?"

I got a little shiver in my gut at that point. It surprised me to realize I still had some feelings for Andy, good and bad.

That shiver turned to the kind of numb feeling that hits when seeing an unbelievable, laws-of-physics-defying accident. Chaplain Nate outlined the chain of events simply, gently, and didn't add any personal feelings or judgments. Maybe that helped.

Andy had basically joined a New Age type of cult, focused on spiritual journeys. Whatever that meant. It started when Andy and his mother had a major falling-out. Whatever it was about, Pastor Hellingar sided with Andy, so Mrs. Carleone left their church. She got swept up by the leader of a group masquerading as a Christian missionary outreach that focused on miracles of healing and prophetic visions. Her new spiritual mentor stepped in and mediated between her and Andy. Then when mother and son were talking again, he took Andy under his wing. Andy's preparation for seminary and ministry, his leadership and musical skills, were just what the cult leader needed. Within a year, Andy was the face and voice of the organization, a clean-cut, intelligent, educated young man who threw everything he had into preaching and teaching and performance. His sincerity could not be doubted.

The honeymoon lasted three years. Then Andy went off the deep end, embracing and revealing all the outlandish, New Age teachings that his mentor had been keeping in the shadows. The traditional, little independent churches desperate for revival were his primary source of income. They pulled back in fear. Andy took everything out in the open and made it desirable, so the revelation didn't hurt the income flow. At first. He was raking in the money, running himself ragged, preaching and performing sometimes twice a day, seven days a week.

His mother became so terrified for him, it triggered a spiritual wake-up call. She reminded Andy of the spiritual foundations that he had abandoned, and they argued. Andy didn't really question what he was doing until his mentor tried to have Mrs. Carleone silenced. Permanently.

Seeing his mother in the hospital shocked Andy back to his senses. He had a collapse and spent a month in a rehab center, regaining his physical health, followed by ten months in counseling. He and his mother went into hiding because of threats on their lives. When he finally regained his health, he was approached by the government to help uncover all the illegal connections that had funded the cult's activities. Andy was now back on the path he had been following in college, getting involved in service activities, and under the mentorship of several spiritual leaders Chaplain Nate had personally recommended.

That gave me a lot to think about. I had plenty of alone time to walk around campus, get reacquainted with the place, and remember. Learning about the turn Andy's life had taken sort of numbed me. I couldn't manage to feel sorry for him, and I didn't feel much guilt, either. Had I hurt him that much, to make him so vulnerable? Or had my leaving just revealed the flaws in his mind and heart? I wanted to blame him and insist, if only to myself, that he had made his choices and brought the whole mess down on himself. I couldn't even hold onto that. Maybe later, when I had processed the whole story, I would feel something.

When the construction teams showed up, I was busy for a few hours getting them settled. A few work-study students were assigned to act as guides and assistants, to help them get around town and campus and find things they needed. They didn't need me, and I was grateful, because Chaplain Nate insisted I come to his place for dinner with his family. He and his wife had two children now. Despite knowing that, it still felt weird to see him drive up to the dorm steps just after six that evening in a van with a "baby on board" sign in the back window and with a four-year-old boy and a two-year-old girl in the back seat. Chaplain Nate explained that he had a few errands to run before he picked me up, so he got the kids out of the house to let his wife have a little peace to finish dinner.

It turned out I did know Bonnie, his wife. She was a part-time music teacher at SCC when I was a student, and still taught now. They had started dating during my sophomore year and kept it pretty low-key and low profile. I was relieved to hear that. With all the time we spent with Chaplain Nate, we would have been pretty oblivious not to notice a lady in his life!

They made things easier for me, talking about old friends and escapades and all the changes on campus. Still, the conversation turned far too soon to Andy. Nate and Bonnie prayed for him. They emailed him regularly, no pressure, just letting him know they cared and they were there for him.

"I believe Andy is going through a time of testing and purification. When he emerges, he will be a valuable tool for the ministry. Once he has regained his first love," Chaplain Nate said.

I nearly choked on a mouthful of chili. I knew he didn't mean me -- he meant God. But still, it was a jolt.

The questions floated up from the back of my mind that night and at unpredictable points over the next few years: If I had gone through with it, stuck it out, swallowed my pride and been willing to sacrifice my dreams and what I was sure God wanted me to do, would we have worked? Would I have saved him? Would I have been sucked down into that cult along with Andy? Would we have been miserable? Would we have found some kind of compromise that would satisfy us both -- or neither of us?

I thought about my wedding dress, hanging in my closet in my solitary, tiny apartment. Time to think about selling it. Time to let go of the dreams and maybe the emotional damage and idols associated with that dress.

Not so easy. The past wouldn't let go of me.

On my third visit for the summer to Blue Bell City, I went to the Student Center to dig through the novels in the bookstore and stock up on colored pens and get a new notebook. A woman followed me from the dorm to the Student Center, hanging back until I bought an iced coffee and settled down in the snack bar.

I didn't recognize her at first when she walked up to my table. She had healthy color in her face. She looked younger. Taller -- no wheelchair. Yeah: Mrs. Carleone. I didn't recognize her even after she started talking, because her voice had changed, too. No whining, or that breathy sound that always made me think of hypochondriacs or wilting Southern belles. A normal, clear, strong voice. She asked me if I was in charge of all those "nice young people helping rebuild the two churches down the highway."

"I'm more of a monitor. I check in with them every once in a while. If they need supplies or something special, they call me, and I get it." Something about her smile, the way she studied me, sent a little chill up my back. "Is there something I can do for you? Something you need, that's why you asked?"

She gestured at the chair facing me. I nodded, assuming she was asking if she could sit.

"You really don't recognize me, Eve, do you?" she said, as she settled down and put her little purse on the table in front of her. "I wouldn't really blame you if you tried to block everything from your memory."

Then I recognized her. That crooked little twist of her mouth, the sudden flash of resemblance to Andy.

"I never told you that I wouldn't share Andy with anyone," popped out of my mouth after about ten seconds of staring. My face had probably lost all color.

Wasn't it weird, what came to the top of my mind, the moment I recognized Mrs. Carleone?

"Yes. I know." She sighed and actually looked ashamed. "Andy knows that now, too."

"Look, that was a long time ago. We both had to grow up. Andy and me," I hurried to say, in case she thought I meant she had to grow up. "Look, I heard what happened, and I'm sorry--"

"No, Eve. You're the last person to need to apologize. I'm here to apologize to you."

It was a good thing I was already sitting down.

"I work for the college now. I'm the RD in your old dorm. My assistant has been helping your team. Mostly because I didn't want to scare you away. Nate didn't tell you when you came up the first time. Maybe he was afraid you'd head for the hills if you knew I was so close."

"Maybe," I whispered.

"I'm proud to say, I'm finally looking after someone else, instead of expecting them to take care of me." She shook her head. "Andy says you suggested something like that."

"I don't remember--"

"You suggested that maybe if I concerned myself with other people, I'd get over my own health problems. You were right. He should have told me that at the time."

"It would have just given you more ammunition to use against me." I shrugged and offered her a smile. A weak one. It wasn't like I was trying to argue or be nasty. I hope.

"No, I wouldn't have listened, back then. I really think I was so cruel because I was jealous. You were young and so full of life and energy, and you were going to take my son away from me. My slave. I harmed Andy just as much as I harmed you."

She rubbed her eyes, and I realized she was crying. Weird. I never would have expected Mrs. Carleone to cry about anything.

"If this were a novel, I'd still have all the letters you sent Andy that summer. I'd give them to him to read, and to give back to you. Well, I don't. I burned them. That was very selfish of me." She shrugged and looked at her hands for a moment, spread flat and palms up on the table.

That gave me a little time to catch my breath and think and try to shove aside a dozen brutal or whiny responses. What I came up with didn't make much sense, but at least it wasn't anything that might trigger that shriek starting to build up inside my chest.

"I don't understand how you got his letters when I sent them to school."

"Simple. I picked up all his mail and sent the packages to him on the road. You were the only one who wrote to him. I should have taken that as a clue to the damage I had done. What kind of a boy, so popular, so active, doesn't hear from his friends over the summer?"

"His friends were all busy on mission trips, too."

"You were busy, but you still found time to write. He never made any attempt to call you, which just made my task easier." She raked her long fingers through her hair and sat back and took a deep breath. "I've had so much time to think about what I want to say, what I need to say, ever since I heard you were coming here. Please, hear me out. Before I lose my courage." She took another breath, sort of shuddering.

"I'm sorry, Eve. Losing you...that argument just broke him. Andy had been drifting for a long time, and neither of us knew it. Falling in love with you gave him an anchor and purpose. I didn't see the healing you offered. I only saw the influence you had over him, and I was jealous. When he lost you, he let go of everything. Turned self-destructive. He turned his back on God because of what I did."

Then she folded her hands in her lap and hit me with the bomb.

"Will you let me tell him you're here?"

Panic clutched at my lungs for a second. "Why? What good will it do either of us?"

I couldn't really untangle all my thoughts until later, in the quiet of my room, but part of that panic was the totally stupid fear that Andy would think I was chasing him. That I wanted to get back together.

That couldn't be good. Not while he was still on the road to recovery.

At least, that was my reasoning, when I was still awake and trying to understand that whole weird encounter, at about two in the morning.

"Nate let us both know when he heard from you. Andy knows what you're doing now, the important work entrusted to you. He cried, so happy to know you were all right and were busy doing what you wanted. Thinking that you hated him, blaming himself for the split between you, has been such a burden on him. And I did it to you both."

"We did it to ourselves, too. We both could have tried to fix things, but we walked away."

Did that actually come out of my mouth? It was like someone else spoke through me. Hard to believe I was so gracious.

Mrs. Carleone told me a little bit about how the threats to her life and Andy's had forced her to break out of the emotional cage she had built around herself. She had regained her life. She had bad spells every once in a while, but she found a lot of satisfaction in looking after "her girls" in the dormitory.

"You were so wise, recognizing what my problem was. If I hadn't been thinking about what a threat you were to the plans I had made for Andy's life, I would have recognized that. I would have wondered what sort of pain had given you that wisdom." She reached across the table to rest her fingertips on the backs of my hands. It didn't feel strange or threatening. "I hope someday, you and Andy can meet face-to-face and...I don't know, fix things? Reconcile?"

"If I was so wise, would we have messed up so badly?" I wanted to say that if I had been all that wise, I would have recognized what trouble Andy was and never tied my life into his, even if just temporarily. My throat tried to close up, and I had the awful feeling that if I said anything more, I would burst into tears.

I had a lot to think about when I got back on the road two days later.

Funny thing. Despite the strain of that encounter, I didn't have an attack. In fact, despite all the driving I did, dealing with arrangements that fell through and solving problems for everyone, that was the most cramp-free, attack-free summer I had had since the summer before I met Andy. And I honestly couldn't decide if that was a good thing or just plain sad.

Part Three: Mason
Chapter 11

Three school years later, I moved back to headquarters. Our college outreach had grown enough to split into multiple teams. Each was assigned a geographical territory. That meant we were home most weekends. I liked the change, the chance to reconnect with friends and settle in again at my former church. Maybe I was getting old?

I was now leader of my team. Ken, from the Chapel Team at SCC, was on the team. He immediately settled into the role of big brother, and I appreciated his support. AMEA came under increasing scrutiny that fall because of our growing outreach and expanded ministries. Some of our teams had to host journalists or photographers or documentary teams. Most of the time, they came from local or national magazines who wanted to do a story about the impact we were having. Some were there to help other faith-based organizations study our approach. Some were definite outsiders. I heard horror stories about teams who found out the hard way that the seemingly friendly reporters were there to dig up dirt. The media decided we were too good to be true, and they were determined to uncover the truth. Even if they had to make it up.

Fall semester, my team got a reporter from *America's Voice*, Harrison Fry. Harrison was a friend. I had met him several times when I worked support for a few AMEA activities, such as pre-crusade support.

Winter semester, we got a freelance photographer, Mason VanderBlass. An old-fashioned name for a guy midway between hippie and preppie. Tall, lanky, with a ponytail and a pencil-thin beard framing his long jawbone. Polo shirt and chinos and loafers without socks -- in the middle of the winter! Big, green-gray eyes. Always laughing, making jokes. He had assignments from several smaller, newer magazines in the region that wanted photo essays on the "experience." Whatever that meant. He had been persistent enough, polite enough, and his credentials and background checked out, so when we headed out on the road after Christmas break, he rode with us.

His professional reputation was solid. I didn't know much of anything about photography, but people at headquarters were impressed by his portfolio. While he seemed to be a church gypsy, and somewhat fuzzy on the basics, no one had anything negative to say about him.

Mason had a way with kids. When he talked with the students, he drew them out with such natural ease and skill. They were talking with him like he was an old friend in ten minutes flat. I timed him a couple times. He would make a great sneak thief or cat burglar. He could slip into a room and snap pictures, change cameras and lenses without disturbing the class in progress. I mentioned that to Chris Hawkes when I made my first weekly report. I treated it like a joke, but he didn't really smile. I trusted Chris to know when someone was a potential problem and to give me enough warning to get my team out of trouble.

I had the feeling right from the start Mason was kind of lonely. When we got back from the first overnight college visit, he just took it for granted we would all head out for dinner once we got off the bus at headquarters. Everybody else had families to head home to. I had reports I wanted to finalize and file that evening, so I could collapse that weekend. Mason didn't argue, and even made the others laugh as he joked around, pretending to whine, sometimes following the other team members to their cars and whimpering. I shouldn't have stood around watching, because suddenly we were the only ones left in the parking lot.

"Tom's Ribs. How can you say no?" Mason twisted his face into a sad, droopy look. It lasted all of three seconds before I laughed. He tucked his arm through mine. "You need to build up your strength. We've got months and months on the road ahead of us. I will look after you, fair maiden. You are definitely fair. Still a maiden, I hope?"

Before I could decide to be insulted and punch him, he grabbed hold of my left hand.

"No wedding ring. Yes, God does still grant miracles." That grin of his was mischief and fun, with something wistful underneath.

I got that fluttery feeling for the first time in a long time, knowing he was glad I was single.

I didn't let Mason talk me into going out to dinner, but he walked away insisting I had promised him a date soon. The guy could talk faster than an auctioneer. How could anyone think straight when they were laughing at and with him?

It was a good thing I resisted him, because when I got in my car, my phone rang. It was Chris Hawkes. He had questions about Mason. I immediately glanced around, to make sure Mason had left and couldn't overhear my part of the conversation. He was driving by me at that moment. He slowed to wave. I waved back, and pointed at my phone. He grinned and kept driving.

I considered Chris a friend. Since we both worked at headquarters, we saw each other at least once a week. I should mention here that Mrs. Allen Michaels was a regular at headquarters, and we were comfortable enough with each other, I got to call her Jennie. That was just the kind of atmosphere we had at headquarters. I trusted Chris, and that was a good thing because I was a little irritated that now, after three weeks, he had questions about Mason. Why? What had he found out? When I asked, Chris admitted he didn't have anything concrete, but he had learned to trust his instincts when facts said otherwise. I understood that. Even though it happened rarely for me, I had learned to listen to that quiet vibration inside me that sometimes said, "Go for it," and other times said, "No way," and sometimes said, "Run for your life."

Chris wanted to know if Mason ever talked about his current church, if I knew about the people he socialized with, and most important, if I believed Mason's story about changing his career. Up until an accident three years ago, he had been just another paparazzi, doing whatever it took to get a picture that would pay the big bucks, and unconcerned when people were hurt. Mason claimed he had left that behind, and he was trying to use his talents to serve God. Chris had a point. If Mason wanted to feed lots of twisted stories to the press, to undermine AMEA, he was in the perfect position to do it. Especially if people trusted him enough to relax around him. Mason was definitely likeable.

I told Chris what I knew and observed so far. Mason was spiritually hungry and asking a lot of questions. Some tended to make people look twice, shake their heads and say, "Huh?" He usually turned such moments into a joke, with him as the butt of it. Who couldn't like a guy like that?

Chris thanked me for my input, asked me to be careful, and to feel free to call him if anything felt wrong or off while we were on the road. I prayed hard on the short drive home, asking God to protect our team.

I did feel a little irritation because I liked Mason. I didn't want to doubt him. I liked him, as a person, and not just because every once in a while, I caught him watching me with this solemn, awed expression that made me catch my breath.

Had a guy *ever* looked at me that way?

*****

Mason took hundreds of great photos, documenting wonderful memories of the students and faculties we'd seen and talked to. Headquarters was impressed with him, and that didn't change when he made it clear he was aiming to get a job working for AMEA.

Then he made the mistake of admitting to several people that he was doing it to stay close to me.

My first reaction was flattered. My second reaction was that squirmy feeling, not quite "no way," but closer to "wait a minute." I pushed the odd sensation aside because I was just too busy to spend time or energy on the slightly uneasy feeling. Besides, I just wasn't used to a guy showing interest. I was the Dateless Wonder once again, too busy for anything even remotely resembling a social life or a romantic one. I forgot about that squirmy feeling quickly enough that I never reported it to Chris Hawkes.

It wasn't like Mason did anything to follow up on those don't-tell-Eve-this-would-just-make-her-uncomfortable confessions.

He did seem a little too nosey (certainly not jealous) when the Hansons re-established contact with me. Nathan had left the Marines and was taking college classes over the Internet to finish up his bachelor's degree, to prepare to enter seminary. More important, AMEA had accepted the donation of the family farmland with the intent of building a combination boot camp and conference center. Royce and Nathan wanted me to know because I had been so helpful in the initial stages. They hoped I could explain things, make the whole process easier to understand, since I had been involved in the Georgia boot camp process.

That was fine by me, but I made sure Nathan and Royce understood I was no longer involved in that division of the ministry, so I might not have up-to-date information. I also called headquarters to make sure it was all right. It was always better to ask and make sure the people with authority knew what was going on ahead of time, rather than have to apologize and scramble for explanations and do damage control.

I got a call back a couple days later, asking if I would be interested in switching back to developmental work. They liked the idea of me acting as the voice and face of the organization during the whole development, planning and building process, since the Hansons were already friends. Yes, I might be interested, but would I have to quit the work I was doing now? My supervisor, DeNita, laughed when I asked her.

"Sweetheart, the boot camp dovetails nicely into what you're already doing with the summer teams. Everyone who's ever worked with you knows you can handle far more responsibility, as long as you feel you're up for it. But to answer your question, no, you won't be leaving the tour team any time soon."

That was good news, but the funny thing -- not funny ha-ha, but funny weird, thought-provoking -- was that I had a fibroids spell soon after that phone call. I had been doing so good, despite my crazy life on the road. The "swoop in, deal with the problem, swoop out" tactic reduced the stress for me. Unpleasant situations never stuck to me because I didn't linger long enough to be affected. If I had an attack, the cramps only lasted a few hours and were easily dealt with by medication. Maybe a few hours lying on a hotel bed with my feet propped up on the headboard and a heating pad on my belly, and I was good to go again.

After that call, I spent the evening in my room in the college guest house, curled up with a book I had been trying to read for months. Mason was sweet but slightly irritating with how many times he checked on me. Could he bring me some dinner? Could he bring me more pillows? Could he bring me some ice cream? Would it help if he massaged my feet? I had to give him a lecture on appropriate behavior. It was bad enough he was constantly knocking on the door. If we were in a dormitory on a Christian college campus, that would have been violating a number of rules. He only got away with what he was doing because first, he didn't step into the room, and second, the rest of the team was just down the hall in the living room of the guest house. That "hey wait a minute" feeling came back for a few seconds. Mason looked like a kicked puppy when I explained that such physical contact wasn't appropriate.

We were representing AMEA. The implications of such intimate contact could be taken the wrong way.

I should have reported the incident to Chris, but it just seemed so stupid, so petty.

"I just want -- I mean, what's wrong with me taking care of you?" Mason said, in a quiet voice that I almost couldn't hear over the laughter coming down the hall. "That's what we're supposed to do, right? I made a promise, you made a promise."

"What?"

Bethany showed up and nudged him aside right then, carrying her tablet with the silly YouTube video that had made everyone laugh. Mason slunk away. When I remembered the conversation later, I felt squirmy enough that I didn't want to pursue it.

*****

Three days later, we had a day off. We were between colleges that were situated close enough together we didn't need to change hotels. All my reports were up to date. The hotel had a pool, hot tub, and a huge game room. Most of the team opted to spend the day goofing off and enjoying the facilities. Mason, Sonja, Ken, and I went to the zoo for exercise and fresh air. It was nice for February, just chilly. We practically had the place to ourselves.

Mason was a hoot, making up conversations between the animals about the people who stared at them all day. Or worse, who read the information signs but never really looked at the animals. He made me laugh like it was his whole mission in life, the reason God made him. We were having a great time, being silly but not obnoxious.

Then suddenly, I was alone with Mason, and that was neither smart nor permitted.

I didn't realize it at first. Mason was doing a bad Mexican accent. We came to Monkey Island. It was basically a big pile of rocks and some trees with a few fake waterfalls and a big, murky moat. Too deep for the monkeys to swim to freedom? Too wide for them to jump across? There were certainly no vines for them to make like Tarzan.

"Hey, Paco." Mason lumbered along, his back hunched so his knuckles almost dragged on the ground. "Look at that hot chick. You think that *hombre* in that funky green coat knows how hot she is?"

Mason wore a camouflage jacket, two sizes too big.

He jumped in front of me, blocking me against the rail that kept children and idiots from jumping into the water. He changed his voice higher, still with a bad accent.

"Hey, no, man. He's *muy estupido*. A guy with brains would grab a girl like that, and he'd kiss her."

Mason put both hands on the rail with me trapped between his arms. He was in a good position to get a knee where it would do me the most good. His goofy look faded, and his eyes got big as he leaned close.

"Well, Eve?"

"Well, what?" My voice cracked. I was scared enough to freeze, forget my training, and my responsibility as leader of the team.

"Do you think I'm smart?"

I could only stare. He stepped closer, so I had to press back against the rail or risk our anatomy touching. Not a smart thing. Not when my knees were feeling wobbly. Something twisted deep in my stomach. Not sure what it was, but it was neither a cramp nor the flu.

"This isn't--"

"Nobody can see us. Nobody but the monkeys," he whispered. "I really want to kiss you. Would that be so bad?"

"Kisses mean something."

"Good. Because you mean something to me."

"Mason--"

"If I don't stake my claim, there's something wrong with me."

Okay, so that wasn't the most romantic thing I'd ever heard. But who wouldn't want a guy to be worried that someone else would steal what he wanted?

Looking back, I can't believe how stupid I was to have that as my first thought.

I froze, trying to decide if I should scream or punch him or wait in hopes he would laugh and admit he was joking around. Ken called my name, and Mason took a step back. I turned, gratefully looking for him and Sonja. The moment passed. I was saved from having to think of the right response.

Proof that God was looking out for me even when I didn't have the sense to ask Him.

We walked around a little more. We took a break from the chill breezes and ducked into the cat and primate house. I didn't realize how chilly it was until warmth wrapped around me. With the expected internal changes. Sonja followed when I went hunting the bathroom.

"Sorry about that," she said, when I came out of the stall and found her sitting on the bench inside the women's restroom.

"For?"

"It looked like you and Mason were having a moment. I was afraid to say something and kind of make it obvious."

"Thanks for *not* stopping the rescue." I rinsed my hands and didn't bother using the hurricane-force hot air hand dryer.

"Seriously?" She laughed and followed me out of the bathroom. "Something about him, you know?"

"Yeah, but we've got our standards and I'm in charge, so..."

Had I left Sonja with the impression that I wanted Mason to kiss me? I was relieved that he hadn't. And to be honest, even more relieved that I hadn't needed to defend myself. I had no curiosity about kissing and no physical attraction to Mason. No need to remind myself about our standards of conduct to guide me away from trouble.

When we met in the hotel dining room, Ken and Mason were a little late. Ken came in first. Mason followed, looking flushed, head bowed, shoulders hunched. He came as close to skidding to a halt as someone could on carpet when Ken sat down opposite me. The only other open chair at the long table was five seats away. Something sparked in Mason's eyes, and a muscle rippled in his jaw. A moment later, he laughed at something Cho said and slid into the chair facing him.

"Didn't take it well, did he?" Morton was sitting next to me, with Lizzie across from him, putting me and Ken at the end of the table.

"Take what?" I said. Lizzie echoed me.

"Mason was getting a little too close when we were at the zoo." Ken shrugged and gave me that slightly sheepish little grin he did so well, a mixture of mischief and cuteness and embarrassment.

"Oh. That." I recalled Sonja's words. Ken had definitely rescued me.

"Look, I know you're not Andy's girl--"

"Andy has nothing to do with this."

"Who's Andy?" Lizzie wanted to know.

"A guy we both knew in college." Ken made a brushing motion, basically relegating Andy to the dusty past. "Eve deserved better when she was with him, and she deserves a whole lot better than--" He tipped his head in Mason's direction. "Lately, he makes my creep-o-meter go off."

Lizzie and Morton's confused looks were almost funny.

"Okay, he's a brilliant photographer, and he's fun, but once he started focusing on you..." Ken shook his head.

"What exactly did you say to him?" I almost got a cramp in my neck trying *not* to look at Mason's end of the table.

"Told him a jerk broke your heart in college, I considered you my little sister, and I'd break his face if he hurt you. Then I gave him the lecture on standards of proper behavior for the tour."

"Oh, just great..." I didn't lose my appetite, but I was close. Still, I couldn't help feeling grateful to Ken for looking out for me.

Mason apologized the next day. He looked appropriately subdued, no games or silliness glimmering in his eyes. He promised me that when we did kiss, I would like it, and I wouldn't be afraid. Then he told me he'd make sure I forgot all about the "bozo" who broke my heart.

That didn't put any flutters of anticipation in my heart. My track record in dating was either abysmal failure or a long, steady stream of, "Nice guy, no spark, let's just be friends."

*****

125

When we got back to headquarters, I learned the basement storage lockers in my apartment building got flooded. Fortunately, I had learned the value of using those plastic bins that could stand up to thermonuclear war and resist the invasion of bugs. Most of what I stashed in my storage locker consisted of books and pounds of family photos in boxes and albums. Mom had asked me to store them digitally, and I usually spent a few hours every weekend scanning, cataloging and labeling, and packing up a box or album to send back to her. Everything was safe from water damage, so I wasn't too worried when I heard about the flood. The water only got about a foot high, and the bins were about three feet deep. No damage, not even dampness.

Sitting on top of everything, however, was my wedding dress. Several layers of plastic bags didn't seem to protect it from the damp. The building manager insisted on paying to have it dry cleaned, treated, and preserved all over again. Honestly? I wouldn't have been upset to have to throw it out, full of mildew. Instead, I got it back good as new. I figured the time had come to try to sell it. I put it in the nice, deep, secure-as-a-bank-vault walk-in closet in my apartment, so it would be handy when I got a response to my advertisement. Then I forgot to advertise. Life, like in the Chinese curse, got interesting.

*****

That Sunday, Mason was waiting in front of my building to drive me to church. I usually walked. My church was only three blocks away, and I liked to get exercise. That day, I got in his car because the sky was gray and threatening more snow. Plus, the team had agreed we needed to encourage Mason to listen to some solid biblical teaching. If he wanted to go to church with me, that was a good sign.

I didn't pay attention when he pulled out of the driveway because a friend in Singles class had texted asking if I could pick up some donuts for the fellowship time. I looked up and opened my mouth to ask if he could take a detour and realized we were already taking a detour. He had turned left when we needed to go right.

"This isn't the way to my church. Where are we going?"

"Church." He gave me that endearing, triumphant-little-boy grin.

"You're going the wrong way."

"My church."

It could be argued that I had agreed to go to *his* church just because I hadn't specifically stated I wanted to go to mine. I responded to my friend's text, saying I was checking out a friend's church this week, sorry, no donuts. Checking out Mason's church would give me a close-up view of the source of his biblical training or lack thereof. For all we knew, Mason was the problem, not his pastor.

He filled the drive with details of what made his church so great. He repeated himself, but I never had a chance to point that out. So, fine, they were involved in all sorts of family-oriented activities. Yeah, it was kind of cool that on Wednesday nights, when other churches had families split to go to all sorts of activities for their age groups, his church had activities that kept families together. It was wonderful that they considered the family the most important element and keeping families together as a unit was a vital step for spiritual growth of all members.

Everybody I met before the service was nice and friendly, and the sanctuary was jammed full. And big. I found out later it had to be big because everyone stayed in the service. No dismissing the children to Sunday school. The family worshipped together.

The concept of the place being family-oriented kind of stuck in my brain. I couldn't figure out why there was the sensation of a yellow alert light flashing in my head. I had to concentrate to focus on the sermon, rather than gnaw on what felt just slightly off here. The senior pastor -- they had four, Pastor Riverfield and his three sons -- seemed to teach from the Bible. At least I didn't catch him tossing scripture that disagreed with what he wanted to believe.

My guardian angel was at work that day, although I didn't realize it until much later. I started cramping near the end of the service. The timing was right, but I was still dismayed because it broke a long stretch of good health. Mason must have seen something in my face because he didn't argue or tease me until I agreed, when he wanted to go out for lunch and I said no. He even asked if I needed to stop at a drugstore to get something. That was sweet of him. I shouldn't have told him that, though.

Babby called when I was settling down with my trusty old friend, the heating pad, *True Lies*, and a carton of mint chocolate chip ice cream. Catching up with her made me feel better faster than my prescription and the heating pad. We laughed and reminisced, and I got to chat with my honorary niece and nephew. Then I told her about Mason and the conflicting messages I was getting about him. I was only half-joking when I commented that I was ready to blame my cramp attack on something at his church. She asked me the name of the church.

"Well, shoot, Evie, there's your explanation right there. That scumbuzzard cousin of yours probably gave you your condition, right?"

"What does Saint Bill have to do with Mason?"

"Mason's church is the one your jerkface cousin was attending when he broke into our apartment. Remember?"

Everything came together like a film of the destruction of a Lego Star Wars battlecruiser running backwards. I didn't know whether to be relieved or freak out.

Mason had asked me to come to church with him next week. I couldn't remember if I had said yes or no. Panic time?

Well, that didn't matter. I would just say no from now on. The last thing I needed was to run into Bill at that church. Maybe I had subconsciously recognized the name and that got me sick? Maybe I had seen Bill, but hadn't recognized him. What if he had seen me and recognized me? I could only imagine all the poison he would start spilling into Mason's ears, to turn him against me.

*****

The first weekend after Easter, I attended a friend's wedding. Mason looked like he was going to burst into tears that I hadn't asked him to go with me. Why would he expect me to ask him to be my date? My first mistake was not to report the incident to Chris Hawkes, because the incident stayed in my thoughts long enough to bother me.

I caught the bouquet, even though I joined the other single girls for fun, not because I believed in luck. However, I made the mistake of showing the team the picture another friend emailed me, of me catching the bouquet. Mason looked like he had just won the big prize at Publisher's Clearinghouse and was set up for life. He just grinned at me, constantly, and every time our gazes met, he waggled his eyebrows. There was this look in his eyes, like he expected me to know what he was thinking, and he expected me to agree with him. I didn't know, I didn't agree, and I certainly didn't like it. So I avoided looking at him whenever I could.

Maybe that encouraged him? Made him think I was shy? Maybe I should have confronted him? I doubt it. By this time, he had his mind made up, and interpreted everything I did and said through his own unreal version of reality.

The night we got back to headquarters after the wedding photo "incident," I got up to my apartment, kicked the door closed behind me, dropped my suitcase and computer bag in the door of my bedroom, and headed for the kitchen to read whatever mail had piled up. Lyndsey, a cubicle neighbor at work and one floor above me in the apartment building, had my keys. She checked my mailbox and put everything on the counter to pile up for me while I was on the road.

Someone knocked. I expected Lyndsey, so I didn't check the security peephole. I opened the door.

"I thought they'd never leave!" Mason wrapped his arms around me and kissed me so fast I nearly fell off my feet. Except he was holding me up. For about five seconds. Until I jerked free.

Then I punched him. Right on the left side of his jaw. Enough to make him take a step back, into the hallway.

I should have slammed the door right in his gorgeous, arrogant, grinning face.

Not because he had assaulted me but because his kiss did nothing for me. No tingles. No fireworks. No bells ringing.

I was too stunned and maybe too polite. I hesitated just long enough for Mason to give me a wide-eyed look, step into my apartment and close the door.

"It's okay, honey. We didn't do anything wrong."

"That is so wrong!"

"Well, okay, so we're jumping the gun, but..." He shrugged and his mischievous grin invited me to join him in enjoying a joke I didn't understand. "We're going out to celebrate."

"Celebrate what?"

I should have said, "No, we aren't, get out," and offered him a knuckle sandwich.

"We're getting married, and we can finally tell everybody."

"We're what?"

He reached for me, and this time I was alert enough to take two fast steps out of his reach. Up came my fist.

"I'm sorry!" He laughed. "I'm just so excited. I forgot. He told me I had to -- let me start over, okay?"

"You can start over by getting out of here."

"Oh, come on!" Another laugh. "It's a sign. You catching the flowers. Then showing everybody. I've been praying for weeks for a way to tell everybody. You've been playing it so cool for so long, I was getting worried maybe you changed your mind."

"Changed my mind about what?"

I yelped when Mason caught hold of my hand. His grip was a killer. He knelt. If I had been thinking clearly, I would have clocked him good with my knee to his chin, and then while he was stunned, either fled my apartment or called the police. Or both.

"Okay, I know we haven't made it official, official. You know." He grinned. "He told me you're kind of old-fashioned and you like to follow all the steps. So here goes." There was something in his eyes. I understood how a mouse felt when a cobra mesmerized it. "Eve, marry me. I promise I'll take good care of you. We're gonna be so good together. It's fate -- no, it's not fate. I know this is a God-thing. You know? Like we were talking about on the tour? God made us for each other. It's perfect."

"You're crazy." I yanked my hand free and took two steps back.

Mason stayed on one knee, otherwise I would have punched him again. I had a horrified vision of the scandal that would result after I called the police to take his unconscious body away, after I kicked and pounded the daylights out of him.

"Yeah, but you love me that way, don't you?" He waggled his eyebrows. "Admit it! You do."

"I hardly know you."

"Trust me. You're going to be crazy in love with me." He hopped up to his feet again and gestured down the hall. "Wear that pretty yellow dress with the purple flowery sweater. You look so good in that."

"No!"

That finally got through his thick skull. I swear he whimpered.

"But we have to celebrate."

"No, we don't, and no, we aren't."

"But we're getting married. We have to celebrate."

"We are not getting married." I planted both hands flat against his chest and pushed. That caught him by surprise, so he stumbled back three steps. I got around him and yanked the door open. He wasn't out of my apartment, but close enough to let me breathe a little easier.

"But -- but--" He gaped a few times like he couldn't come up with the words to fight with me.

"You can't just walk in here and assault me and expect me to say yes when I hardly know you. Forget about being in love with you."

"I love you enough for both of us."

"Nice try, Romeo, but your timing sucks."

For some reason, he thought that was funny.

"I know the perfect place to get married. You know the Music Mound, down in the park? With all the old willows and the river wandering through and the daffodils and...well, the daffodils will be dead by the time we get all the arrangements in place, but it'll still be gorgeous."

"I am not marrying you."

"But honey--"

"I am not your honey. We hardly know each other." What I said next came from a strange mixture of desperation and guilt, because he looked so sad and doggone it, I did like the guy. Even though he was seriously creeping me out. "I refuse to get engaged to anyone I've known less than a year."

"A whole year?" His voice cracked, and he looked so stricken, I almost felt sorry for him.

"Ask me when we've known each other for a whole year." Maybe that was mean, because I planned to call headquarters and tell them to get Mason banned from the tour.

It suddenly struck me that Mason shouldn't have even gotten to my apartment without me buzzing him through the security door. He had to have followed me home. The front door took so long closing on its new pneumatic hinges, he probably had time to get in behind me without me seeing him. I never thought to look behind me when I crossed the lobby. Why did I need to? Wasn't I safe in my own apartment building?

Obviously not.

"That's nine months from...okay." Mason took a deep breath and calmed down, and a determined glow filled his eyes. "A year from the day we met. I can handle that. We're going to be together for the rest of our lives." He laughed and reached for my hand. I took two steps back. "But -- but we have to celebrate."

"Celebrate what?"

"We're -- well, we're engaged to be engaged." He grinned again.

There was something very wrong with a guy who could morph back and forth between so many emotions so fast.

I was so focused on getting him out of my apartment, I didn't pay much attention to that tight feeling through my chest, the twisting in my gut that warned of trouble. I should have clarified that just because I told him he had to wait a year to ask me didn't mean I promised to say yes.

Mason must have decided he had won and he could be generous now. He at least gave the impression of listening when I said I was exhausted and just wanted to take a shower and relax with a good book. When he left, he promised me that in three months, I'd be begging him to marry me. Later, I realized he had given up promising that I would be in love with him.

*****

God was kind, and we had a week off from tour. Mason left me alone but sent me flowers every day. A daisy or tulip or carnation wrapped in green tissue paper waited on my desk when I came back from lunch. By Wednesday, my co-workers were teasing me about my boyfriend. I debated telling them about Mason just to get them to stop. I should have asked them for advice.

By Thursday, I was irritated enough that I didn't care how he reacted when my request came through and he was banned from the team.

Then Jennie Michaels came to my office to ask me to lunch. She wasn't Mrs. Allen Michaels, she was a friend. How could I refuse when she stopped in? I should have known something was up when Chris Hawkes pulled up to the front steps of the admin building to pick us up instead of us taking either my car or Jennie's.

I ate lunch at the Michaels' house. How's that for being on top of the world and held in high esteem by my ultimate boss?

Well, God was and always would be my ultimate boss, but Dr. Michaels was as close as I'd ever get while in this body!

The Michaels kept their house separate from the ministry, a place where he could just be a husband and father and grandfather. Funny, I never thought of him as a grandfather. But there were pictures of the grandchildren all over the place, and the backyard was full of big plastic slides and playhouses and other equipment. The Michaels' house existed for the comfort and amusement of the grandchildren.

It was just the four of us. We talked about the campus tour, the good feedback, and ideas for additions and changes the other teams were sharing. Recruitment for the summer missions teams had gone up another twenty percent from last year. That good news segued into the next topic.

AMEA would be expanding the summer mission projects to include touring music and drama groups. The camp being planned for Coshocton would focus on music and drama. They wanted me to supervise the

131

construction phase and put staff together to run the camp. We would establish the training program and organize the campgrounds for retreats and conferences throughout the year. I would spend this summer as the traveling troubleshooter and spot-checker, like I had been doing, but in the fall, I would move to Coshocton to be on-site. I would be the face and voice of AMEA, and the boot camp would be my baby. With the help of a big staff, of course, but still *my* baby.

Dr. Michaels asked me if I wanted to do it when he could have just ordered me. The great thing about him has always been that he knew how to make people feel comfortable. There was no fear that if I said no or asked for time to think it over, he'd be insulted or upset.

The whole time, Chris just sat there, giving me this satisfied grin like it was all his idea. Knowing him, he probably did a little lobbying to make me the first choice.

Jennie put her hand on mine once the general overview of the plan had been presented and squeezed. "So, are you interested?"

"If she isn't interested, there's something wrong with her." Chris had this wonderful laugh that rumbled like an entire mountain was shaking. Too bad, in his job, he didn't get that many opportunities to laugh.

"I'll have to think about it," I said, even though inside I was already jumping up and down and shouting *Yes*! "And pray about it. I know you have, but I still need to be sure this is what I'm supposed to do next."

"We'd be disappointed if you answered yes immediately." Dr. Michaels put his big, warm hand on my other hand. "Whatever you decide, it'll be the right decision."

My head was so full of all the possibilities, I wasn't careful when I got back to the office. My phone rang, and I picked it up instead of checking first who was calling.

Mason wanted me to go to church with him Sunday morning. Instead of reminding him that I had said no every time he asked me, I told him I had commitments at my own church, so I wouldn't be going to his. He said okay, he understood, and left it at that.

Sunday, I rode to church with Lyndsey. When I got home, there was a note tucked under my windshield wiper. I couldn't figure out from his scribbles if he was bewildered or having a snit fit.

Where are you? Are you angry at me? What did I do? I'm going to church. Don't go anywhere until I come back. We have to talk.

Why should we talk, when obviously he wasn't listening?

I seriously considered taking off again, so I wouldn't be there when he came by. I didn't, though, because that would be childish. I made myself lunch, changed into sweats, and planned not to answer when Mason buzzed to come in.

Chapter 12

Mason never showed up.

The whole situation reminded me of Charles and Andy -- one showing up when we didn't have plans, the other not showing up when he said he would. Of course, that made me think of my wedding dress.

I needed to sell that dress. My frustration put crazy scenarios in my head, part comedy, part nightmare. The worst one was Mason finding out I had that dress in my closet and arranging our whole wedding in secret. He would have to kidnap and drug me to make me go through with it.

Granted, I did find it hard to believe someone would be so desperate to marry *me*, specifically, that they would risk a prison sentence.

With my luck, Mason would show up as I was putting the dress in my car to take it to the consignment shop. He would decide I was bringing it home, not getting rid of it.

No. Too risky. The dress was staying in my closet. I could leave it behind for the next tenants when I moved out.

I needed to take more steps to put distance between me and Mason. I called Morton and Ken and told them what had been going on, and they agreed to back me up. I emailed DeNita and asked for a meeting first thing Monday morning. Morton and Ken wrote to her to back up my request to have Mason removed from the tour team. I nearly cried when Morton admitted he had filed a report about Mason's behavior toward me and how I was handling the situation with discretion and maturity.

The meeting went well. Morton and Ken helped my credibility. I had been afraid someone might accuse me of imagining things or blowing them out of proportion. We learned my previous request had been received and discussed. The decision would stand to allow Mason to travel with the team. The situation that had originally led to outsiders traveling with AMEA teams still existed. We needed good PR.

DeNita and her supervisors promised Mason would not be invited back. Oddly, they reported that despite telling several people he was applying to work for AMEA to stay near me, no application had been filed yet. That was little comfort. Even knowing any application he did file wouldn't be considered.

Then I got some news that shoved my grumbles to the back of my mind. Mini bombed into my office just after lunch on Monday with Tony in tow. She looked great in dress jeans and a red-checked blouse. The country girl look suited her. So did Tony.

They were in town to interview for a job living on-site year-round at the Georgia boot camp. Tony and Mini wanted to get involved in youth missions work. When they started investigating opportunities, the boot camp job was at the top of the list of job matches. Before I knew it, we were talking like there had been no gap of years. We made plans for dinner.

Mason was just coming into my apartment building that evening as I stepped off the elevator to leave to go pick up Mini and Tony. I braced for him to scold me for not being there Sunday morning when he came to pick me up, and never thought to ask how he got into the building. He just smiled, handed me a single white rose, and announced with great delight that he had big, mysterious plans for a fun evening out on the town.

I couldn't feel sorry for him, because he wasn't listening or learning from his mistakes.

"You should have called ahead. I'm going to pick up some friends from out of town."

"Well, call and tell them you changed your mind."

"Why should I lie?" I asked him.

"Because you want to be with me!"

"If I wanted to be with you, then I *would* be changing my mind, so it wouldn't be a lie, would it?"

He blinked like he couldn't follow my train of thought. For a moment, I wondered if he was on drugs. Then he grinned. Did he think he was cute and that was going to get him out of trouble?

"Honey, I'm sorry. Guess I've been acting like an idiot lately, huh?"

"A selfish idiot."

"Guess you're ticked at me, huh?" He sighed and gave me that big-eyed, wounded look. It no longer made me want to laugh. "You want me to go away?"

I hesitated to answer because my first reaction was to shout, "Yes, go away forever." Followed quickly by a surge of exhaustion and a longing to just curl up on the sofa with a pizza and a movie, and vegetate. However, I had plans with Mini and Tony, and they were waiting for me.

"It's okay. You don't want to be seen with me." He let out a fake sob, which got a grin from me no matter how hard I tried to resist. "I'll go away. And I promise, I'll make it up to you."

I refused the rose. Mason walked out the door. I ran for my car, fighting down the image of him following me.

He did.

Mason caught up with us in the parking lot of the restaurant and attached himself to us, so charming and eager to meet my friends. What was I supposed to do when Tony invited him to sit with us? I couldn't say no and look like an ogre, could I?

I had to admit, Mason was charming. He came very close to dominating the conversation, but he was full of stories about our college tour. He was a good PR man. Who wouldn't want to work for AMEA after an evening spent listening to Mason?

Mason ruined things when we left the restaurant. He insisted on driving me back to my apartment to save Tony and Mini the trip. The problem was, I drove. He knew that, since he had followed me. He pouted when I reminded him of that. Then he suggested that he drive me home, and Tony and Mini could follow us. Tony watched Mason, narrow-eyed, until he vanished in the darkness of the parking lot.

"Sorry," he said.

"For what?"

"You weren't exactly thrilled when he showed up, but I didn't catch on until after I invited him to sit with us." He snorted. "After Mini kicked me a few times under the table."

Mini giggled and went up on her toes to kiss his cheek. "You're above average when it comes to noticing things, Babe," she said. "Don't worry." Then her smile faded. "But do we need to worry about you, Eve?"

"It's an ongoing situation that should be fixed soon. Prayers would be appreciated, though." I nearly confided in them about Mason insisting we were going to get married.

When I went to bed, I lay awake a long time, staring down the hall at the light coming through the balcony and flooding my living room. So many thoughts churned through my head. Mason wasn't a cute, mischievous boy anymore. He had crossed over into creepy.

*****

The next morning, I woke up with spotty bleeding, two weeks early. I was leaking through double protection before lunchtime. Not a good sign. I called my doctor and she said to come in right away. I told a few friends at work who knew about my health problems, and they promised to pray for me. I was halfway to my doctor's office when her nurse called my cell phone and told me to go to the hospital instead. The doctor wanted to have me do a series of tests and exams to find out what was wrong.

I could tell her what was wrong -- stress in the form of the guerilla warfare groom, Mason.

My doctor was a saint, and I thanked God for her several times through that long afternoon and into a late evening. Multiple ultrasounds. Blood tests. Discussions about my routine, eating habits, and yes, emotional problems. I didn't get home until nearly eleven because my doctor consulted with several colleagues with more experience. "Inconclusive" just didn't satisfy anyone. The topic of a hysterectomy came up, which just signaled how bad my condition had become. I hadn't considered a hysterectomy since my first really bad bleeding spell in high school. Mom fired the gynecologist who recommended it. Granted, he was callous enough to remark, in my hearing, that I "would never need the equipment, so why not avoid years of misery?"

For about five minutes, waiting to get in to see a doctor I didn't even know, I seriously considered it. Yet...I was still young, medicine was constantly coming up with new treatments, and I did have hope that someday, I would meet a man who I wanted to give me a baby. Explaining that reasoning to my doctor wasn't so difficult. Out in public with so many medical staff walking by, feeling like the entire hospital knew my business? That made it hard. Especially when another doctor stood there and listened in and told me I was being silly and idealistic. A hysterectomy was the wise choice. It would make my life so much simpler. In his opinion, anyway. Why did men think they knew so much more than women about the pros and cons of having a uterus?

Either the flare-up had run its course, or the prayers of my friends worked. My bleeding stopped before the doctors could determine the trigger. The fibroids were measurably smaller in the final ultrasound. I went home with a new prescription and a note from my doctor to take the day off work if I didn't feel better in the morning.

I was feeling better as I stepped out of my doctor's office. A nurse I didn't know, who had passed me in the halls several times during the afternoon and evening, scrambled to get on the elevator with me. She leaned against the opposite wall, crossed her arms, and glared at me the entire ride from the third floor to the lobby. I was tired enough to ignore her. She wouldn't let me, though.

"You do realize, don't you, this is God's punishment?"

"Excuse me?" I had a vague idea of hitting the stop button and getting out of the elevator. Her tone was clearer to me than her words.

"If you would submit to God's will for you, you wouldn't be having these problems. You're denying your proper position as a woman, so that's where God is striking you." She gestured at me with her chin, and her gaze landed on my aching abdomen.

"It's none of your business--"

"It would serve you right to have that hysterectomy. Even if it wouldn't be fair to your husband."

"I don't have a husband, and it's none of your business!" My head ached from the volume I managed to produce.

Her eyes widened and for a few seconds she looked afraid instead of pissy. Her face went white, then turned red, and she opened her mouth. I just knew she was about to yell. The door binged and opened. I staggered out, focusing on getting away from that crazy woman. Later, when I thought about registering a complaint with the hospital, I couldn't remember more than her hair, her angry eyes, the color of her scrubs. I hadn't seen her nametag. Her voice and her words stuck with me, waking me up from sleep a couple times.

Despite my restless night, when I got up, I felt good enough to go to work. Until I found a note shoved under the door. With a border of big red and pink hearts. Somebody decided to chew me out for staying up late and ruining my reputation as a nice girl.

At least the note wasn't composed of letters cut out of the newspaper. I figured the note had been delivered to the wrong apartment. Some nosey old woman had decided to lecture the party girls in our building and targeted me by mistake. But what if it wasn't a mistake, and some wacko was watching me? One late night out, and suddenly I was the Whore of Babylon?

Now I felt ick again, but I didn't want to stay home. I was safer at work, surrounded by my friends and co-workers. There was all that work I had to do to prepare for my job change and more school tour trips. I felt even more inclined to stay home, though, just thinking of the last two weeks I would have to endure working with Mason, dodging his attempts to get close to me.

I did go to work, and I did feel better once I had to focus on other things. I even managed to go out to lunch with Mini and Tony without feeling like my painkiller had me floating six inches above the floor. When I came back to the office, there were five messages on my phone from Mason, first telling me when he was coming to pick me up for lunch, then asking why I hadn't come to the front door, then asking where I had vanished to, and then asking why security wouldn't let him into the building. I was grateful no one was telling him anything. His last two messages were loud enough that Amy, in the cubicle next to mine, overheard. She told me I needed to report Mason to security. Before I knew it, I was spilling the weirdness to her, and several others overheard. Including DeNita. She called in her supervisor, and -- glory, hallelujah -- they changed their decision to let Mason finish up the tour.

There was still the problem, though, of him using everything he had learned about AMEA against us if he got angry. That was the whole reason for letting him finish the tour and kind of ease him out and away. Far away. Like to the moon, perhaps?

Lyndsey came up with the brilliant solution. First, don't boot him from the tour team. He really was a good part of the team and had been a blessing when he wasn't stalking me. Mason would go on the tour, but I would stay home. I could use my recent health problems as the excuse.

I was close to tears by the time the plans had been made and everyone necessary had been brought up to speed and agreed to their part. AMEA was the best place in the world to work because of the people who came to my defense and aid without being asked.

My nerves knotted up again when I got home and found three notes shoved under my door that night. One accused me of being a liar and a covenant breaker. Covenant? Who, outside of Sunday school or Old Testament study, used the word anymore? The second called me a liar and a coward and a sluggard. Again, with the Old Testament language? The third told me I would be worse than a murderer if I went ahead with my hysterectomy because I would be killing the children that God had decreed were my duty to give my husband.

I was still standing in my open doorway -- well, to be honest, leaning against the door -- reading the notes and trying to wrap my brain around it all when Lyndsey came down from her apartment to check on me. Later she said I looked like I had lost about a gallon of blood. She bustled me into my apartment, shut the door, and made me sit down. Then she made tea for both of us and got me to tell her what was going on.

"Notice something?" she said, after she had looked over all three notes several times each. She held out the one with the hearts. The one that accused me of being a covenant breaker. I couldn't see any other difference, but she pointed out the font and the paper was different.

"So you're saying I've got two wackos harassing me?"

"Either that or Sybil."

We talked for a while, and I let her make dinner for us. I was a total slug, stretched out on the couch with the heating pad on my stomach. We agreed I needed to take this to security at work and let them involve the police and our building manager. Because we worked for AMEA, there was always the chance some wackos would target us. Other employees had been followed when they left work, and attacked by people who couldn't get into the building to cause damage. We had security in the lobby of the building, patrols in the parking lot, and security cameras focused on the streets.

Just having a plan of action made me feel better.

I had another note stuck under my door when I got up the next morning. I was feeling pretty good, ready for a normal day at work, until I saw the bright pink heart. The writer ordered me to stop wasting my time on people who weren't worthy of my notice.

Mason called me at work. He wanted to take me out to dinner and "straighten out" our relationship. I told him no. I had a dinner meeting to prepare for my summer assignment.

A note waited under my windshield wiper when I came out after ten that night. No hearts on this one. I tried to look calm when I walked back to the building and asked the guard on duty at the door to help me. I would have run, but my legs were too wobbly for that. I was standing at just the right angle to see the guard's computer screen and the flagged notation with Chris Hawkes' name on it, giving my problem special priority. Oh, great...

This new note warned me that lying about my work obligations so I could sneak around and cheat just compounded my sins. I wanted to find the person who wrote the note and scream at him -- I was sure it was a him -- that I hadn't left the building since I arrived at nine that morning. Who did he think he was, calling me a liar and accusing me of crimes I hadn't committed?

While I waited, the guard checked the security videos for the two cameras that showed the section of the parking lot where my car sat all day and the adjacent streets. As far as they could tell, no one came onto the property and approached my car. Which meant that someone who *belonged* in the building during the day had put the note there and managed not to be seen as he walked past.

Not a good development.

I left the note with the guard to pass up the chain of command. He walked me out to my car and asked if I would feel better if someone drove me home and picked me up in the morning. I thanked him and declined.

Another note waited under my door when I got home from Bible study on Friday night. I was tired and headachy from the long day, and threatened cramps were haunting me despite the muscle relaxer my doctor had sent over. My adrenaline shot up, scouring away that dragging feeling, when I read the note.

Now the creep claimed that I belonged to him and I had no right to go out at night.

I was so tempted to leave a note sticking out from under my door, telling him women stopped being property hundreds of years ago. Not smart. Best to ignore him and not give him the attention he wanted.

My first mistake was reading the note before I even stepped into my apartment. I was still standing there when Mason stepped off the elevator. He reached to hug me, spouting apologies for not showing up at Bible study like he had promised. When had he promised me? When did I invite him? While I was evading his arms, he took the note out of my hand, read it, crumpled it, stepped past me into my apartment, and tossed it into the wastebasket. My second mistake was stepping aside so he could get into my apartment.

"Who's telling you not to go out?" His eyes had angry sparks, but he tried to smile, and I had the impression he was trying to make a joke of it. Maybe to comfort me?

Honestly? It felt good to have someone angry on my behalf.

"I have no idea. If I did, I could do something about it."

"Aw, honey, don't worry." He put an arm around my shoulders. I slid free before he could tighten his grip. He sighed, but grinned like we were playing a game. "You know I'll take care of you. Whoever this jerk is, he's just blowing hot air, that's all. Come on, you and me, we'll go out and have a good time and teach him he can't tell you what to do."

"Mason, I am wiped. I'm still not feeling completely back to normal, it was a crazy hectic day, and it's late. I just want to go to bed."

His mouth flattened for a few seconds, then he shook his head and summoned up a smile. "You're sure? Of course you're sure. That's just smart. Yeah, promise me you'll go straight to bed."

The weirdest part was that he didn't argue with me and left almost immediately.

Mason told me to lock my door, turn off my phone, and go to bed. He insisted that if I wasn't feeling completely well in the morning, I should call him, and he'd take me to the doctor. He wanted to take care of me. It was his duty.

Since when?

I thanked him and avoided promising him I would call. I locked my door, deadbolt and regular lock and the chain. Wednesday, Lyndsey had commented on seeing Mason in the building and agreed it was a little strange how easily he got inside. What if he had stolen my keys from my purse while we were on tour, copied them, and that was how he was getting in? I almost hoped there was a flaw in the security system. Accusing him of stealing my keys would just make the situation worse.

If he did have my keys, that meant he could get into my apartment. While he would probably think it was romantic, I did not want to wake up to find him keeping watch in my doorway or even sitting beside my bed.

Creepy.

*****

Mini and Tony got the job at the Georgia boot camp. To get away from Mason's daily phone calls while the tour finished up, I flew down to Georgia to make preparations for their move. He didn't have my cell number, just my office number. I stayed two weeks and helped Mini and Tony get settled. Then I did some preliminary work for the Coshocton boot camp. We were busy with getting permits, landscape studies, water flow studies, and environmental impact studies. Plus PR work with the churches in the surrounding area. Always better to be totally transparent before we moved in, rather than having to deal with ugly rumors and hurt feelings after work had begun.

My stalkers stuffed notes under my apartment door every day. Lyndsey checked my apartment regularly to pick them up. She wore gloves, put them in a zipper bag to protect all evidence, such as skin cells and possible fingerprints, and turned them over to security, for Chris Hawkes' special attention. The security team monitoring the parking lot found a note left under my windshield wiper two days after I left. They had my keys, so they moved the car up to the front row where they could keep an eye on it. No more notes were left. Somehow, that wasn't encouraging. I wanted my critic to be stupid enough to get caught.

Whoever was putting the heartless notes under my door probably lived in the building and was well-connected to the gossip chain because he knew I was out of town. After three days, those notes stopped. All the other notes were bordered with hearts and scolded me for hiding, for breaking my promises, for sneaking around and abusing the love that I did not deserve. The second week, the notes changed to threats. All sorts of eternal punishment, administered by the angels, if I didn't keep myself pure. I belonged to him.

Creepy to the max.

I had four nasty notes under my door when I got back from Georgia on Saturday night. I only read the first. I didn't want to know what the other ones said. The first was bad enough.

According to my anonymous lunatic, I was a whore because I left town without his permission. Now he knew I'd been out of town. The previous letters had all been scolding me for hiding from him. He warned me that if I didn't repent and live in isolation and make myself worthy of him, he would punish me. He said he would punish my boyfriend for daring to violate the purity that was reserved for him alone.

Again, angry more than scared. What boyfriend? Anyone paying close enough attention would know Mason wasn't my boyfriend. Just because he wanted to marry me didn't make him my boyfriend.

I remotely checked my office phone. Lyndsey had arrived by then with dinner, to report any Mason sightings and what she had heard at work. I put the replay on speaker. Mason had left multiple voicemail messages, expressing his concern, and promising to protect me. He wanted us to get married as soon as I got back from Georgia, so he could protect me full-time. We would go away somewhere that no one could find us.

"Wait a second. I know we all had instructions not to tell anyone *where* you went, so how did Mason know you went to Georgia?" Lyndsey asked.

"Same person who helped put the notes on my car without security catching them. Someone inside. What gets me is how he knows mister hearts is threatening me."

"He knows the creep."

"What if he is the creep?"

"Why would he do that?"

"Scare me."

"Well, yeah, but...well, duh." She leaned back and slouched a little. "If you're not scared, you're not going to let him protect you. So what are you going to do?"

"Certainly not marry him."

I had to take this brainstorm higher up the chain. I had done a lot of praying about the whole situation in Georgia, and I did a lot more that night after Lyndsey and I agreed to ride together to church.

Chris Hawkes went to my church, so I didn't have to wait until Monday morning to talk to him. Lyndsey and I went to the early service to avoid Mason coming by to pick me up. If my theory was right, he knew I was back in town, and I wouldn't put it past him to try to follow up on my increased terror -- hah! -- and swoop in to take advantage of my sleepless night and convince me to marry him.

Why did the guy want me to marry him? Wasn't it clear I didn't love him?

That Sunday, Chris went to the early service and sat two pews up from me. Before I could approach him after the service, he turned around, met my gaze, and signaled for me to wait for him. So he knew I was there the whole time. He didn't seem surprised when I told him what Lyndsey and I had theorized. Something cold in his eyes chilled me as he filled me in on what he had been doing while I was out of town. I was so glad he was my friend.

Chris had consulted with a friend who was a fingerprint expert. Three people were sending me the notes. Two sets of fingerprints on the heartless notes, one set of prints on the heart-bordered notes. He also got permission from the building manager and put a hidden security camera in the hall to watch my door.

"So now you know who's doing it?" For some weird reason, I felt a little disappointed.

"Why are you letting them keep doing it?" Lindsey added.

"Ever heard about giving someone enough rope to hang themselves?" Chris said.

"What are you going to do?"

"That depends on how much courage you have. I'm working on a theory, and the less you know, the less warning the conspirators will have when the trap finally closes on them."

*****

Chris asked me to go out for lunch on Monday. By myself. And eat outside. He promised I would have a shadow. I suspected a trap was involved. So I stopped at a deli for a sandwich and a bottle of iced tea, and went to Riverside Park.

My phone rang. Nathan Hanson was calling to let me know about the progress of the property transfer and rezoning, and getting cooperation from the local churches. We chatted about his classes, and I told him about some of the pre-sem students at SCC. We laughed. He had a proposal for when I moved down to Coshocton. They had a number of outbuildings on the land they were keeping. His father wanted to renovate an old cottage within walking distance of the farmhouse, and be my landlord. I thought that sounded lovely. Spending more time with Royce Hanson was one of the benefits of my new job.

We chatted about the jobs I had had, working for AMEA even before I graduated from college. I told him some of the horror stories of juggling multiple VBS programs or being caught between the sports rivalries among different churches and denominations.

"Maybe when you're down here you'd want to take over our Bible school program," Nathan said.

"I think I'm going to be way too busy."

"Don't take this the wrong way. I know how they live in a goldfish bowl, but you'd make an incredible minister's wife."

"That's the cruelest thing I've ever heard." I laughed. "I'm strictly a backstage person. I'd freeze the minute I stepped into the spotlight. Ministers' wives take too much abuse and criticism. I couldn't stand it."

"You'd be a breath of fresh air."

"Oh, no thanks. I was warned in college to stay away from ministers, seminary students, and especially pre-sem students looking for wives."

Nathan tried for a few more minutes to convince me that I could do wonderful things for any church lucky enough to have me as their minister's wife.

"Okay, if you're so sure, just who do you have in mind for me to marry?" I challenged him.

Silence.

"Nathan?"

"Well...how about me? I mean, have some pity on me, Eve." His laugh sounded a little ragged. I had a mental image of this big, tough ex-Marine swaying on his feet, playing with the brim of his hat, and afraid to look me in the eye. "I can't go to seminary without a wife. It's like a law of nature."

"You're not asking me to marry you. Nathan..." I had to laugh, but there wasn't much humor. "For one thing, I am not leaving AMEA. Not until I get word directly from God that's what He wants me to do."

We chatted a little longer, until we both got over that awkward moment. I breathed a sigh of relief when I could finally turn off my phone and finish my sandwich.

"Who was that?"

I yelped and choked on the bite of sandwich I had been about to swallow. Mason stomped around the side of the bench to face me. I had the awful feeling he had been standing behind me, listening. I had to wonder how much he had overheard of Nathan's side of the conversation, not just mine.

"Who was that? Who are you cheating on me with?"

"Cheating on you?" I stood up and had to restrain the urge to throw my iced tea bottle at him. "To be cheating on you, Mason, I would have to have a commitment to you. And I don't. I will never marry you. How many times do I have to say it?"

"You have to marry me."

"No, I don't!"

"You have to. It's all arranged. Everything is settled."

"No, nothing is settled. I will not marry you. Not ever. Do you understand?"

"You have to. He promised."

"I don't love you!"

"Yes, you do. He told me you did. He told me you were crazy about me."

"Who told you?"

His eyes got big, and he looked over my shoulder. I started to turn, to see who got him scared all of a sudden, but it occurred to me that it was a trick. As soon as I turned my back on him, Mason could grab me. But he didn't. He ran. I looked over my shoulder and wasn't surprised to see Chris approaching.

"If you'd waited just another minute, I might have found out who's been behind all this craziness. Some idiot has Mason convinced I'm in love with him. Somebody promised me to him."

"Uh huh. I have a theory."

"Are you going to tell me?"

"In good time."

*****

Wednesday, on Chris's orders, I flew home to Mom without telling anyone. I had orders for her not to answer the phone or let anyone know I was there. It sounded weird until Mom got inundated with phone calls from, of all people, the remaining Millers. Many of them had died off in the years since they cut us off over Dad's estate. They were all asking about me, what I was doing, where I was working, what I was up to. Mom didn't answer the phone, so we got to listen to the messages they left. Why were they interested in me after so long?

Saturday, Chris called. Someone had trashed my apartment during the night. The attacker stood on the lawn under my second floor balcony and shattered all the windows and sliding door with the equivalent of a potato gun. He filled my apartment with stink bombs and paint bombs and rocks. There was no telling yet how much damage had been done, how much could be salvaged, or what had to be thrown out.

The building manager had called Chris after he called the police. Chris got there first and found three more notes, accusing me of lying, pretending to be out of town, hiding from him, and "whoring" in my apartment. All the heart-bordered notes came from Mason. The extra cameras inside and outside the building caught him doing the bombing.

Even now, I shudder to think of what would have happened if I had been in my apartment. If I had fled in a panic, would Mason have been waiting to pretend to rescue me? Or punish me?

Tuesday, my plane landed at seven. Chris met me in the baggage claim area. I nearly screamed when I felt an arm go around my waist, but I looked up into his eyes and never felt so relieved in my life.

"Play along," he whispered -- and kissed my cheek.

Okay, I had seen enough spy-type movies to guess what was going on. Chris was playing to an audience. I guessed Mason was there, that he had followed Chris to the airport. The only way he could have done that was if Chris let him. For what purpose?

"I was going to take a taxi," I said, when we had my bags and headed down the long walkway to the parking garage.

"Back to headquarters, to get your car in a dark parking lot." Chris glanced back over his shoulder. "Besides, your car isn't there anymore."

"What did you do with it?"

"We towed it after the fire died."

"Mason torched my car?"

"His inside man. Mason was elsewhere at the time. Ordering wedding invitations."

I was too furious about my car to consider that other bit of news. I seethed and thought until we were settled in Chris's car and heading for the gate out of the lot.

"It's been interesting, following him around town, putting together the wedding."

"Since when do guys plan the weddings?"

"With your brother and sister-in-law's help, of course."

"I don't have--" I felt sick. If I had eaten anything on the plane, I might have ruined the upholstery in Chris's car. "Bill's still pretending to be my big brother. How did he meet up with Mason?"

"Bill used to attend the same church. They've started their own church. Your wedding is supposed to be the first celebration in it. Kind of a christening."

I felt colder than if I had jumped into a snowdrift in a dripping wet nightgown. It all made nauseating sense. When Mason insisted I "had to" marry him, someone had promised I would, that someone was Bill. Had Bill convinced Mason that I actually *wanted* to marry him?

Maybe I could plead insanity after I killed both Bill and Mason with my bare hands?

Chapter 13

"What makes those loonies think I would show up for a wedding I never agreed to?"

Chris hesitated, and that worried me. He gave me a somber, searching glance, his face half-lost in the shadows of the car. "It's going to be kind of ugly before it starts to get better."

"There's more?" I could almost laugh, except I had a growing cramp that threatened to wrap around my lungs.

"He set up a menu with the caterer. Another member of the new church. And he bought you a dress."

"I already have a dress. It doesn't make sense that I would ask him to buy me another one."

This was starting to sound and feel like a really bad psychological thriller. Was I going to find out Mason had a cabin somewhere in the mountains, with the bodies of ten dead wives decorating it inside?

"You have a dress?" Chris frowned at me.

"I was engaged in college and bought a dress. I still have it. At least, I think I do. How bad was the damage in my apartment?"

"I supervised the inspection. If I didn't see the dress, then it wasn't in the damaged area."

"Oh, that's a big comfort. I've been planning on getting rid of it for years."

"Be thankful you didn't. We can use that as evidence."

"Evidence?" Now I got that shiver down my back that curled around in my gut.

"Mason and Bill are telling everyone involved in planning the wedding that you've given them specific instructions for everything. Including the dress. If you *already* have a dress, and you can prove you've had it for years--"

"It still has the sales receipt stapled to the bag."

"Good girl."

"How can their church -- sorry." I tried to smile. "I should stop interrupting and just let you tell the story."

"Asking questions means you're thinking and not just letting all of this sweep you away."

"Okay. Good. Points in my favor." That got a tight little chuckle from him.

"We're still asking questions, getting the chain of events, the timeline. Our first big mistake was assuming that the lack of cooperation from

Mason's church, when we started investigating, was because they're one of those churches that have decided AMEA is a cult."

"Us? How about them? One interpretation of their doctrine is that men can't get into heaven unless they're married."

"Close, but...well, we've been talking with the pastoral staff. We discovered that the closed doors and mouths were more from shame than refusal to help. Bill and Mason pretty much instigated a church split." Chris gave me a sideways look, and one corner of his mouth twitched.

I could nearly ignore the cramp that stole my breath for a second. He wasn't implying what I thought he was implying. Was he?

"The process of approving marriages involves the whole church. The groom doesn't just buy the bride from her father. Or older brother. Or only living relative, who is worried about her mental and spiritual health."

"Yeah, that sounds like Saint Bill." Another twist in my gut. "Did you say buy?"

"Bill sold you to Mason to settle some huge debts he had racked up with a few failed businesses. Mason is independently wealthy. He paid off all Bill's debts after he met you and decided you were the one for him. The church leadership learned that money had been exchanged and contracts signed without your knowledge. Not something they condone.

"The truth came out when Bill and Mason refused to bring you in for the meetings to go over the contract and start courtship counseling. The two conspirators got called up before the elders, scolded, and were forbidden to proceed."

"And when he didn't get what he wanted, Bill did what he's always done, and left the church. Did he have a big public meltdown and accuse them of heresy? Maybe he threatened to sue them for emotional damage and spiritual blackmail, to get back all the money he tithed?"

"Standard procedure?" Chris looked amused but not so much that I could be irritated with him. I nodded, and he sighed. "The big break in the investigation came when you remembered that woman at the hospital who scolded you about having a hysterectomy."

"Just that she talked to me, but not her name. Who?"

"Bill's wife."

"Figures."

"They live in your building." Another sideways look at me.

"Those are the two sets of prints on the other notes?" I slouched a little in my seat. "So now what? Are you setting a big trap or something, picking me up? I assume that kiss meant Mason was watching? He isn't going to ram us on the highway and try to kidnap me, is he?"

"The trap has been baited. A couple members of their church work for us. They're so angry over how those two have torn their church apart, they want to help us. They've been pretending to be on Bill and Mason's side, feeding them inside information."

"You're enjoying this too much." I couldn't help grinning when Chris snickered and took his hand off the steering wheel long enough to pat my hand, resting on the seat between us.

"Believe it or not, this whole mess might just build some bridges between that church and us. In this day and age, Christians need to stand together, not keep sabotaging each other. First, we get those nutcases handled. We have to give them enough rope to hang themselves. Then we can press charges, bring legal action against them. Our friends have been feeding them information about your schedule. That's how Mason knew you were coming in tonight."

"Uh huh. And that kiss was to make sure he followed us?"

"More like to stir the pot. Mason makes regular visits to psychiatric hospitals whenever his grasp of reality gets shaky. Whenever he believes he loves a woman who never seems to love him back, he convinces himself she's in danger. He has to kidnap her to rescue her." Lines formed around Chris's mouth, and a steely light touched his eyes. "His records are unavailable through privacy laws, but we've gathered enough information to be worried that he's on the verge of a psychotic break. He hasn't been violent before."

"The bombing of my apartment."

"Exactly. We suspect Bill has been playing mental games with Mason. From what we've gathered, Bill does that a lot. He has a history of driving people apart, telling them different stories to keep them from getting together and comparing the lies. People who take the time to talk quickly realize that he's been manipulating them for his own profit."

"Like he did with our relatives for years. So…you think Bill is driving Mason into violence? Why?"

"We have testimony from a number of people, including Bill's ex-fiancées, that he's convinced he's the heir to your father's estate. You and your mother have stolen what rightfully belongs to him."

"He wants Mason to kill me?" Funny, how I couldn't really react to that with any feelings whatsoever. "Wait -- fiancées? More than one?"

"Four. He leaves a church when things don't go his way. In at least three instances, his fiancée, always the pastor's daughter, starts having second thoughts."

"He doesn't want them, he wants the inside track on authority. Wouldn't it have been easier to go to seminary and earn his degree and start his own church?"

"Too much work. No money. He can't get scholarships, and he builds up so much debt, no one will loan him any money."

I was feeling a little queasier with every mile we drove and every new revelation. I was almost disappointed to get to my apartment building without any kind of attack along the way. Chris revealed the next phase of the trap. I had surgery scheduled with the same doctor who had recommended I have a hysterectomy. Bill's wife, Helen, worked for him, and overheard enough to assume I was going to have one. She certainly proved she was the right wife for Saint Bill.

Chris recruited several friends from church who worked at the hospital. With my doctor's help, they dropped enough chance remarks and left enough misplaced files around for nurse's aide Helen Miller to snoop and learn I was scheduled for an elective hysterectomy in the morning. Elective was so much more "sinful" than needing one because I might just bleed to death. Yesterday, after our friends on the inside let them know I was coming home, Bill and Helen had pretended to be me and Mason, and applied for a marriage license. Then Helen stole drugs from the hospital pharmacy. All caught on security cameras.

Mason had told quite a few people we wanted at least five children. He had to prevent that hysterectomy. Maybe the deal would be off if I had the operation. If he followed true to form, he would try to "rescue" me with a kidnapping tonight.

Lyndsey and two female security guards were waiting for me in an unoccupied apartment on the first floor, where I would be staying while my apartment was being cleaned up. They made sure Bill and Helen didn't see them come in and get into place. As far as anyone knew, I was alone once Chris dropped me off.

Funny thing -- that night was the best sleep I had since the whole mess with Mason began. A large part of that came from trusting in Chris and his team, and knowing that soon Mason and Bill would both be out of my life. With extreme prejudice. I did a lot of heavy-duty praying before I went to bed. What else was there to do? We couldn't sit up and have a pajama party, even though both security guards were friends. I was supposed to be alone and vulnerable.

Yeah, vulnerable, with Chris Hawkes and AMEA security and a whole squadron of angels protecting me.

The self-righteous trio stepped onto the patio of my borrowed apartment armed with stolen hospital tranquilizers, ropes, and a sledgehammer. Chris, his team, and the police were waiting. The moment Bill raised the sledgehammer, he was caught and stopped. There was very little noise. I heard nothing of the minor ruckus.

By 3am, Wednesday morning, it was over.

Bill and Helen were so desperate to put all the blame on Mason, they contradicted each other's stories. Mason snapped. He gave the authorities everything they needed, including all sorts of documents with my forged signature. They weren't even good forgeries.

*****

I didn't go to work the next day. I alternated between semi-comatose periods when I stared at the TV without knowing what was on, eating without tasting anything, and ridding out my apartment like a madwoman. The cleaning team Chris had brought in had tried to salvage everything, but there were a lot of things I just didn't want anymore. I was going through a phase that some nomadic co-workers described as preparing for immediate evacuation. I was compelled to figure out what I truly I valued in life, to rid myself of anything that would keep me from traveling light and fast. If I couldn't take it to Heaven with me, did I really want or need it?

My co-workers decided to have a shower for me to replace the things that had been damaged beyond repair. It just proved once again how much of a family, the good kind of family, we were at AMEA.

Jennie Michaels and Chris and DeNita all insisted I needed a couple days off. During that time, I learned the rest of the details of the bizarre picture. Helen's cousin, Geoffrey worked in HR at AMEA. He had a fake resume that stood up to the standard investigation process, thanks to some illegal connections. It fell apart once Chris started investigating anyone associated with Bill and Helen. Originally, Geoffrey had infiltrated AMEA to get Bill a job and to sabotage me. I had to be punished for refusing to do my duty and pull every string to benefit Bill.

Geoffrey got access to my schedules and personal information. Helen and Bill moved into my apartment complex to spy on me. Bill was already grooming Mason to latch onto me while turning over control of his bank accounts to his future in-law. Then Geoffrey learned about the plan to let outside journalists and photographers travel with the college teams. He manipulated the assignment process, and ensured no one learned about Mason's mental problems.

All the conspirators were going away for a long time. Unfortunately, they didn't lose access to the outside world. Bill repaired his broken connections with the rest of the Miller clan, and they went to work making Mom's life miserable again. All this was her fault. That was their go-to explanation for any disappointment, problem, or failure.

Jennie Michaels came by to see me when I was on the phone with Mom one day, getting the low-down. I had her on speaker so I could work on sorting while we talked, so I introduced the two of them. It turned out Jennie had asked Chris to keep her updated on all the fallout. She knew about the Miller clan's treatment of Mom, because it tied into Bill's actions and choices. She asked how Mom was doing, and she had a suggestion.

I would be moving to Coshocton once my cottage was ready on the Hanson farm. Mom needed to get out of town and beyond the reach of the Miller clan for a while. To benefit both of us, Mom could help me with the move. She could stay with me for a month or two, to help me settle in. We both could use a vacation after all the stress we had been through. AMEA, of course, would include her travel expenses as part of my move, since Mom was helping me.

Everything got settled quickly. I had a brilliant idea once Jennie left and it was just Mom and me on the phone again. Maybe Mom should move down with me? I had the plans for the cottage, and there was plenty of room for both of us. Move away, leave all the nasty memories behind, and start over.

"It isn't really moving that far away," Mom said with a chuckle. I had grown up in northeast Ohio, and Coshocton was only a few hours south.

"It's still getting away. Most of what I'll be taking with me is clothes and books. Mason did a real number on my furniture, and most of my dishes are shards. Most of our furniture will be yours, unless you want to get rid of all that old stuff and start fresh."

That was what we did. Mom agreed with me: get rid of lots of things that would remind us of the past and start out fresh. We would have fun, decorating from what she referred to as Salvation Army Classic, hitting antique and secondhand shops. When friends and co-workers stopped by to help with the cleanup process, I asked them to move everything out to the pad in the apartment complex where bulk waited to be hauled away on trash day.

My living room was wasted. My bedroom was about half-salvageable. I had been wishing for a new wardrobe, but certainly not that soon or that drastically.

Ironically, everything in my storage closet was fine, not even a whiff of stink bomb. Not a splatter of paint. Nothing on my wedding dress. I wondered if I should consider it a good luck charm, however twisted that was, or finally get rid of it. Why haul it to Coshocton, after all, to hang in my closet and torment me?

Mom urged me to keep it. Ironic, in the final analysis.

I did go through a few periods of mentally and emotionally kicking myself. How could I have not seen through Mason sooner? But my friends and co-workers came through. When they seemed to sense I was ready to bang my head against the wall and call myself stupid, helpless, or oblivious, there was always someone around to tell me I shouldn't blame myself. Who could really know what the dividing line is between irritating and psycho dangerous?

I still blamed myself. The residue of the mental and emotional abuse of my childhood kept me vulnerable. Predators and psychos had a sense for people who were ripe for victimization. If I had had a better self-image, I might not have been attractive to Mason. I might have fought back sooner.

I wouldn't have been so delighted to be desired, to be pursued, that I was blind to the danger signs.

Bottom line: a portion of my problem *was* my fault because I had been neglecting praying and turning it all over to God. I mean, yes, I'd done some heavy-duty praying, but it was sporadic, whenever I got a feeling of something being wrong. I hadn't been consistent and regular. Would things have turned out any differently if I had been praying all this time? If I had turned to God and asked for His guidance from the moment I realized Mason was interested?

Talk about adding to the guilt.

When the courts finally processed all the charges against Mason, Bill, Helen and Geoffrey (and their counterclaims against me), my main concern was that I never had to see any of them again. The legal department at AMEA promised to keep everything as quiet as possible and reduce the requirements for my presence at the proceedings. Can I say grateful?

Bottom line: God wanted me to be single. That was pretty obvious. As soon as Chris gave me back my wedding dress, which was being logged for evidence, I decided I would put it up for sale.

In a way, the whole dress situation could be symbolic of holding onto preconceived notions and dreams that were just plain bad for me.

Yeah, I definitely needed to sell that dress.

*****

Just when I thought things were calming down, I had another bad attack. Fortunately, Mom was in town, helping me prepare for the move. She held my hand and ran down the street to get treats for me. She got to meet all my friends and co-workers. She spent several hours in deposition with the AMEA lawyers, relating the abuse Bill had loaded on me since childhood.

Mom read me the emails from friends when I was so sick, curled up the couch, I couldn't read. She read an email from Mrs. Carleone. Since that summer of revelation and healing at SCC, we had written to each other occasionally. Maybe three emails a year. Bonnie and Chaplain Nate had lots of friends at AMEA. They heard I was sick, and they told Mrs. Carleone. I braced myself for some concern, maybe a gentle inquisition from Mom, because I hadn't told her we were in contact. She didn't say anything other than, "How nice of her." So of course, I had to tell her everything.

"Have you thought of writing to Andy, clearing the air with him?" Mom said.

"Mom...it's complicated."

"Uh huh. And did you ever think that part of this problem is tied in with your not forgiving him?" She gestured at me. Specifically, at the warm herbal pack I was holding to my stomach. "That advice you gave him about his mother's problem was applicable. How about for you, too?"

I at least had the integrity and maturity not to even open my mouth and protest that I had forgiven him. At least, I thought I did.

Gee, when had my Mom gotten so incredibly wise? Yeah, and part of growing up was admitting that I kind of looked down on her for the mess of her life. Marrying Dad. Putting up with the Miller clan. *Not* dumping

Michelle L. Levigne

Dad years ago. I had learned from her mistakes. Or at least I thought I did. Maybe I had learned the wrong things from her mistakes? Because if I was honest -- and that was good for my mental, emotional, spiritual and even physical health -- Mom and Dad were pretty happy. When Bill wasn't around. When the rest of the family wasn't criticizing and invading. How come I had focused more on the misery than what made the misery at least semi-bearable?

So about the time my doctor reported my fibroids were shrinking again, I put together a short note for Mrs. Carleone to pass on to Andy. I apologized for hurting him and being unwilling to trust him. I didn't make excuses, and I didn't expand on it. I told him I was glad that he was back on the right spiritual path, listening to God, and trying to find his ministry. I told him I was praying for him.

Andy didn't write back.

I was relieved.

Mrs. Carleone wrote back, though, and told me Andy cried when he read my note. She said they were good tears.

Part Four: Nathan and Drew
Chapter 14

What with one thing and another, I didn't put the notecard with, "For Sale: Wedding Dress. Never Used," on the bulletin board at church or at work very long. I only got two phone calls of interest before it was time to head to Coshocton. My new cottage not only had enough room for Mom to move in with me, but a huge storage closet with plenty of room for that dress and the mementos, photos, and bits and pieces we couldn't let go.

After a month in Coshocton, I was pretty sure I was going to be losing my roommate.

I had seen love at first sight in books and movies, but never in real life, until that moment.

Royce got that funny, two-by-four between the eyes look when he walked up to the back of the little rental moving truck, reached to take a box from Mom, she turned around, their eyes met, and history was made. Mom blushed and they just grinned at each other for a few seconds. I had never seen Mom blush in my entire life, up until that moment. Then Mr. Hanson stammered and did a version of "Awwww, shucks, weren't nothin', Ma'am," when she thanked him for taking care of me and setting up the cottage so nicely for us.

Nathan showed up about then with his sisters, nieces, nephews, and baskets of food for the moving-in party. They basically rescued Mom and Royce from just standing there for the next hour.

I was kind of relieved, even though it freaked me out a little, seeing Mom look a little goofy from time to time. She wouldn't feel cut off and alone while I was at work. Royce offered right away to take her around to meet the community. He was combination guard dog and faerie godfather for both of us. From day one, we had the perfect relationship. He brought over fresh vegetables, eggs, and milk every other day. We filled his cookie jar, and had him and Nathan over for dinner at least twice a week. We went to church with them. Royce and Mom were together for hours at a time, every day, rain or shine. I had never known Mom liked walking so much. When I commented on it to Nathan, he laughed and said the same thing about his father.

*****

I spent the summer getting to know the community, setting up the AMEA office space, and doing some on-the-road troubleshooting and spot-check work. We rented space in one wing of the massive church the Hanson family attended. Several people asked me and Mom if we were attending their church just because we felt an obligation, living on the edge of the Hanson farm and having the office there. They assured us they wouldn't feel insulted if we found a church home that was more comfortable. Which went a long way toward making us feel comfortable.

In September, the construction on the boot camp finally began with clearing the acreage and doing some landscaping by moving lots of dirt around. The first step was creating retention basin ponds and small hills and ridges to divide the property into areas devoted to specific purposes. Headquarters sent me a small staff to move into the office. They were there to oversee construction and start the process of recruiting and hiring the staff to run the camp year-round. The facilities wouldn't be sitting idle, after all, when boot camp finished. We would have conferences and retreats throughout the year. The property would also be available to local churches for things like music festivals and multi-church fellowship events. Since this boot camp was going to focus on performance ministries, specifically music and drama, part of the property would have an amphitheater, and that opened up lots of options. We were all excited as we set up the office and started making lists and creating our recruitment campaign. The sky definitely wasn't the limit.

October came and the office staff was filling in, including my old friend from college, Ken. The foundations had been poured for all the buildings. We got a little negative feedback from people who seemed to be offended that AMEA was "invading" the area. We had half-expected some churches to be upset because either they weren't consulted or they just didn't like Allen Michaels, but the advance teams and the crusade in the area a few years ago had been good PR. The trouble came from a college professor who was a loud advocate for socialism and for defending young minds (his words) from "the opiate of religion." He was especially offended by the music and drama focus of the boot camp, insulted that AMEA would use those avenues to "infect" the rising generations with "emotionally and mentally defective teaching." It was okay for socialists and New Age gurus to use those venues to reach people, but Christians were forbidden?

People who weren't connected to AMEA or even to churches got ticked at this guy's nasty campaign to turn the surrounding communities against us. Threats of legal action to rescind all our permits stayed just that -- threats, empty talk. Once the tidal wave started, more people decided he was a loudmouth with a greasy grasp of facts and reality, and he lost a lot of momentum. We knew better than to hope he would tuck his tail between his legs, toddle home, and shut up. At least the uproar had quieted for a while.

Then headquarters let me know they had at long last chosen my co-leader for the office and boot camp. Drew Leone would be director/coordinator for the musical groups we would train and send out next summer. He had a strong background in touring music ministry. We were going to start small, just four musical/drama groups this first year, and only touring the States. Once we had worked out the anticipated bugs in the program and the numbers had grown, we would move north and south, crossing the border into Canada and Mexico with Spanish-language and French-speaking teams. Then, eventually cross the ocean. Big dreams when just four teams seemed pretty ambitious for our freshman year. The goal was to have our recruitment campaign together and start hitting the high school and college kids when they returned to school after Christmas break. We missed all the advertising deadlines for magazines for January, and even February, so to make up for it, we'd have to go directly to the Christian schools.

The day Drew arrived, we had his apartment all set up, furnished, with linens, cleaning supplies, and groceries. Ken volunteered to wait at the apartment to meet Drew, give him his keys and such, and then show him around town on his way to the church and our offices.

I got an email from Mrs. Carleone that morning, and wished I hadn't. It put ideas in my head that were getting in the way of finishing my preparations before Drew showed up. She said if I got angry enough never to talk to her again, she would understand, and she apologized. Then she told me I needed to know that the threat from the cult had been so bad that she and Andy had needed to take on new identities. She admitted it was foolish to even stay in Iowa, much less work at SCC, but the cult leaders were after Andy, not her. Then she warned me that Andy was coming to see me. He wanted to work with me. Mrs. Carleone (whatever her name was now, she hadn't told me) wanted me to keep in mind that Andy was right with God now.

I had no idea what to think or feel. I didn't have time, with my new co-leader about to show up. For about ten seconds, I played with the similarities in the names, but I just thought I was being paranoid. Why would Andy go to such lengths, just to see me? It was ludicrous.

Yes, I was grateful Mrs. Carleone feared I would be so angry I would cut off contact. Hadn't I healed more since writing that letter to Andy, to try to clear the air and heal us both?

I was still processing that email when Kurt Green walked into the office. He looked a little flustered, a little angry, and asked if Drew had shown up yet. When I said no, Kurt asked if we could speak in my office.

AMEA had rules about individuals of the opposite sex meeting behind closed doors. If I had another member of the staff with me, I could have closed the door. Kurt and I went into my office, and I left the door open enough for someone to see us, and we kept our voices down.

"I'm sorry, Eve," he said, dropping into the chair facing my desk. "You're going to feel like you've been ambushed. The guy lied to me. Technically, he didn't, but..." He shrugged. "I just found out. Ned and

DeNita know what's up, and I warned them we might have to do some damage control. The thing is, until this morning, I really liked the guy. I thought the two of you would work well together."

"You're talking about Drew?" That was kind of a no-brainer, but I needed to make sure we were talking about the same guy. "What did he lie about?"

My gut instinct knew, that shivering feeling inside. My brain just didn't want to accept the signal.

I'm not exaggerating to say a cold gust of air wrapped around me. We had an outside door, opening onto the parking lot. Someone had come in, most likely Ken and Drew, and the breeze swirled through the office on windy days.

"Hey, Eve?" Ken called.

"I'm here for you," Kurt said.

"You're not going to tell me, are you?" I hadn't sat down yet, so I stepped back around my desk and headed for the door.

"He lied about his name and his past. The guy was in the next best thing to Witness Protection--"

Then I knew, before Ken stepped into the door and pushed it open all the way, and I saw Andy Carleone standing behind him.

Correction: Drew Leone, who had to change his identity to hide from the cult wackos who wanted to punish him for reclaiming his soul and his spiritual integrity.

Fortunately, there was too much to do and too many people in the office for us to react to each other. The moment Andy (Drew, I had to think of him as Drew) identified himself as the new music team director, my staff swarmed him with messages and paperwork. I didn't have a moment's peace to think and react. It was go, go, go. I dove into my work, and every time it got quiet in the outer office and I had a break in my reports, I would freeze, afraid to look up and see Andy (Drew, his name was Drew now) standing in my doorway, giving me that poor, pitiful puppy look that had worked so well, too many times, to get me to forgive him for being a thoughtless, oblivious jerk.

He never did come to see me. I found out later that Kurt took Drew aside once the first big rush of meeting him and getting him settled had quieted down. I got a warm feeling when I did learn about it, knowing that my big brother was looking out for me. Kurt lectured him on lying, or withholding important information, or whatever it technically was.

Drew's response was basically, "Would you have let me come here if you knew?"

Kurt's was, "No." Then after he thought about it, he added, "I don't know. Because the guy I've come to know isn't the guy who broke Eve's heart. Are you?"

And Drew said, "I hope not. I hope I'm the guy I should have been when we were together." Kurt left soon after that talk, after asking me to wait to see how the whole situation felt before I talked to our supervisors about any changes.

I felt slightly betrayed. Hadn't he told me just an hour ago that he was there to support me? Now he wanted me to test the waters and see if we could work together? Yet if Kurt, who was so defensive of me, thought I should wait, maybe I should.

Ken avoided me, which was a good thing, because by then I had put together enough pieces to figure out that he knew Drew was coming, and he cooperated with keeping the secret from me. I found out later that they had been back in contact for a few years. Ken had been counseling him, helping him get straightened out, and keeping Drew updated on me. Was I supposed to get a warm, fuzzy, "awwwww" feeling from that, or a squirmy, creeped-out feeling? Ken later admitted that if he had known Drew would get the posting, he never would have spied on me. He was there through the whole Mason mess, after all. He knew I needed some protecting and coddling. He was my protective big brother, too.

God was kind, and I never had to face Drew in private for the remainder of the day.

Mom was on a date with Royce when I got home. Even though I *needed* to vent to her, I really didn't *want* to talk to anyone. I just wanted to stew for a little while. I settled in to unwind and let my brain go into neutral by watching *Terminator* and inhaling some chocolate peanut butter ice cream.

Where was Arnold when I really need him to cream something -- or someone?

Mom knew something was wrong almost as soon as she walked in the door with Royce. The empty ice cream carton and the opening credits of *Terminator* 2 were a big giveaway.

"What happened with Drew?" she asked, settling on the big green steamer trunk we used as a coffee table. That was an easy guess because she knew my co-leader was arriving. She looked over my head. I was sprawled on the couch, and turned around enough to see Royce standing in the doorway.

"Drew is Andy."

"Oh…honey." She scooted off the trunk onto the side of the couch and wrapped her arms around me.

"I'm not going to cry. I'm not really sure what I'm thinking or feeling. I just need time to…let it sink in maybe." Then I told both of them about the whole weird day.

I didn't hesitate to spill all of that in front of Royce. He was like a father to me -- forget the fact he was dating my mother, still getting that goofy look in his eyes and inspiring the same blushes and starry-eyed expression in her.

I needed to get out and get some fresh air, even if the night had taken a chilly turn. I had become just as much of a fanatic about long walks as Mom and Royce. At least mine could be explained by needing to check on the newest developments in the camp. I excused myself, changed into my thickest sweats and my hiking boots, and headed outside.

Royce told Nathan, and he came to look for me. Nathan looked out for me like a big brother by this time, which made sense. If things kept going the way they were, he was going to be my stepbrother. He didn't say anything when he caught up with me, walking the perimeter of the future pond, except to ask if I wanted some company. We walked for another twenty minutes or so in silence.

"Need some diversionary tactics?" he asked, when we were clearly heading back around the perimeter of the camp toward home.

"Like what?"

"Officially, this guy is here to set up the music camp, hire the staff, start recruiting, right?"

"That's all he's going to do. Right."

"We need to make sure if he has any other ideas, he can't make any progress."

"Like what?"

Nathan saluted, and my cold face actually ached from the grin I couldn't resist. "Reporting for guard duty, Miss Miller, ma'am."

"What? You're going to stand outside my office door and require a password whenever anybody wants to see me?"

"I was thinking more along the lines of preemptive action. If you're dating somebody, this guy can't make any moves on you."

"You and me. Dating." I wasn't sure what to say. It wasn't the worst idea I had ever heard, but I knew better than to phrase it that way. "I have to warn you, it sounds like the plot of a lot of romance novels."

"Would it be so bad if something did…develop…between us?" His smile was kind of crooked, kind of amused, kind of awkward.

"With your dad and my Mom all kissy-face and probably heading for a Christmas engagement?"

"Ah. Yeah. Don't know if that could be considered incestuous, but…" He shrugged, and then he laughed. "Could be a lot worse."

"I've had a lot worse. You're a vast improvement over what's been showing interest in me lately."

"I'll take that as a compliment, ma'am." He tipped an imaginary cap to me. We were both smiling as we came up the driveway to the cottage.

*****

Drew was sitting on my front porch swing at eight the next morning, when I came back from another walk. I needed a walk every morning to make it possible to spend the next ten hours mostly sitting behind a desk.

"I'm not leaving, Evie," Drew said, standing up as I approached the cottage front door. He had obviously seen me coming up the gravel drive and sat down to wait for me.

"If you want to stand on my porch all day, that's fine. I have to go to work."

"I meant here, Coshocton, the office, the organization."

He took a step back and leaned against the porch post. Most guys, after making a statement like that, would have stepped forward, an unconscious intimidation tactic. *He* would have done it when he was Andy Carleone. The difference made me relax a little, which made no sense.

"We need to talk. Yes, I ambushed you. Mom told me, Ken told me, Kurt told me. Here's the thing. We were a good team in college. I want that again. I've grown up an awful lot in the last few years. I needed to. And I know you're probably a lot more grown up than me." He flashed that charmer smile I knew so well from college.

Funny, but my heart started racing, just like in college. The good days, not the hurting ones.

"Let me prove myself. Prove God's been changing me. So we can work together. I'd like to be friends again, but if all you'll give me is friendly co-worker, I'll settle for that."

"Promise?" I thought of Nathan's offer last night to protect me with a fake dating relationship.

"I'll try. I have a lot to make up for. A lot of bridges to repair. You can trust me. I mean, with Ken glaring at me all the time, and with Kurt checking up on me, I don't dare push the limits." He grinned.

The wind chose that moment -- or maybe it was God -- to blast right around both of us, hard enough to make me stagger a little. Drew shivered and tugged his coat around himself.

Then Mom came to the door. I had the feeling she had been watching for me to come up the drive and had been listening to us.

"Neither of you needs to catch a cold with a long week ahead of you. Either invite the boy in for some coffee, or get to work early and talk."

I invited Drew in, which surprised him. I figured that was a sign of change. He didn't just assume he'd be welcome inside.

"You drink coffee now?" he asked, following us into the kitchen.

"The fat-free, sugar-free, instant packaged variety," Mom said with a chuckle. She lifted the lever on the electric kettle, hooked two mugs with her other hand, and set them on the island counter down the center of the big, made-for-cooking-feasts kitchen Royce and Nathan had built for me. Then she took several different flavors of cappuccino and instant coffee mixes from the shelf under the counter. She was out of the kitchen before the water started rumbling in the kettle.

"No chaperone?" he asked, glancing around.

"Earshot is fine," Mom called from the living room.

We both had to laugh. Drew settled into one of the stools set around the island counter, and I leaned back against the sink to wait for the kettle to heat.

"I was pretty much straightened out, but I was still drifting. Your note, sent through Mom, and hearing what you'd been going through...that was the kick in the butt, really the kick in the head that I needed. All I could think about was that I let you down."

"No, you didn't," I had to say. That didn't mean something inside of me wasn't trying to shout yes, all my problems were his fault. Because he hadn't been there like he had promised.

"Would that wacko have targeted you if we were married? I've run into creeps like your cousin all the time. They're cowards. Sexist slime who expect women to be easy prey. He wouldn't have targeted you if you had had a husband to stand between you and him. Even if you didn't need anyone to defend you."

"Bill always held onto his version of reality, no matter how much evidence he had that it wasn't real." I thought about telling him that I had needed plenty of defense and defenders. God had always provided. It was on the tip of my tongue to tell him I would have loved to see him face down Bill, maybe knock him flat. I remembered how he had tried to get between me and those idiots playing mud football back in college, and ended up breaking his arm. It was easy to see Drew as my defender, despite all his flaws.

I didn't say anything, though. I knew better than to give him any encouragement. Even if he was here first to get the music camp established, there was all that history between us.

He tried to laugh. "Come on, Evie, say something."

"You flatter me, kind sir." I had to move or start shaking, so I opened up the refrigerator. "Have you had breakfast yet?"

"Always taking care of everybody else." He grinned, but it was a shaky grin.

The water rumbled louder, and then the temperature control clicked in and turned off the kettle. He got off the stool and stepped around the counter to pour the hot water while I pulled raisin bread and yogurt and pre-cooked sausage out of the refrigerator. Something easy to prepare and fast to eat. I still had to get a shower before heading to work.

"I knew you'd take care of me, no matter what kind of a mess I made." He was talking fast, like he was nervous. A nervous Drew was a totally new experience for me. "I think that's why I latched onto you from the beginning. You'd take care of me, instead of making me take care of you. I was so sick of living my life to please Mom... You were better off without me. Are you happy?"

"Happiness is relative, isn't it? It comes and goes."

"That sounds like the New Age garbage I was selling. Are you doing what you wanted, what you planned on doing, when we were together? Are you still close to God, working hard, and feeling good about it?"

"Lately, I haven't felt all that close to God. That's my own fault, I guess."

"Sometimes God is silent to make us listen," he offered with a sad little smile.

"Chaplain Nate said that." I slid the sausage into the microwave and tapped the controls, and then I couldn't delay facing him again. I turned around and leaned against the counter while he stirred the coffee for both of us. "How did you get the job so fast? I know the vetting process. They're twice as careful now."

"I was getting a lot of counseling from the field office where I was. I started to do volunteer work to pay back the time and effort the staff put into me. They were my references and vouched for me, all the classes I took, the spiritual gifts and maturity assessments I took. They saw my work close-up. I was giving the kids music lessons and had a coffee house band organized. They recommended me for this posting. Mom advised against it when I told her. This is your baby. I had to talk her into letting me try, and promised her ten ways from Friday I wouldn't hurt you."

"Wow," slipped out. I knew Mrs. Carleone had changed a lot since that whole ugly mess back at school, but for her to defend me against her adored son? Yeah, we all had changed in the last eleven, going on twelve years.

"Yeah. Wow. Ken gave me a lecture when I asked for his help. He about took my head off and played basketball with it for a few hours before he handed it back to me."

I had to laugh at that image, and that seemed to take some of the tension out of the air for both of us. Drew's smile wasn't quite so strained.

"He advised me to confess to some of your friends at headquarters when I was up there for interviews. You have a lot of people who love you." His voice got raspy the last dozen or so words.

We both jumped when the microwave timer went off. I pulled out dishes for us, and we settled on either side of the counter.

"So, I'm finally where I should have been when we broke up. Ready to serve." He picked up his cup and saluted me with it, almost slopping creamy brown foam over the side. "I should have followed you, like you asked. Just think what kind of a team we would have been all these years."

"Thinking about what might have been is a waste of time." Where was all this wisdom coming from so early in the morning?

"True." He sipped, studying me.

His gaze had more power to it, less distracting cuteness, without a heavy fringe of hair falling into his eyes. The glasses weren't Clark Kent anymore and weren't just frames. He looked like he had been through the wringer -- we both had -- but I had the growing suspicion I was going to like Drew Leone a whole lot more than Andy Carleone. Was that going to be a problem, or would that help?

"You weren't too happy to see me yesterday, no matter how polite you were. It's got to hurt, having to hand over part of your project to me, of all people."

"It's my baby. It'd hurt no matter who headquarters sent out."

"Yeah, but the fact that it's me makes it twice as hard. You can trust me, Evie. I'm straight and clean. I swear it."

I wanted to trust him. I knew he'd passed a lot of tests for AMEA to send him to us. The people at headquarters who knew what I had been through also knew Drew's connection to me. They had to know what he had done, the mistakes he had made -- and the growing he had done since those awful days. They had to trust that God was going to do good things with this uncomfortable situation. They had to trust that Drew, having some visibility doing heavy-duty promotion in the next few months, wouldn't catch the notice of the wrong people and bring the cult on the warpath again. Who was God testing in this, and who was He teaching something new?

It was one thing to *say* I would trust God in this and wait for Him to bring something good and useful out of all our past tangles and pain. Actually *doing* it was something else altogether. I doubted my ability to relax, trust God, and give Drew a chance. Yet what choice did I have? I held onto the sermon from a few weeks ago, reminding the congregation that God never let anything happen to us that was too hard. It might hurt, and we might have bumps and bruises and a lot of strained spiritual and mental muscles, but it wouldn't destroy us, unless we needed to be destroyed so God could remake us.

Not an encouraging thought right at that moment. I held onto the rest of the lesson as Drew and I dug into our breakfast before it got cold. We both had to go to work, after all. Together.

*****

Nathan took seriously his idea to pretend dating to protect me from Drew. I didn't realize it until he walked into the office just before lunch that same day to take me out. As if we had a date. Ken, Drew and I were in the front office, talking about Chapel Team. We were laughing about the time some jerk sabotaged Drew's guitar, thinking he was sabotaging Curtis's, because Curtis had supposedly stolen this guy's girlfriend. Nathan walked through the door just as Drew apologized.

"For what?" I looked over his shoulder, caught by the gust of cold air coming in, and saw Nathan. Something in his smile, a little crooked, a little...not bashful, but close, put a funny extra thump in my chest.

"I promised you so many times in college I'd teach you to play guitar, and I never did." Drew slapped Ken across the chest. "How come you didn't beat up on me to treat Evie better?"

"The girl was a saint back then and didn't complain about you nearly as much as she should have," Ken growled, teasing.

"Back then?" I said. "So, I'm not now?"

"Of course you are. Except when you're hungry," Nathan said, stepping up and resting a hand on my shoulder. "I know I'm a little early, but can you leave for lunch now, or do you still have things to do?"

"Uh…" I knew better than to look at Drew like I was interested in his reaction. "No, I think I'm good. Let me grab my coat."

Ken had introduced Nathan and Drew by the time I came out, and they were talking about giving Drew the "grand tour" of the campgrounds. Nathan asked me what I had a taste for.

"Do you still like Greek?" Drew asked. "Do they have a good gyros place around here?"

Nathan cocked an eyebrow at me, and I had to think fast to muffle a groan. He wasn't going to play jealous boyfriend, was he? That was the last thing I needed.

"Funny, that was where we went on our first date," he said, then gave Drew instructions to get to a Greek restaurant about twenty miles away. I just prayed Drew hadn't been looking at me, or if he had, I didn't look as off-balance as I felt.

"Does that place exist, or did you give him all those directions hoping to get him lost?" I asked as we headed across the parking lot to his truck.

Nathan laughed and hooked his arm through mine. He didn't look back to see if anyone was watching us. I paid attention, and we went the exact opposite direction of where he told Drew to go. Ten minutes later, we were pulling into the parking lot of the new Aladdin's. Nathan turned off the engine, let out a deep breath, then gave me a sideways look.

"You do still like this stuff? I hope so, because I love it. The more we have in common, the easier it'll be to convince him we're for real."

"Yes, I still love it." I decided not to bring up the jealous boyfriend problem. Not now, at least.

We were sitting in a back booth and had given our order when he asked me if I had a guitar.

"No. Why?"

"Do you still want to learn?" Mischief sparkled in his eyes.

"You play?"

"Before I decided to go into the Corps, my sisters and I had a little bit of a soft rock band. We've got a couple guitars sitting around in storage."

By the time Nathan dropped me off at the office, we'd made arrangements. Twice a week we would meet in the choir room at church to have lessons at lunchtime. When I got home that night, Nathan had already dropped off a guitar and several lesson books. Mom just shook her head when I told her what was going on.

"I'm not trying to make Andy jealous." My face got hot at that slip-up.

I'd been able to think of him as Drew most of the time because he was visibly different from the bozo I thought I loved in college. "Just the opposite. Besides, it was Nathan's idea, not mine."

"That's what I'm afraid of. Royce would be delighted if the two of you got serious. What if Nathan does get serious?"

"He's got too much common sense. Besides, he already asked me to marry him, and I turned him down."

That got such a wide-eyed look from Mom, I had to laugh. Then I explained the circumstances around what had just been a joke between us. Mom didn't think it was as funny as I did. She told me she was going to tell Royce what we were doing, so he wouldn't be hurt when Nathan and I eventually broke up. We would have to break up.

"Especially if people start putting pressure on you to make things official," she added. "I know you've got too much self-esteem to fall for the trap of marrying someone you don't truly, fully love."

"Mom, Nathan is my friend, not my boyfriend. There's a difference. Besides," I added, as she headed into the kitchen to answer the oven timer, "he's going to be my stepbrother. I can't marry my brother."

She laughed. I noticed she didn't deny the implied, pending wedding for her and Royce.

*****

After less than two weeks, the team had coalesced into a smoothly functioning unit. Part of that was due to the care and time that headquarters put into choosing the right people for the team. Part of that came from the hard praying we were doing.

Who wouldn't like Drew? He'd always been a hard worker. He was still a people person. Everybody in the office, the construction workers on the farm, the folks in the church where we rented our offices, everybody liked him. The only time he ever talked about the past was when Ken brought up SCC. I was pretty sure he did that to remind Drew he had a lot to make up for. In some ways, talking about our past was healthy, like taking a bandage off a cut to give it air and make sure nothing was going bad under the surface. Pretending there was nothing between us wouldn't have done that. Besides, everyone in the office knew Ken and I had been in college together. They had heard Ken and Drew talking about SCC. It would have been weird if Drew and I didn't talk about school.

The hardest part of those first few weeks was resisting the temptation to think about what might have been. If I had married Drew, would we have had children by now? We might have been happy. A baby might have made him straighten up and commit to God a whole lot faster than the road he had taken.

"Might have been" always has been and always will be a waste of time and energy.

Chapter 15

Thanksgiving approached. Mom and I decided to invite everyone in the office who didn't have a family or whose families were too far away. I didn't really think about Drew, but I just assumed he would drive to SCC to spend the day with his mother.

Like a self-proclaimed wit at SCC used to say, never assume anything because it makes a you-know-what out of you or me.

Tuesday afternoon, Drew volunteered to run a few errands that would have him driving all over the place, including as far as Columbus. He returned with his mother, who he'd picked up at the airport. She was staying just for Thanksgiving. She hadn't warned me. Maybe she thought I was angry with her?

Mrs. Carleone -- correction, Mrs. Leone, looked even better than she had when we met at SCC five years ago. She laughed when Ken just about dropped his jaw on the floor at the sight of her. Well, it was nice to know Drew hadn't told him, either, that she was coming or even that she was out of the wheelchair for good. We had a nice little reunion there in the front office. What could I do? I invited her and Drew to join the gang on Thanksgiving day. Mom approved.

I had a lot of work to do to host Thanksgiving dinner for nearly twenty people in our cottage. Royce and Nathan had given us a big living room specifically so we could host meetings, but still, it was going to be tight. We had to borrow chairs and folding tables from the Hanson house to fit everyone. I was glad to be too busy to brood and tie myself into knots. This was my first big dinner party. Somehow, arranging dinner for so many, even with everyone bringing something to eat, was more exhausting than arranging the college tour or summer camps or the dozens of other jobs I had performed for AMEA over the years.

All in all, Thanksgiving was a lot of fun.

Everybody brought a dish or two, but I had to arrange seating, set up tables, and cook the turkey. I settled for really sturdy paper plates, which meant the cleanup was greatly reduced. The last guests left around eleven. The day would have been a few degrees better if I hadn't caught Mom and Mrs. Leone in serious conversation a few times. They weren't arguing, because they whispered and laughed over some things, and they hugged when Drew and his mother left around nine.

Royce and Nathan stayed to help with the cleanup, which meant basically washing up the serving dishes. They took the garbage bags out to the shed and set the borrowed folding tables and chairs in the cart they used for hauling things around on what remained of the farm. Best of all, I caught Royce and Mom sneaking kisses a few times. If he didn't propose at Christmas, I was going to be very disappointed.

All in all, it was a wonderful, noisy, happy day, and it didn't feel weird having Drew and his mother included in the fun and warmth and family feeling.

I would be dishonest if I didn't admit that I noticed and kind of enjoyed, in a weird, am-I-nuts kind of way, Nathan and Drew giving each other a few somber, assessing looks.

*****

The Hanson girls wanted to go shopping on Black Friday, and they invited Mom and me. I was tired, and I had never enjoyed huge crowds fighting for deals. Forget about the enhanced craziness of getting up at 4 in the morning to get to the shopping centers by five or six when the doors opened. I opted out, and teased Mom that she needed time to get to know her future daughters-in-law. She blushed a little, so I was pretty sure things were just as serious between her and Royce as I hoped.

I got up at the decadent hour of 9am on Friday. The silence of the cottage, combined with my exhausted satisfaction over the day before, made me philosophical.

Time to sell my wedding dress. Hauling it around the country had been like holding onto a grudge. Sure, there were good dreams and plans wrapped up in it, but a lot of painful memories too. I had to let go of the past completely, good and bad. That meant getting rid of the dress. I pulled out some index cards and wrote up a simple For Sale announcement on them, to post on the community bulletin boards at church. There were six bulletin boards where people could post notices with things for sale or services offered or wanted. I'd give the lovely people in my church the opportunity to snatch up the dress first. If I didn't get a response in two weeks, I would put an ad in the paper.

Sunday I got permission from the church office, then went around to the bulletin boards and put up the cards with white thumbtacks, per church policy. *For Sale: Wedding Dress. Never Used.*

Monday morning, Drew took them down and slapped them all down on my desk at 8:30.

He was angry. That shook me. Then it struck me as funny.

"Is this the dress you bought for me?" He braced with both arms on my desk, very quiet, mouth pressed hard and flat and his eyes bright like they were filled with lightning.

Funny, but I kept looking at his mouth. Which made no sense because I had no interest whatsoever in his mouth. Except when he said something intelligent and useful, of course. Certainly not for kissing.

"No, that's the dress I bought for myself. It wouldn't fit you."

He stared for about ten seconds, then he tipped his head back and

168

laughed. Short and sharp, but at least he laughed. He dropped into the chair in front of my desk.

"Why? Why sell it now, after so long? You're going to get married someday, Evie. I'm surprised you aren't married. A lot of guys smarter than me should have snatched you up years ago."

"No, just guys crazier than you." I shuddered.

"Hey." His voice went soft, with a funny strain in it like he might cry. "I'm sorry. That lunatic is the last thing I'd want to remind you of." He reached across the desk and caught hold of my hand. "How are things? All that mess. Is it settling down? Are you able to forget?"

"Not with lawyers and other people checking in with me every couple weeks." I sniffed a little and didn't really mind. For once I was near tears and Drew was there to comfort me instead of causing those tears. "It's going to drag on for a couple years, at least. So much dirt is getting dug up, and the lawyers are trying to keep me from having to come back and testify. Then there's the whole mess with Dad's side of the family, trying to blame me and Mom."

"Want to talk about it? Want me to call my friends in the gangs and have them arrange for this jerk and your jerk cousin to be..." He waggled his eyebrows. "Y'know...silenced?"

I laughed, but it came out a snorting kind of gulp-sob.

Honestly? I liked having Drew standing up to defend me, even if there really wasn't anything he could do. Legally, anyway. Just the fact he wanted to, and he was angry and worried on my behalf. That felt good.

"So...the whole idea of marriage scares you now?" Drew didn't look me in the eyes when he said that.

"No. At least, I don't think so." I pulled my hand free and sat back. "But that dress has a lot of weird memories and lost dreams all wrapped up in it. If I ever get married, I want to start fresh. No baggage."

"I don't know. Seems like wearing it would make you feel strong. A winner. Just because you hit two bad apples in your love life--"

"Three. And you shouldn't really mix metaphors."

He wrinkled up his nose at me.

"Three is better than some people ever get. Don't give up."

"Holding onto lost dreams and painful memories isn't good, either."

"I remember how we fought over that dress." He leaned back in his chair like he was settling in for a long talk.

"We didn't fight. You were upset. Our ideas of a simple wedding didn't match." It was weird, but nice, sitting there, looking at him. He really was my friend again. Like we had gone back to those first few months at college.

He sighed. Gave me a crooked grin. "You're going to think this is crazy ... What if we start over, Evie? What if we got back together?"

There were so many things I wanted to say. Some of them were funny, some were angry, some were scared. Finally I settled on: "We're both entirely different people from who we were in college. You're feeling nostalgic."

"Then let's get to know each other. I like the girl I see now. We're heading toward where we should have been. I want that. Partnership, the best kind."

"What about what I want? What about my plans and what I'm interested in?"

"That's what got in the way before."

"Fine. Blame it on me. I don't care. Because I don't want you any more than I want that dress."

"That wasn't what I meant." He stood and took a backward step toward the door. Amazing -- a man who knew he needed to leave without being told. Drew really had grown up. "We're both to blame, and you know it. We could have been great. We were a great team, back then."

"We're turning into a great team now. We'll stay a great team, as long as we don't let personal stupidity get in the way. Drew, please…we have to work together. Why can't friends be enough?"

"Because I want you to love me again."

"I'm not even sure I loved you the first time."

He inhaled, hard and loud, and just stood there for a few seconds, not even blinking.

Then he blinked and shook his head and exhaled. He tried to smile.

"Well, I probably deserved that." He shrugged and turned halfway to the door. "Give me a chance?"

"Drew, don't make me tell my friends at headquarters that *you're* stalking me now."

He really had changed -- Andy would have gotten angry. Drew just got stern and sad.

"That's the last thing I'd want to do. Scare you. I'm sorry."

I sighed. "Me, too."

He shrugged and turned and left. I was grateful. I had work to do, after all. Before I could start typing, I heard a footstep and turned to the door. It was Nathan.

"You okay?"

"Oh, great -- you heard that?"

I said a quick prayer that the rest of the office hadn't arrived yet. That was the last thing I needed -- everyone realizing just what Drew and I had done when we knew each other in college.

He gave me what I thought was supposed to be an evil grin. For an ex-Marine, he didn't do it too well. He was too farm boy wholesome in a square-cut, chiseled features kind of way. "I'm pretty good at breaking fingers or legs or necks, if you need it."

I laughed. Nathan was a dear. I was so glad he was going to be my brother. "No, it's not that bad."

"Then what about that stalking you mentioned?"

"A problem solved." I could see he wasn't about to let it drop or accept my explanation.

"Didn't sound that way to me. The guy wants you back."

"The girl I used to be isn't coming back."

"He doesn't seem to know that. We stick with our plan, spend more time together. Besides, your duties as girlfriend include helping me shop for my sisters and their kids."

"True." We shared a smile.

Nathan picked me up at lunch, and when we came back, he talked loudly about our plans for shopping that evening, so everyone in the office knew what we were doing.

*****

Sunday, as usual, Mom and I sat with Royce and Nathan in church. We were on our way down the aisle to our usual pew when Nathan caught my arm and made me slow down.

"Enemy at six o'clock," he said, and hooked his free thumb over his shoulder.

I had to assume he was gesturing at Drew, lurking somewhere in the crowd, trying to find seats before the service. I didn't see him until just before the prelude music stopped. I looked over to the right, answering a greeting from a friend sitting in the pew behind us, and saw Drew sitting in the same row with us, on the other side of the aisle. He met my gaze and nodded solemnly, then his gaze flicked past me. I didn't look, but I caught a glimpse of Nathan looking down the aisle.

That was the start of something that, yes, I have to admit kind of felt good. When I wasn't squirmy. When I wasn't relieved, and yet slightly disappointed. And a little peeved with myself.

Nathan followed through on his campaign to protect me by making it very clear we were together.

The problem was that as far as I could tell, Drew didn't need warning to stay away. That shouldn't have been a problem, because it was what I wanted. He kept our relationship a friendship that focused on our work, but sometimes slid into references to our college year. Ken was usually part of it, so how could anybody construe me and Drew laughing together as anything but memories?

Nathan did. Or at least, his reaction was clearly the defensive response of a boyfriend who felt threatened.

And yes, it felt good when I got "those looks" from women at church and in the neighborhood. The ones congratulating me on having snagged one of the most eligible bachelors in the church. The ones that were amused at how defensive he was -- those looks came from the women who could see just as clearly as I did that Drew was not competing with

Nathan.

For example:

Drew bought coffee, hot chocolate, and chai for the whole office at a special coffee shop that was off the route he took to get to work in the morning. He did it to celebrate another item being checked off our task list. Nathan then brought me my favorite chai every day for a week. Drew went out for lunch for everybody in the office. Nathan then took me out for lunch, twice, and walked back to the office with me after our guitar lessons. Drew offered me one of his beginning guitar lesson books. Nathan bought me a strap for the guitar I had borrowed. Drew asked me for advice for his mother's Christmas present. Nathan overheard, so he stopped in to talk about gifts he wanted to get for his sisters' children, and ask my opinion and help. That would have been fine, except that Nathan took care of spoiling his nieces and nephews on our first shopping trip.

My car died, and I hitched a ride to work with Mom and Royce, who were going out shopping. They called about four that afternoon to say their wandering from one outlet mall to another took them so far away, they wouldn't get home in time to pick me up. Nathan would drive me home. That was fine. Except Nathan talked -- in front of the whole office -- about taking me to see a friend who owned a dealership. My job was too important for me to ride around in an unreliable car. He announced we were going to look at cars, then go out for dinner.

None of the cars in his friend's lot suited me. I really did love my car, and I was more interested in keeping it than finding something new and having to break it in.

I finally gave Nathan that little talk about the jealous boyfriend routine being unnecessary. Drew wasn't treating me any differently from anyone else in the office. Nathan gave me "the look" that guys have been using since the Tower of Babel -- the one that said I wasn't seeing clearly, and he, the man, knew better.

When Nathan drove me home, Mom and Royce had returned. Drew and four guys from the Singles group at church were out front of the cottage, working on my car.

Nathan stayed around to help. Drew welcomed him without hesitating. I thought about making hot chocolate for them, just to have an excuse to be out there and make sure Nathan didn't embarrass both of us. Then I thought I might just be more embarrassed if I was out there, to witness what he did or said.

The five of them fixed my car so it ran better than ever. That was fine for my budget, but something happened when I wasn't there, and I didn't dare ask. Ken reported to me the next Monday that word was going around the church that Nathan and Drew had some rivalry going. They were civil, almost friendly, but it was clear there was a rivalry.

The funny thing -- and the frustrating thing -- was that no one thought they were competing over me!

Just clear evidence only Nathan thought Drew was trying to win me back.

I was irritated, but I couldn't figure out who irritated me more. Nathan for being oblivious and making me feel a little ridiculous?

Or ... and this made me feel especially stupid ... was I irritated with Drew because he *did* listen to me and he *didn't* try to win me back?

Yeah, stupid, huh?

Ken was the only one who could see what was going on. He thought it was hilarious. When he asked me how long I was going to let the game go on, I wavered between laughing and punching him.

"So, what happens if Nathan decides it's for real?"

"Nathan has too much common sense."

"You're a cruel woman. Serve you right if people decide the two of you are wasting time and the whole church puts together a --"

He stopped with a stricken look. It took me a moment to catch on to what he was thinking, and thankfully didn't say. I wanted so much to turn it into a joke, that I would be grateful if someone arranged a wedding for me so I didn't have to do any work. But I couldn't get the words put together, much less say them.

"Sorry. I did not want to remind you of that," he said after a moment.

I told him it was all right, I was grateful for his concern, but I wasn't worried.

Back in the shelter of my office, I thought about my wedding dress. Definitely, time to get rid of it. Putting it up for sale again would certainly make it clear to everyone in the church that I had no intention of walking down the aisle with anyone any time soon.

*****

Christmas Eve was Friday that year. We had our office Christmas party Thursday afternoon, with Friday off for last-minute errands or to travel. We had the entire week off between Christmas and New Year's. We drew names for a gift exchange, and I got Drew's name. I didn't mind because I knew the perfect gift for him. A new strap for his guitar and a stack of music staff books for writing songs. It was a gift between friends. Just friends. With a long, finally comfortable past.

He loved it. His mouth dropped open, and I thought for a moment he would hug me. Then he laughed and ran to his office and brought out his gift to me.

Drew gave me two gerbils. A parachute made of a black plastic garbage bag with dental floss strings was attached to one side of the cage, and two G.I. Joe helmets were held on top with twist ties.

I nearly screamed, and then laughed. Soon the whole office was laughing as Ken, Drew, and I reminisced about Spiritual Emphasis Week and the craziness and the fun we had. We kept trying to talk over each other. Every other sentence started with, "Remember the time," or "Remember So-and-so?" And we laughed.

The laughter stayed with me through cleaning up after our party, putting away everything for a week's absence from the office, and walking out to the parking lot. Everyone said multiple Merry Christmases and Happy New Years, and those of us with brushes ran around helping the others clear a couple inches of snow off our cars. I laughed as I got in the car and saw the cage and gerbils sitting on the front seat.

About five minutes later, right after I turned down the long country road to get to the farm and my cottage, the road got blurry. I wove over the yellow line and then nearly went the other way into the ditch. I blinked and realized tears were trickling hot down my cheeks. I spotted an access road off to the right that the farmer there used to cross the road from one side of his property to the other. I pulled in and sniffed and wiped at my face. My gerbils just sat there in their cage, half-buried in cedar shavings, watching me, their little noses twitching and black eyes never blinking. I put the car into park.

Then the gusher came.

It didn't last long, and I got out of the car and scooped up some snow from the hood to cool my eyes. I did not need to worry Mom. What I needed was time to think. Something had changed. I could feel it. I just couldn't figure what the change was. Maybe it scared me enough I didn't want to think about it.

*****

What can I say about Christmas? It was my first family-style Christmas that was the way Christmas should be: Kids running around, excited and silly. Relaxing around the table and then in front of the fireplace, groggy from too many Christmas goodies. Games and Christmas music. Lots of talk. Lots of laughter. Feeling wanted and welcome, not just tolerated. The noise. Until then, my favorite Christmases had always been quiet ones, just Mom and me.

The Hanson family knew how to celebrate Christmas and listen to what God wanted from people who claimed to follow Him.

They were going to be my family, and that was the best Christmas present of all.

Because Royce proposed to Mom.

Then Ellie, Nathan's oldest sister, took the gloss off the moment. She wondered aloud which coming holiday would have another engagement. She wasn't a master of subtlety by any means, because she was looking right at me. Her sisters hushed her, but they giggled and smiled at me or at Nathan. For about ten seconds, I played with the idea of being their sister-in-law, rather than stepsister. Then I put the thought away, firmly, in the same mental box that held my resolution to sell my wedding dress.

"Sorry about that," Nathan said. We were in the kitchen refilling the glasses of egg nog.

"Well, it just means you're putting on a convincing act."

"What if it wasn't an act?"

"Nathan..." I was glad to have my back to him, as I put the eggnog carton back in the refrigerator. Too bad I couldn't walk the carton all the way out to the extra refrigerator in the garage. I had to face him again. "You don't love me, and I don't love you. We're just friends. You're helping me out, and I appreciate it, but..." I couldn't think of any words, period. It wasn't a matter of finding the right ones that wouldn't hurt him.

"But that's not a good enough foundation for marriage?" He smiled, shrugged, and didn't look hurt.

Stupid me, I was kind of disappointed. I wanted a guy, a nice guy, a sane guy, to be a little hurt that I didn't love him. Maybe I wanted to be able to love Nathan, to feel romantic and a little giddy.

"But with enough time, when we know each other better, maybe?" Nathan said, his voice threatening to drop to a whisper. "There are lots of kinds of love. I could learn to love you like you deserve to be, and you could learn to love me."

I almost told him the same thing I told Mason, that I wouldn't consider a marriage proposal until I had known a guy for a year. I didn't want to even think of Mason, and anyway, I had known Nathan for a few years now. Instead, I settled for humor as a defense.

"It'd be totally immoral for us to fall in love. You're going to be my brother, soon. I can't date my brother," I said and picked up my tray full of eggnog glasses.

"How about I check my academic advisor on that? Since we're not blood relatives, there might be a way around that." He laughed and followed me out into the big farmhouse living room. I laughed too.

He was joking, wasn't he?

*****

The whirlwind started Monday morning when we all got back from our Christmas break. We dove into our recruitment efforts and the final phase of preparing the boot camp for our first summer. I was so busy, it took until the following Friday to realize I was free from Nathan trying to drag me away to lunch or just stopping in to "check up on you, see how you're doing." The constant chaos probably worked like a repulsion field, driving him away before he could approach. A chute had opened, dumping one crisis after another on us. I had to cancel my guitar lessons, and it was a relief.

Our enemy the professor had returned to his campaign to get the entire state of Ohio to condemn us as a threat to the mental and emotional health of the youth. The construction constantly ran into problems of one kind or another. Nathan, who was in charge of site security, got permission from headquarters to hire more security personnel for the night shift. The breakdowns, missing equipment, and landslides had to be sabotage, rather than just human stupidity and bad weather, right? Building permits that we thought were in order all of a sudden no longer existed. The Planning Commission was on our side, but one historical society after another suddenly decided that the Hanson property *might* be part of some historical site that had been forgotten for decades. Or the building supplies weren't arriving on time. Or another nearby church suddenly decided they had been insulted because AMEA didn't consult more with them or get them more involved. This went beyond the typical inter-church sports rivalry or fiddly denominational differences. Satan was on the attack, and too many people were listening to his lies. We pulled in the big guns, meaning we called everyone we knew to double down on praying. Between Ken, Drew and me, we had at least half the alumni at SCC and most of the current campus population praying for us.

Thank goodness Mom was there to keep me steady and handle the details of ordinary living that I couldn't, like cooking, laundry, getting exercise, and eating properly.

We put in a lot of late days, and despite the crises and self-righteous naysayers creating roadblocks, there was something wonderful in the whole experience. I didn't mind staying out past ten many nights and sliding home through an ice storm.

I liked the feeling of accomplishment and satisfaction I got after all the day's crises had been put to bed and resolved. I liked working around the conference table in the main room. I liked eating take-out pizza, burgers, and lukewarm tea. I liked sharing my responsibilities with Drew.

This was the Drew I had planned to marry so many years ago, but mature and wise and able to defuse any tense situation with common sense and humor. That quiet, cold anger never made an appearance. This was the dedicated worker I knew he could be, always putting God first. I knew I could always admire and support him, but he had grown beyond the potential I had seen in him. Now he had become a man who could support me in turn, free of the old-fashioned stupidity that insisted I had to put my brain on hold and defer to him just because of our different anatomy.

We were deluged with applications, query calls, and letters for the music boot camp. We had two tables set up like an assembly line to fill the envelopes with information packets, application forms, lists of paperwork, and health forms. Whenever we got a request, the letter and envelope went to those tables. It was more efficient to fill packets and mail them once a week, rather than every day.

Drew figured the avalanche of audition CDs and flash drives would start by the end of January. That was his territory, and I was glad to turn it over to him. He was off by eight days. The deadline to get audition recordings in was the end of February, and we averaged about six packets a day, five days a week.

The last day of January, the insanity had slowed down enough that Drew asked us to listen to some auditions with him, and the whole office was able to do that. No one was working on something on a tablet or running back and forth to the copy machine, or responding to email. The ones he played for us all sounded polished and professional. I didn't think about how false that had to be. These were teenagers who were supposed to send in simple recordings just to demonstrate their musical range and what instruments they played.

"It's too slick," Jarod said, after we had listened to the fifth audition disc. "Like the guy's been recording since elementary school."

"Exactly." Drew tapped his mouse to turn off the playback. "We'll get two kinds of singers and musicians applying for the touring groups. The ones who want a ministry and the ones who see this summer as just a step in their career ladder. Big difference."

"A difference in the heart," Brenda said, nodding. "So, you're only going to choose the kids who do it simply? No backup tapes, no special effects, no music at all?"

"The only possible answer is 'it depends.'" Drew winked at me. "I had some experience with both kinds when I was touring in high school and college. You want the ministry kids. They're willing -- most of them -- to have fun. There are a few holy rollers who think it's a sin to enjoy life."

"Baptized in bad vinegar." I recalled some griping sessions on the Chapel Team. "What was it Lizabeth said? Saved, sanctified, freeze-dried and waiting to go home?"

After that, when our workload permitted, Drew included all of us in listening to and assessing the auditions. He wanted everyone's input. Sometimes the recordings were funny. Sometimes, we couldn't tell them from the music we heard on the local Christian station. Which, we all basically agreed, was a warning sign, but we had to be careful not to vote against someone just because they were outstanding. Drew wanted heart and soul, not glitz and Broadway.

I was proud of him. That made no sense, because I wasn't there through the whole process that made him the man he was now.

*****

February turned into March. We made decisions, we sent rejection and acceptance letters, we inspected the slow work on the camp. Drew and I spent a lot of time walking around in knee-high boots, nearly knee-high in the mud, making plans for how our camp would be next year. He held my hand a lot, not always to help me keep my balance in the slick, sometimes icy mud all around us. I liked holding his hand.

We made plans for five, ten years into the future--the two of us a team, training youth for ministry work, running the campground, and organizing programs to bring people in all during the year to make good use of the grounds.

Chaplain Nate, Bonnie, and their kids came out during spring break to look the place over. Everything he said, the look in his eyes, his quiet smiles of satisfaction, let us know he thought it was God's will for us to be together as a ministry team. We complemented each other. Drew had the wild ideas, and I had the ability to make them workable. I could see the problems, while he saw the possibilities. He could get me to look ahead, to imagine and believe, while I brought him back down to earth. Between us, we could make things happen.

I could go on like that forever.

Nathan, however, had his own ideas of how I should spend my "forever." The big dummy hadn't been listening to me at all.

What is the saying about telling a lie often enough it becomes reality?

I blame part of the whole blow-up on wedding fever. We spent Easter at the Hanson farmhouse with all the sisters and brothers-in-law and grandchildren. They were all calling Mom "Grandma" already, and she was loving it. The girls especially were begging, "Please, Grammy, can't I be your flower girl?" They were precious. We were having great fun looking at catalogs full of dresses. Mom still hadn't picked out her dress, and they were talking a May wedding, and here we were, April. Mom laughed and admitted that while she couldn't justify wearing white again, my dress was very close to what she had in mind.

"Why don't you wear mine, Mom?" slipped out of my mouth before I realized I was going to say it.

The next thing I knew, the five of us were trooping out of the house and down the gravel lane to the cottage. I was a good five inches taller than Mom, so the girls insisted that I model it for them, and we could decide if it could be hemmed up to fit Mom. I stood on Mom's little footstool so the train could be displayed. It wasn't a lot of train, just a foot of extra material in the back, but the effect was nice.

Nathan walked in on us while I was reaching to take the headpiece and veil that Gina had dug out of the closet and insisted I wear. He demonstrated just what bug-eyed meant. His sisters laughed and teased him about bad luck seeing the dress before the wedding. Then the big dummy stayed there, leaning against the wall, while we discussed what it would take to adjust the dress for Mom. The girls all agreed they liked the style. They wanted to know the story of the dress. I admitted I had bought it when I was engaged, in college.

"So let me get this straight," Nathan said. Most of us jumped. We had forgotten he was there. "You were planning on marrying me in a dress you bought for some other guy?"

I nearly came back with the line I gave Drew back in November: I had bought the dress for me, and it wouldn't fit him. But I knew, without even looking at his face, that Nathan wouldn't see the humor in it at all.

"Nathan, we're all part of the secret," Mom said. "You're being a dear and helping Eve discourage Drew from restarting their relationship. No need to keep playing the role here."

"Maybe it's time to stop the game," Gina added. "I mean, if the guy hasn't done anything yet--"

Nathan sighed and stepped forward to rest his hands on the back of the sofa, which sat between him and us. "Why not, Eve?"

"We already talked about this." I stepped down off the footstool and talked slowly, to keep the trembling in my chest from affecting my voice. "You don't love me, and I don't love you. Not the way people should love each other when they get married." I looked at Mom, and she had that teary look in her eyes, as if she knew what I was thinking, so I said it. "Not the way you and Dad loved each other, so you could put up with all the garbage his family put you both through."

"And you agreed that we could learn to love each other," he said, his voice taking on some frost.

"Nathan, don't," Shari said.

"Don't what? It's time Eve got her head on straight and took a long, reasonable look at what we've got here. We're good together. We like each other. We have a lot in common. I'm going to seminary. I don't have any problem with you keeping your ministry. Not like some guys you've had the bad luck to run into."

"Oh, Nathan, don't," Mom said.

"So what if we don't love each other that way? What use is it? Fireworks die down. Mom and Dad were all fireworks and roses, and look what they had when the fun was gone. They could barely stand each other."

"Nathan!" Gina cried. "You don't know what you're talking about. You were twelve when Mom died."

"Yeah, I was. I could see how much they fought and how much they hated each other once the fun was gone and they had to deal with real life. Eve and me, we're good at real life. Mom and Dad would still be miserable if she hadn't died when she did. I will never make a mistake like that."

Chapter 16

"Well that's something we have in common," I said. My chest felt like it was filled with ice. "I'm never going to make a mistake of marrying someone who doesn't agree with me on the things that are important."

"Romance isn't important."

"Nathan, you're talking like a fool," Royce barked, startling all of us. He had come in without any of us noticing. From the aching, disappointed expression he wore, he had heard enough.

Any other time, I would have laughed at how big, tough, ex-Marine Nathan hunched his shoulders and kind of folded in on himself under the look his father gave him. I couldn't laugh, though. I could barely breathe.

"Excuse me. I need to get out--" I picked up my skirts and fled into my bedroom.

The cottage had a short hallway from the bedrooms to the back door off the kitchen, so when I made my escape about ten minutes later, I didn't have to go through the living room. They were all still there, talking. I told myself that the old saying about bad luck, seeing the dress before the wedding, might just apply here. Enough to use that as an excuse not to marry Nathan?

A bubble of laughter escaped me. I was already pulling the door closed behind me, so I didn't think anyone heard me. Definitely, I was on the verge of losing it.

I just hoped the bad luck of seeing the dress didn't apply to Mom and Royce. He had seen me in the dress, not her.

Like I had been doing a lot since we first moved down to Coshocton, I went walking through the muddy campgrounds. I needed the solitude and the feeling of putting lots of distance between me and that whole crazy, ugly scene.

It was nice to know the girls and Royce were all on my side.

I hoped they could straighten things out before I came back, because how in the world were we going to get through Mom and Royce's wedding if things were awkward between me and Nathan?

It was about four in the afternoon by that time. I had a few more hours of strong, warm sunlight for walking. Would it be so bad if I stayed out past dark? How long would I need to keep walking until everything got settled back on the farm? How long until everything was settled inside me, too?

The atmosphere of the half-finished camp settled me like few things had in my life up until then. Often lately, it was my source of satisfaction and peace. I would walk around the property and talk to God, and it was far enough away from people that if I yelled at God or broke down crying, nobody but God would hear me.

And the funny thing was that God heard me before I even started praying -- or yelling, or whining, or whatever my prayer was going to be. God heard and sent comfort and the beginning of an answer, even if it wasn't quite concrete in my conscious mind at the time. And not exactly what I thought I wanted or needed.

I went into every cabin, whether just a cement slab, or walls without a roof, or nearly finished. I walked all the trails to all the reflection sites, where we would have benches and little shelters so campers could have private devotions or just sit and think in peace and quiet. I walked down to the pond that would eventually have fish and turtles and ducks. I walked around and made mental notes, because I hadn't even brought my cell phone with me. Despite trying to focus on the camp, I couldn't get my mind completely off that afternoon's weirdness.

Maybe there were people out there who were more messed up by family stupidity than I had been?

Somewhere in all the swirling tangle of my thoughts, I had a weird one. Totally dangerous. What if Drew had walked in on us while I was modeling the gown? What if he had joked about the bad luck of seeing the dress, and then started talking about us getting married anyway? What would his reaction have been if I said that he didn't love me and I didn't love him?

Okay, I did love Drew. Lots of different kinds of love. All of them healing him and me, because he had to know I cared. More than cared. That stupid gerbil cage and all the little things he did for me every day. Maybe there was more than friendship and partnership and respect involved? I liked him a lot. I was angry when people were nasty to him, and I hurt for him when he was upset or something went wrong.

Then in the middle of all these revelations, Drew showed up. As if thinking about him made him appear.

"Hey, are you okay?" He ran down the slope from the main building, where he had parked his car, and skidded to a stop. "What are you doing out here?"

"You don't want to know. Believe me."

"How long have you been here?"

"Not long enough."

"Eve."

He got that look on his face that he wore when that idiot in the mud football game came after all us girls on the sideline. Angry and protective.

Yeah, I wanted Drew Leone to be my knight in shining armor. That realization was kind of shocking, because until about three hours ago, if someone had asked me, I would have told them no, I didn't need a knight,

I didn't want one.

He slung his arm around my shoulders. "What's wrong?"

Honestly, I didn't mean to tell him, but it just sort of spilled out. Mom still needing a dress. Looking at my dress. Nathan making that stupid comment about me marrying him in a dress I bought for someone else. Then admitting he didn't care if we loved each other *that* way.

"Thank You, God!" Drew tipped his head back and closed his eyes. "Whatever You want from me, God, You got it!"

"You're an idiot." I punched him -- softly -- and tried to pull free of his arm around me. He held on tight, and I felt something heavy inside melt. I was so glad he was there, it hurt. "What are you talking about?"

"I've been sitting back and waiting. Doing things your way. Keeping it just friends, and hating it. And I've been praying since December that Nathan would show you what a loser he is so you'll dump him."

"He's not a loser. He's been pretending to be my boyfriend to keep you from..." I sniffled and came closer to crying than I had been since I fled the cottage.

"Stalking you?" He waggled his eyebrows.

Incipient tears turned to snorting laughter, ending on a choked gasp.

Drew turned me around so I faced him, and he rested both hands on my shoulders and shook me once. As if he needed to get my attention? "Don't be mad, but I'm glad this happened. He isn't good enough for you."

"And you think you are?" I could almost laugh.

"I know I'm not, and that's the difference. Nathan thinks he's good enough and won't work to make sure you're happy."

"I think the only times I've ever been happy are when there isn't a man in my life."

"Yeah, well, that's because you aren't hooked up with the right man."

"That means you aren't the right man. We were hooked up." I couldn't believe I stood there bantering with him with only six inches of air between our noses. "Or have you forgotten?"

"No, I haven't forgotten. And yeah, we weren't hooked up right. You like me now, don't you?" He leaned in closer so our noses almost touched.

"Drew...right now, you're about the best friend I have in the whole world."

Yes!" He raised his hands and did a funny little dance like a quarterback after a miracle touchdown. "Progress! Thank You, God!" He yelped when I turned to leave -- flee, really -- and he grabbed my hand. "Don't go yet, Eve. If I kiss you, would you punch my lights out?"

"Are you asking me to punch your lights out? Because you don't have to kiss me. I'll do it for free."

"Women." He wrapped an arm half around my shoulders, half around my neck -- and started walking. I had to walk to keep from being dragged.

The nice thing about this new, mature Drew was that he knew when to change the subject. By the time he got me back to his car, we were talking about my inspection of the camp. He took me to Aladdin's, and we sat there until the place closed at eight. It was Sunday, and it was Easter. We didn't talk about the whole meltdown and problem with Nathan. We talked about the camp and the music teams and some new ideas he had for boot camp and training. He had a notebook in his car, and we spent that time making notes and deciding our plan of attack for the rest of the spring.

I liked working with Drew. I could do it forever.

He really was my best friend. I needed him to tease -- and to be glad Nathan and I weren't together.

God sent him. That was the only explanation. Drew had no reason to come out to the camp, but he was bored and the Singles group Easter luncheon was a fizzle, so he came out to the camp to check something, and there I was, needing him.

Maybe ... I needed him to try to win me back again? Maybe I wanted him to sweep me off my feet?

Or was that what he had been doing all along, but I was too self-absorbed or paranoid or stupid to realize it?

*****

Mom was waiting when I got home, and she seemed pleased that Drew had essentially come to my rescue. She filled me in on some things that had come out during that semi-argument with Nathan. His mother had suffered from a brain tumor for years before she died, and there was nothing the doctors could do about it. Radiation and drugs didn't shrink it, and they couldn't remove it without killing her. The tumor changed her personality. Nathan had conveniently forgotten how vicious she was toward him, as well as Royce. The girls were older and had a better understanding and clearer memories of what was going on. In the last six months or so before she died, when she was blind and bedridden, she and Royce had peace and regained their first love. They were happy together. Even in the shadow of death.

In front of everybody, Royce had told Nathan that he was a fool if he married a girl he didn't love with everything he had. If he couldn't give all his heart, if he wasn't willing to risk his heart, then he had no business asking a girl to give him the rest of her life.

The next day, I had a call from Kurt Green. He asked how Drew and I were doing, if we were still a good team, if all the pressure had revealed any problems that needed to be fixed before boot camp started. I told him everything.

"You're kind of my big brother," I told him. "Do you approve?

"Approve of what, exactly?"

"Well, mending things, I guess. Trying for more than this great partnership we have now."

"No, Eve. Don't mend. Start all over again. Make sure the foundation is right."

*****

The next few weeks were unusually quiet, considering how much work remained to prepare for our first year of boot camp. Mom and Royce chose the last Saturday in May for their wedding. I worried that there wasn't enough time to put the wedding together. More important, I wanted things to settle and try to create a new, non-dating normal between me and Nathan. I really did want us to be friends. God was good, and we were talking and able to enjoy the family dinners at least three nights a week while we worked on putting the wedding together.

Drew gave me plenty of breathing room, even as he took over my guitar lessons. With the nicer weather, we had our lessons outside during lunch, on the picnic tables set up at the far end of the parking lot. Where everyone could see us. We did have our image and reputation as AMEA employees to keep up. Drew was my hero for making a real effort to go on as if nothing had changed. He could have gloated, but he stayed out of sight or said as little as possible whenever Nathan came into the office to handle boot camp security business.

The changes were little things. Like when he stopped at the coffee shop for treats for us, I always ended up with an extra cookie, or sprinkles on my whipped cream. Or he made sure I got the last dumpling when we got Chinese. Or an extra container of olives when we had Greek food at work. Little things. Things other people might have missed. But I didn't.

And oh yeah, he managed to hold my hand under the table, during meetings, without anyone guessing. I know no one guessed, because Ken at the very least would have winked at us or given me a thumbs up sign, or some indication that he approved.

Drew missed the wedding, even though he was invited. He had to go to Georgia to meet with Mini and Tony and some of the trainers who had been working with the college students. He was gone for more than a week, and I missed him. How could I miss a guy when we talked several times a day on the phone, and sent dozens of texts? Strange, but true.

Friday finally came. I planned on sleeping late that morning, still enjoying having the cottage all to myself. Mom and Royce (I had to remember to start calling him Dad) were due back from their honeymoon on Saturday. I had hoped to sleep late because I wouldn't go straight to the office. Drew was coming into the airport, and I needed to drive up to pick him up. Why waste time going in to work, getting my computer booted up and beginning a task, only to stop after half an hour and head out again?

I woke up at five and couldn't go back to sleep. Was I excited about Drew coming back?

Since I was awake, I decided to make a batch of brownies for the office. Drew loved brownies. Especially mine, with all the chocolate chunks and cream cheese and the chocolate syrup drizzled on top while it was hot from the oven.

When I pulled up in front of the baggage claim area at the airport, the sidewalks were jammed with people trying to flag down taxis. Drew burst out between two huge guys wearing dreadlocks. He grabbed the handle for the back door of my car, flung his duffle bag and computer case in the back, and slammed the door shut almost before I realized he was there. Then, he opened the passenger door and jumped in while I was still putting my foot down on the brake.

"Drive, woman! Get me out of this loony bin!" He slammed the door.

I turned to say something smart, but the look in his eyes made the words catch in my throat. I floored it. Drew had this ability to convey a thousand emotions in a single glance. Happy and hungry and sad and exhausted and relieved. My heart thundered in my ears all the way through that stupid knot of access roads around the airport.

"Did you miss me?" Drew broke the silence first.

"Oh, yeah, more than--" I gasped when he rested his hand around the back of my neck, and his fingers kind of twined through my hair. Little shivers went through me.

"I missed you." He gave my neck one last squeeze and took back his hand.

Good for my driving. Bad for keeping those weird, wonderful feelings going through me.

"Your old buddy, Mini, had some interesting stories to tell about when you were roommates."

"Uh huh. I trust Mini."

"Meaning you don't trust me?"

"I know you too well."

"That can be taken several different ways." He snorted a laugh.

We talked about Georgia and boot camp all the way back to the office. Andy went quiet when I pulled into the driveway, and looked around the parking lot. There were no cars behind the church other than the ones belonging to our staff.

"No visitors, huh?"

"No. Who were you looking for?"

Maybe Drew expected Nathan to take advantage of his absence? Maybe Drew was jealous? Insecure about our relationship? I liked that thought, which was silly, arrogant, and selfish. And made me feel so good.

We transferred his luggage to his car, which had been parked behind the church for security. He caught hold of my arm just before I could step away from that side of the building, which had no windows.

He kissed me.

What could I say about it that wouldn't sound adolescent?

Andy had practiced since the last time we kissed?

Or maybe we had both grown up, and this kiss had been a long time in coming.

And okay, I admit it. I wanted him to kiss me.

It was nice. And more than nice. It had me going up on my toes to get a little closer to him, and I felt this funny little vibration in my throat, like I would purr.

Very nice.

And far too short of a kiss.

"Guess you did miss me," Drew whispered as he pulled away.

He grinned at me, and there was so much of the old, fun, mischievous Andy in his eyes, I could only laugh.

Then we went inside and got to work, and neither one of us said or did anything all day to lead anyone to believe anything had happened.

We worked late that day because there was so much last-minute work to do with camp nearly upon us. I had been watching the calendar, counting down the days, and marking items off my long-term checklist since I moved to Coshocton, but it was still hard to believe that in two weeks, boot camp would be open for business.

I knew we would be ready, logistically. But I constantly prayed: *Will we be READY, Lord?*

If we're not there yet, how about some miracles?

Please, Lord, whatever happens this summer, let this all be for Your glory and service. Help us all to step back and take our egos out of gear and turn it all over to You.

Sometimes, I would stop and look across the office at Drew, bent over the long worktable or sitting at his computer and talking on the phone, and I would add, *Please, Lord, am I too old to hope that Drew plans on kissing me again? Soon?*

*****

Saturday, Drew came to take me to breakfast. We had a work morning planned, transferring a lot of the office to the administration building at the camp. I had gone for a long, sweaty walk around the camp, and he caught me when I was feeling icky-stinky-sticky. He laughed at me when I nearly panicked. I was even wearing shorts with holes in them and my sneakers that should have been thrown out months ago. My face was unwashed and my teeth unbrushed.

Andy kissed me anyway, even when I warned him away.

"I've seen you a lot worse. Remember some of those late-night studying binges in college?"

"Ugh. Don't remind me. I had no sense of fashion."

"You were always cute to me."

"Do I kiss you or write you off as a hopeless schmoozer?"

"Dumb question." Then he kissed me, very briefly, turned me around

187

and gave me a shove toward the bedroom. "Hurry and get dressed, and we'll go out for breakfast, okay?"

It was really the last private time we had together for the next week. Mom and Dad Royce came home that afternoon, and there was a family dinner. Sunday afternoon was a dedication service for the campground, with all the local pastors and their churches invited. Since this was a big PR push, Drew and I and our staff were going in ten different directions, answering questions and giving tours. When I got back to my cottage, it was nearly midnight. I went into a coma and nearly slept through the alarm on my phone. Being late would not have been a good start to the last week of preparation work.

*****

Drew didn't kiss me, or even hint that he wanted to kiss me, for the following week.

We really had no chance, no privacy. There were all those last-minute fires to put out. When we weren't working late at the campground or packing up the office to move out of the church, we were passed out in our own, separate beds.

Drew didn't make a single move, didn't say one word to make me think Saturday and the closeness and caring would continue. Oh, he gave me plenty of longing looks. Along with twisting his face into crazy masks while he was on the phone, expressing what he couldn't say to various idiots who decided to throw a monkey wrench into the works at the last minute.

Sunday, with our first invasion of staff and campers due to arrive Monday noon, he held my hand through the whole service. The only time he let go was to open up the hymnal or his Bible to read along with Pastor Jenkins. After the last hymn, he put the hymnal away and took hold of my hand again. He pressed small pieces of something hard into my palm. He wove his fingers through mine and wouldn't let me pull free until the closing prayer ended.

I nearly yelped when I saw what it was.

The pieces of my gumball machine engagement ring.

Drew had kept it all this time.

We didn't say a word to each other on the way out the door. We smiled and responded to everyone who asked about how things were going with the camp. I kept the pieces of the broken ring safe in my fist.

"Would you let me replace that ring, Eve?" Drew said, when we got to my car.

"Replace it."

"With a real one."

"Real is what you believe it is. Kind of like the *Velveteen Rabbit*." I smirked at him. Making a joke was the only way I could handle the churning, light-headed feeling. "I kind of liked my old ring."

"That was training wheels for the real thing."

"Seems to me we did an awful lot of falling off that bike."

"I love you," he whispered. "And when you think you love me, tell me, and I'll replace this ring with a real one."

How did any woman respond to something like that?

When the Singles group invited us to join them for lunch, we agreed. At least we could be together. My only other option was to spend Sunday dinner and afternoon with Mom and Dad Royce and Nathan. It was kind of expected. I certainly couldn't invite Drew to join us. I didn't dare be alone with him in my cottage. Not when I needed to think, to process this big step. This big, glorious, terrifying, exhilarating, please-God-I-want-this-but-is-it-right step. With the noisy Singles group taking up the entire back room of Astoria's restaurant, we could sit next to each other without feeling uncomfortable. We could talk to everyone else, and even talk to each other, and feel no strain. And maybe hold hands under the table when we weren't eating. Just being together could sometimes be more than enough.

Lovely thing, distraction. It gave me time to think of a response to one of the most important questions in life.

It most definitely was not easy.

Forget about trying to carry out an engagement with an entire boot camp to run and both of us being on the road troubleshooting for the rest of the summer. That was the easy part, as far as I was concerned.

Facts: We were good together. We liked each other. We worked well together. The last few months proved how well we worked together, how much alike we thought.

And there was no question about giving up the ministry God had given me, to be Drew's wife.

I finally had time to think, alone, late at night with a Rex Harrison film festival on TV and a carton of caramel caribou ice cream. I grabbed a notepad for think-writing and making lists. If the time came that I had to choose between ministry and motherhood, I wouldn't mind. That was if I could be a mother. Checking with my doctor was somewhere on that list but far down. There were more important questions to ask and answer before that. I had been able to work around my fibroids and adjust my life to try to prevent attacks. For the first time in my life, I saw them as enemies, rather than inconveniences. But if this change in my life, if our renewed relationship and love and all the things that came with them were from God, then my health problems wouldn't get in the way.

More important, Drew and I were already such close partners, if the day came to change ministries, it was a decision we would make together.

Then, after sighing over *The Ghost and Mrs. Muir*, I did something risky, something many Christian leaders tell us not to do.

I asked God for a sign.

The next morning, with the official start of boot camp only four hours away, I decided to get some fancy flavored cream for a treat, on my way to work. There was no road between my cottage and the official driveway entrance of the boot camp, just a gravel path that we could travel by golf cart, bikes, or tractor, if need be. I had to go out the gate of the farm and down the county road half a mile to go through the gate that proudly proclaimed I was now entering Camp Sower. I went the long way around and hit the Munch'n'Go.

There in front of the store was a bank of coin-op machines. I swear, I never saw them before. One was full of plastic bubbles with costume jewelry. I remembered that Sunday in college at the mall, when we stood there in front of similar machines.

Drew watched me when I came into the main room of the administration building. He didn't say anything as I went to the coffee room. That was the wrong move. His silence made me even more aware of him, and everyone probably wondered what was wrong. Drew and I always chattered when we first got into the office. We always had new ideas, something to talk about. Besides, there were all the registration packets to set up for the incoming counselors and campers, tables to set up, and a dozen other details.

The silence hit like a sour note.

When I said his name, his head whipped around so fast, he almost gave himself whiplash.

"You know the Munch'n'Go down the road? They have these gumball machines. Ought to check them out."

"Why?" He grinned, but looked nervous.

"Training wheels." I waggled my fingers on my left hand.

He went white, then he clenched his fist and made a little pumping motion -- until he realized Laura, Brenda and Mike were watching him. I smirked and went into my office. About an hour later, Ken leaned in and just grinned at me, then went away snickering. Well, Ken knew the story of my first engagement ring, after all.

After lunch, I had a blue glass ring sitting on my desk.

I noticed Drew had a big bulge in his back pocket. I wondered how much money he spent to get me a ring just like my first one.

That was love.

*****

We spent the summer apart because of our duties, Drew traveling with the big music-drama team and me troubleshooting. He woke me up with a phone call every morning, and I called him every night before I went to bed. We emailed and texted, sending each other pictures of everything we saw while traveling. We were married at the end of September in a quiet, simple ceremony in the camp amphitheater.

I didn't wear the dress I bought to marry Andy Carleone. The man I fell in love with for real this time was a different man, and I was a very different girl. The dress was dry cleaned after Mom's wedding and put away for safekeeping, for another family wedding someday. Whether it would be my niece or my daughter, it was all in God's hands.

END

About the Author

On the road to publication, Michelle fell into fandom in college and has 40+ stories in various SF and fantasy universes. She has a bunch of useless degrees in theater/English/film/communication/writing. Even worse, she has (or had) nearly 100 books and novellas with multiple small presses, in science fiction and fantasy, YA, and sub-genres of romance.

Her official launch into publishing came with winning first place in the Writers of the Future contest in 1990. She was a finalist in the EPIC Awards competition multiple times, winning with *Lorien* in 2006 and *The Meruk Episodes, I-V*, in 2010, and was a finalist in the 2018 Realm Award competition, in conjunction with the Realm Makers convention.

Her training includes the Institute for Children's Literature; proofreading at an advertising agency; and working at a community newspaper. She is a tea snob and freelance edits for a living (MichelleLevigne@gmail.com for info/rates), but only enough to give her time to write. Her newest crime against the literary world is to be co-managing editor at Mt. Zion Ridge Press. Be afraid ... be very afraid.

www.Mlevigne.com
www.MichelleLevigne.blogspot.com
@MichelleLevigne